HEIDI

Johanna Spyri

Harper Press
An imprint of HarperCollins*Publishers*
77–85 Fulham Palace Road
Hammersmith
London W6 8JB

This Harper Press paperback edition published 2011

Johanna Spyri asserts the moral right to be identified as the author of this work

A catalogue record for this book is available from the British Library

ISBN: 978-0-00-744942-2

Printed and bound in Great Britain by Clays Ltd, St Ives plc

MIX
Paper from
responsible sources
FSC® C007454

Find out more about HarperCollins and the environment at
www.harpercollins.co.uk/green

Life & Times section © Gerard Cheshire
Classic Literature: Words and Phrases adapted from
Collins English Dictionary
Typesetting in Kalix by Palimpsest Book Production Limited,
Falkirk, Stirlingshire

10 9 8 7 6 5 4 3 2 1

History of Collins

In 1819, millworker William Collins from Glasgow, Scotland, set up a company for printing and publishing pamphlets, sermons, hymn books and prayer books. That company was Collins and was to mark the birth of HarperCollins Publishers as we know it today. The long tradition of Collins dictionary publishing can be traced back to the first dictionary William published in 1824, *Greek and English Lexicon*. Indeed, from 1840 onwards, he began to produce illustrated dictionaries and even obtained a licence to print and publish the Bible.

Soon after, William published the first Collins novel, *Ready Reckoner*, however it was the time of the Long Depression, where harvests were poor, prices were high, potato crops had failed and violence was erupting in Europe. As a result, many factories across the country were forced to close down and William chose to retire in 1846, partly due to the hardships he was facing.

Aged 30, William's son, William II took over the business. A keen humanitarian with a warm heart and a generous spirit, William II was truly 'Victorian' in his outlook. He introduced new, up-to-date steam presses and published affordable editions of Shakespeare's works and *Pilgrim's Progress*, making them available to the masses for the first time. A new demand for educational books meant that success came with the publication of travel books, scientific books, encyclopaedias and dictionaries. This demand to be educated led to the later publication of atlases and Collins also held the monopoly on scripture writing at the time.

In the 1860s Collins began to expand and diversify

and the idea of 'books for the millions' was developed. Affordable editions of classical literature were published and in 1903 Collins introduced 10 titles in their Collins Handy Illustrated Pocket Novels. These proved so popular that a few years later this had increased to an output of 50 volumes, selling nearly half a million in their year of publication. In the same year, The Everyman's Library was also instituted, with the idea of publishing an affordable library of the most important classical works, biographies, religious and philosophical treatments, plays, poems, travel and adventure. This series eclipsed all competition at the time and the introduction of paperback books in the 1950s helped to open that market and marked a high point in the industry.

HarperCollins is and has always been a champion of the classics and the current Collins Classics series follows in this tradition – publishing classical literature that is affordable and available to all. Beautifully packaged, highly collectible and intended to be reread and enjoyed at every opportunity.

Life & Times

Story and Fable

There has been some contention surrounding Johanna Spyri's most famous story *Heidi*, published in 1880. In 2010 a scholar discovered a book written by a German author and published in 1830 titled *Adelaide, the girl from the Alps*. *Heidi* also tells the story of a girl whose full name is Adelheid and who lives in the Alps. It seems that Spyri, who lived in the German speaking part of Switzerland, borrowed the basic premise for her book from Adam von Kamp, the original author, unless it is pure coincidence. Peter Buettner, at The University of Zurich has shown that the plots in both books essentially run parallel and there are further similarities in important passages. Curiously, Buettner's own great-grandfather illustrated Spyri's first edition of *Heidi*, and Buettner was researching a PhD on book illustration when he stumbled across von Kamp's book. He tactfully suggested that Spyri was 'inspired' by the original version, which she probably recalled from her own childhood as it was published when she was three years of age.

Putting aside the Adelaide/Adelheid controversy, it is undoubtedly true that Spyri's *Heidi* has become part of Swiss culture and that Spyri has become a Swiss icon, for she wrote a good many other children's stories besides and was a skilled author. *Heidi* highlights Spyri's sense of nationalistic pride and love for the Swiss landscape – indeed, to the Swiss she personifies their feeling for their country. In the tale, Heidi finds herself orphaned at the tender age of five and sent to live with her grandfather, who has a shack in the mountains and lives as a recluse. Her innocent enthusiasm for life penetrates her grandfather's self-reliant toughness and he begins to love her despite himself. Her aunt then takes her away to be companion to an invalided girl, Klara, in Frankfurt, Germany. Heidi grows so homesick that she falls ill and is subsequently returned to be with her grandfather, who is so overjoyed that he visits the local village for the first time in years. Heidi's tonic-like influence is felt by all other characters in the story and her cheerful optimism and youthful exuberance rubs off on whoever she meets. Even Klara learns to walk again in Heidi's company – a modern day miracle.

The allegory to the story of *Heidi* is that childhood honesty is a disarming and inspiring phenomenon that brings out the best in people who might otherwise wallow in their own misgivings about life. There is also the idea that the Alpine environment is clean, healthy and life affirming, which is why Heidi yearns to return there when she is sent to Frankfurt to keep Klara company. Spyri insinuates that Heidi is like a delicate flower that, when removed from its natural habitat, begins to wilt and die.

Heidi has already suffered the awful fate of being orphaned, so her plight captures the concern and imagination of the reader from the start. That she then has such an effervescent personality makes her almost angel-like and the story takes on a spiritual quality, as if Spyri is using Heidi, advertently or inadvertently, as a conduit between the Christian god and the people she encounters in the story. Thus, all who are touched by Heidi become cured of their afflictions, whatever those happen to be. *Heidi* is therefore a kind of folktale that can be transposed into different settings.

Interestingly, the U.S. author Eleanor H. Porter used the basic *Heidi* plot in her own title *Pollyanna* in 1913. In Porter's version, the girl is the orphaned daughter of Christian missionaries who is sent to live with her austere aunt. The girl's charm and honesty once again penetrates those with whom she comes into contact, until the whole community falls in love with her. When she is struck by a motorcar and believes she will never walk again the townsfolk rally around her to provide support and she ultimately learns to walk again.

Thus we have a folk story tradition set in motion, from von Kamp's *Adelaide*, to Spyri's *Heidi*, to Porter's *Pollyanna*. They are all different versions of the same story or fable with the same message: that there is an intrinsic goodness to be found in Christian children that can reach past the idiosyncrasies, the prejudices, the eccentricities, the stubbornness of people, thereby breaking down the barriers that they place between one another and making the world a better place. It is an instruction to aspire to benignity in a world where malignity is so often the outcome of adult behaviour.

About the author

Spyri suffered a personal tragedy in 1884, when both her husband and their only son died. Finding herself alone in the world, she busied herself as a writer and benefactor until her own death in 1901. In the remaining years she wrote about 50 further children's stories, but none had the same success as *Heidi*. As a humanitarian, Spyri was concerned with child welfare, and this is most evident in her later writings. At the time, childhood was often disregarded and children were treated as prototype adults who needed to have their imperfections and flaws beaten out of them – often quite literally. Spyri attemped to re-educate society into realizing that childhood was an important and necessary developmental stage that needed to be encouraged and embraced. She wanted to break the cycle of previous generations, where parents had been treated with contempt as children and were perpetuating that treatment in how they raised their own offspring. Spyri's works have consequently become documents of historical interest as they offer a profile of Swiss society in the late 19th century.

Switzerland had a civil war in 1847 and remained

politically turbulent for decades after. This had undoubtedly affected society, and the wellbeing of children was not high on people's agenda. Spyri though, came from a privileged background and was able to concern herself with matters that the layperson had little time for. Spyri also championed the cause of Swiss women. One of her early stories tells of a woman who is being abused by her alcoholic husband. The story was a nod to the received idea at the time that Swiss wives should accept their lot in life and suffer in silence. It seems that Spyri's own marriage was not a loving one and her husband was a workaholic who may have treated her unkindly behind closed doors. She had both antenatal and postnatal depression, which only served to darken her overall take on married life. After the loss of her husband, Spyri gained a renewed sense of mental freedom. She took to travelling and as her self-esteem and confidence grew she became quite outspoken about her views on the rights of women and children.

Spyri was raised in a Christian household and found renewed faith during her depression. This faith remained resonant for the rest of her life and the Christian doctrine on morals and ethics is a constant theme in her writing. Her own grandfather was pastor in the village church, which was across the road from her childhood home. It may be that Spyri saw a parallel between her relationship with her own grandfather and that between Heidi and *her* grandfather. There is certainly an underlying theme about reconnection that Spyri addresses in *Heidi*, perhaps because she realized the full importance of her Christian faith later on in her life.

In addition, it seems that Spyri's depression had a lot to do with moving to Zurich. She had spent her formative years in rural Switzerland and she disliked the city life that came hand in hand with her marriage. It seems reasonable to conclude that the character of Heidi represented Spyri, for she too became unwell when placed in an urban environment. Thus, Spyri took to living in the past through her imagination, with Heidi as a quasi-autobiographical character. Many people have a romanticized recollection of their childhood, because of the relative safety and freedom of responsibility. It becomes a confabulation – a blend of real memories and imagined memories that make it an attractive realm psychologically.

HEIDI

CONTENTS

INTRODUCTION

Unassuming in plot and style, "Heidi" may none the less lay claim to rank as a world classic. In the first place, both background and characters ring true. The air of the Alps is wafted to us in every page; the house among the pines, the meadows, and the eagle poised above the naked rocks form a picture that no one could willingly forget. And the people, from the kindly towns-folk to the quaint and touching peasant types, are as real as any representation of human nature need be. Every goat even, has its personality. As for the little heroine, she is a blessing not only to everyone in the story, but to everyone who reads it. The narrative merits of the book are too apparent to call for comment.

As to the author, Johanna Spyri, she has so entirely lost herself in her creation that we may pass over her career rather rapidly. She was born in Switzerland in 1829, came [6]of a literary family, and devoted all her talent to the writing of books for and about children.

Since "Heidi" has been so often translated into English it may well be asked why there is any need for a new version. The answer lies partly in the conventional character of the previous translations. Now, if there is any quality in "Heidi" that gives it a particular charm, that quality is freshness, absolute spontaneity. To be sure, the story is so attractive that it could never be wholly spoiled; but has not the reader the right to enjoy it in English at least very nearly as much as he could in German? The two languages are so different in nature that anything like a literal rendering of one into the other is sure to result in awkwardness and indirectness. Such a book must be not translated, but re-lived and re-created.

To perform such a feat the writer must, to begin with, be familiar with the mountains, and able to appreciate with Wordsworth

> The silence that is in the starry sky,
> The sleep that is among the lonely hills.

The translator of the present version was born and reared in a region closely similar to that of the story. Her home was originally in the picturesque town of Salzburg, and her father, Franz von Pausinger, was one of the greatest landscape painters of his country and generation. Another equally important requisite is knowledge of children. It happens that this translator has a daughter just the age of the heroine, who moreover loves to dress in Tyrolese costume. To translate "Heidi" was for her therefore a labor of love, which means that the love contended with and overcame the labor.

The English style of the present version is, then, distinctive. It has often been noticed that those who acquire a foreign language often learn to speak it with unusual clearness and purity. For illustration we need go no further than Joseph Conrad, a Pole, probably the greatest master of [8]narrative English writing to-day; or to our own fellow-citizen Carl Schurz. In the present case, the writer has lived seven years in America and has strengthened an excellent training with a wide reading of the best English classics.

Many people say that they read without noticing the

author's style. This is seldom quite true; unconsciously every one is impressed in some way or other by the style of every book, or by its lack of style. Children are particularly sensitive in this respect and should, therefore, as much as is practicable, read only the best. In the new translation of "Heidi" here offered to the public I believe that most readers will notice an especial flavor, that very quality of delight in mountain scenes, in mountain people and in child life generally, which is one of the chief merits of the German original. The phrasing has also been carefully adapted to the purpose of reading aloud — a thing that few translators think of. In conclusion, the author, realising the difference between the two languages, has endeavored to write the story afresh, as Johanna Spyri would have written it had English been her native tongue. How successful the attempt has been the reader will judge.

Charles Wharton Stork
Assistant Professor of English at the
University of Pennsylvania

PART ONE

Heidi's Years of Learning and Travel

CHAPTER 1

Going up to the Alm-Uncle

The little old town of Mayenfeld is charmingly situated. From it a footpath leads through green, well-wooded stretches to the foot of the heights which look down imposingly upon the valley. Where the footpath begins to go steeply and abruptly up the Alps, the heath, with its short grass and pungent herbage, at once sends out its soft perfume to meet the wayfarer.

One bright sunny morning in June, a tall, vigorous maiden of the mountain region climbed up the narrow path, leading a little girl by the hand. The youngster's cheeks were in such a glow that it showed even through her sun-browned skin. Small wonder though! for in spite of the heat, the little one, who was scarcely five years old, was bundled up as if she had to brave a bitter frost. Her shape was difficult to distinguish, for she wore two dresses, if not three, and around her shoulders a large red cotton shawl. With her feet encased in heavy hob-nailed boots, this hot and shapeless little person toiled up the mountain.

The pair had been climbing for about an hour when they reached a hamlet half-way up the great mountain named the Alm. This hamlet was called "Im Dörfli" or "The Little Village." It was the elder girl's home town, and therefore she was greeted from nearly every house; people called to her from windows and doors, and very often from the road. But, answering questions and calls as she went by, the girl did not loiter on her way and only stood still when she reached the end of the hamlet. There a few cottages lay scattered about, from the furthest of which a voice called out to her through an open door: "Deta, please wait one moment! I am coming with you, if you are going further up."

When the girl stood still to wait, the child instantly let go her hand and promptly sat down on the ground.

"Are you tired, Heidi?" Deta asked the child.

"No, but hot," she replied.

"We shall be up in an hour, if you take big steps and climb with all your little might!" Thus the elder girl tried to encourage her small companion.

A stout, pleasant-looking woman stepped out of the house and joined the two. The child had risen and wandered behind the old acquaintances, who immediately started gossiping about their friends in the neighborhood and the people of the hamlet generally.

"Where are you taking the child, Deta?" asked the newcomer. "Is she the child your sister left?"

"Yes," Deta assured her; "I am taking her up to the Alm-Uncle and there I want her to remain."

"You can't really mean to take her there Deta. You must have lost your senses, to go to him. I am sure the old man will show you the door and won't even listen to what you say."

"Why not? As he's her grandfather, it is high time he should do something for the child. I have taken care of her until this summer and now a good place has been offered to me. The child shall not hinder me from accepting it, I tell you that!"

"It would not be so hard, if he were like other mortals. But you know him yourself. How could he *look* after a child, especially such a little one? She'll never get along with him, I am sure of that! – But tell me of your prospects."

"I am going to a splendid house in Frankfurt. Last summer some people went off to the baths and I took care of their rooms. As they got to like me, they wanted to take me along, but I could not leave. They have come back now and have persuaded me to go with them."

"I am glad I am not the child!" exclaimed Barbara with a shudder. "Nobody knows anything about the old man's life up there. He doesn't speak to a living soul, and from one year's end to the other he keeps away from church. People get out of his way when he appears once in a twelve-month down here among us. We all fear him and he is really just like a heathen or an old Indian, with those thick grey eyebrows and that huge uncanny beard. When he wanders along the road with his twisted stick we are all afraid to meet him alone."

"That is not my fault," said Deta stubbornly. "He won't do her any harm; and if he should, he is responsible, not I."

"I wish I knew what weighs on the old man's conscience. Why are his eyes so fierce and why does he live up there all alone? Nobody ever sees him and we hear many strange things about him. Didn't your sister tell you anything, Deta?"

"Of course she did, but I shall hold my tongue. He would make me pay for it if I didn't."

Barbara had long been anxious to know something about the old uncle and why he lived apart from everybody. Nobody had a good word for him, and when people talked about him, they did not speak openly but as if they were afraid. She could not even explain to herself why he was called the Alm-Uncle. He could not possibly be the uncle of all the people in the village, but since everybody spoke of him so, she did the same. Barbara, who had only lived in the village since her marriage, was glad to get some information from her friend. Deta had been bred there, but since her mother's death had gone away to earn her livelihood.

She confidentially seized Deta's arm and said: "I wish you would tell me the truth about him, Deta; you know it all – people only gossip. Tell me, what has happened to the old man to turn everybody against him so? Did he always hate his fellow-creatures?"

"I cannot tell you whether he always did, and that for a very good reason. He being sixty years old, and I only twenty-six, you can't expect me to give you an account of his early youth. But if you'll promise to keep it to yourself and not set all the people in Prätiggan talking, I can tell you a good deal. My mother and he both came from Domleschg."

"How can you talk like that, Deta?" replied Barbara in an offended tone. "People do not gossip much in Prätiggan, and I always can keep things to myself, if I have to. You won't repent of having told me, I assure you!"

"All right, but keep your word!" said Deta warningly. Then she looked around to see that the child was not so close to them as to overhear what might be said; but the little girl was nowhere to be seen. While the two young women had talked at such a rate, they had not noticed her absence; quite a while must have elapsed since the little girl had given up following her companions. Deta, standing still, looked about her everywhere, but no one was on the path, which – except for a few curves – was visible as far down as the village.

"There she is! Can't you see her there?" exclaimed Barbara, pointing to a spot a good distance from the path. "She is climbing up with the goatherd Peter and his goats. I wonder why he is so late to-day. I must say, it suits us well enough; he can look after the child while you tell me everything without being interrupted."

"It will be very easy for Peter to watch her," remarked Deta; "she is bright for her five years and keeps her eyes wide open. I have often noticed that and I am glad for her, for it will be useful with the uncle. He has nothing left in the whole wide world, but his cottage and two goats!"

"Did he once have more?" asked Barbara.

"I should say so. He was heir to a large farm in Domleschg.

But setting up to play the fine gentleman, he soon lost everything with drink and play. His parents died with grief and he himself disappeared from these parts. After many years he came back with a half-grown boy, his son, Tobias, that was his name, became a carpenter and turned out to be a quiet, steady fellow. Many strange rumors went round about the uncle and I think that was why he left Domleschg for Dörfli. We acknowledged relationship, my mother's grandmother being a cousin of his. We called him uncle, and because we are related on my father's side to nearly all the people in the hamlet they too all called him uncle. He was named 'Alm-Uncle' when he moved up to the Alm."

"But what happened to Tobias?" asked Barbara eagerly.

"Just wait. How can I tell you everything at once?" exclaimed Deta. "Tobias was an apprentice in Mels, and when he was made master, he came home to the village and married my sister Adelheid. They always had been fond of each other and they lived very happily as man and wife. But their joy was short. Two years afterwards, when Tobias was helping to build a house, a beam fell on him and killed him. Adelheid was thrown into a violent fever with grief and fright, and never recovered from it. She had never been strong and had often suffered from queer spells, when we did not know whether she was awake or asleep. Only a few weeks after Tobias's death they buried poor Adelheid.

"People said that heaven had punished the uncle for his misdeeds. After the death of his son he never spoke to a living soul. Suddenly he moved up to the Alp, to live there at enmity with God and man.

"My mother and I took Adelheid's little year-old baby, Heidi, to live with us. When I went to Ragatz I took her with me; but in the spring the family whose work I had done last year came from Frankfurt and resolved to take me to their town-house. I am very glad to get such a good position."

"And now you want to hand over the child to this terrible

old man. I really wonder how you can do it, Deta!" said Barbara with reproach in her voice.

"It seems to me I have really done enough for the child. I do not know where else to take her, as she is too young to come with me to Frankfurt. By the way, Barbara, where are you going? We are half-way up the Alm already."

Deta shook hands with her companion and stood still while Barbara approached the tiny, dark-brown mountain hut, which lay in a hollow a few steps away from the path.

Situated half-way up the Alm, the cottage was luckily protected from the mighty winds. Had it been exposed to the tempests, it would have been a doubtful habitation in the state of decay it was in. Even as it was, the doors and windows rattled and the old rafters shook when the south wind swept the mountain side. If the hut had stood on the Alm top, the wind would have blown it down the valley without much ado when the storm season came.

Here lived Peter the goatherd, a boy eleven years old, who daily fetched the goats from the village and drove them up the mountain to the short and luscious grasses of the pastures. Peter raced down in the evening with the light-footed little goats. When he whistled sharply through his fingers, every owner would come and get his or her goat. These owners were mostly small boys and girls and, as the goats were friendly, they did not fear them. That was the only time Peter spent with other children, the rest of the day the animals were his sole companions. At home lived his mother and an old blind grandmother, but he only spent enough time in the hut to swallow his bread and milk for breakfast and the same repast for supper. After that he sought his bed to sleep. He always left early in the morning and at night he came home late, so that he could be with his friends as long as possible. His father had met with an accident some years ago; he also had been called Peter the goatherd. His mother, whose name was Brigida, was called "Goatherd Peter's wife" and his blind grandmother was called by young and old from many miles about just "grandmother."

Deta waited about ten minutes to see if the children were coming up behind with the goats. As she could not find them anywhere, she climbed up a little higher to get a better view down the valley from there, and peered from side to side with marks of great impatience on her countenance.

The children in the meantime were ascending slowly in a zigzag way, Peter always knowing where to find all sorts of good grazing places for his goats where they could nibble. Thus they strayed from side to side. The poor little girl had followed the boy only with the greatest effort and she was panting in her heavy clothes. She was so hot and uncomfortable that she only climbed by exerting all her strength. She did not say anything but looked enviously at Peter, who jumped about so easily in his light trousers and bare feet. She envied even more the goats that climbed over bushes, stones, and steep inclines with their slender legs. Suddenly sitting down on the ground the child swiftly took off her shoes and stockings. Getting up she undid the heavy shawl and the two little dresses. Out she slipped without more ado and stood up in only a light petticoat. In sheer delight at the relief, she threw up her dimpled arms, that were bare up to her short sleeves. To save the trouble of carrying them, her aunt had dressed her in her Sunday clothes over her workday garments. Heidi arranged her dresses neatly in a heap and joined Peter and the goats. She was now as light-footed as any of them. When Peter, who had not paid much attention, saw her suddenly in her light attire, he grinned. Looking back, he saw the little heap of dresses on the ground and then he grinned yet more, till his mouth seemed to reach from ear to ear; but he said never a word.

The child, feeling free and comfortable, started to converse with Peter, and he had to answer many questions. She asked him how many goats he had, and where he led them, what he did with them when he got there, and so forth.

At last the children reached the summit in front of the hut. When Deta saw the little party of climbers she cried out shrilly: "Heidi, what have you done? What a sight you are! Where are your dresses and your shawl? Are the new shoes gone that I just bought for you, and the new stockings that I made myself? Where are they all, Heidi?"

The child quietly pointed down and said "There."

The aunt followed the direction of her finger and descried a little heap with a small red dot in the middle, which she recognized as the shawl.

"Unlucky child!" Deta said excitedly. "What does all this mean? Why have you taken your things all off?"

"Because I do not need them," said the child, not seeming in the least repentant of her deed.

"How can you be so stupid, Heidi? Have you lost your senses?" the aunt went on, in a tone of mingled vexation and reproach. "Who do you think will go way down there to fetch those things up again? It is half-an-hour's walk. Please, Peter, run down and get them. Do not stand and stare at me as if you were glued to the spot."

"I am late already," replied Peter, and stood without moving from the place where, with his hands in his trousers' pockets, he had witnessed the violent outbreak of Heidi's aunt.

"There you are, standing and staring, but that won't get you further," said Deta. "I'll give you this if you go down." With that she held a five-penny-piece under his eyes. That made Peter start and in a great hurry he ran down the straightest path. He arrived again in so short a time that Deta had to praise him and gave him her little coin without delay. He did not often get such a treasure, and therefore his face was beaming and he laughingly dropped the money deep into his pocket.

"If you are going up to the uncle, as we are, you can carry the pack till we get there," said Deta. They still had to climb a steep ascent that lay behind Peter's hut. The boy readily took the things and followed Deta, his left arm holding the bundle and his right swinging the stick. Heidi jumped along gaily by his side with the goats.

After three quarters of an hour they reached the height where the hut of the old man stood on a prominent rock, exposed to every wind, but bathed in the full sunlight. From there you could gaze far down into the valley. Behind the hut stood three old fir-trees with great shaggy branches. Further back the old grey rocks rose high and sheer. Above them you could see green and fertile pastures, till at last the stony boulders reached the bare, steep cliffs.

Overlooking the valley the uncle had made himself a bench, by the side of the hut. Here he sat, with his pipe between his teeth and both hands resting on his knees. He quietly watched the children climbing up with the goats and Aunt Deta behind them, for the children had caught up to her long ago. Heidi reached the top first, and approaching the old man she held out her hand to him and said: "Good evening, grandfather!"

"Well, well, what does that mean?" replied the old man in a rough voice. Giving her his hand for only a moment, he watched her with a long and penetrating look from under his bushy brows. Heidi gazed back at him with an unwinking glance and examined him with much curiosity, for he was strange to look at, with his thick, grey beard and shaggy eyebrows, that met in the middle like a thicket.

Heidi's aunt had arrived in the meantime with Peter, who was eager to see what was going to happen.

"Good-day to you, uncle," said Deta as she approached. "This is Tobias's and Adelheid's child. You won't be able to remember her, because last time you saw her she was scarcely a year old."

"Why do you bring her here?" asked the uncle, and turning to Peter he said: "Get away and bring my goats. How late you are already!"

Peter obeyed and disappeared on the spot; the uncle had looked at him in such a manner that he was glad to go.

"Uncle, I have brought the little girl for you to keep," said Deta. "I have done my share these last four years and now it is your turn to provide for her."

The old man's eyes flamed with anger. "Indeed!" he said. "What on earth shall I do, when she begins to whine and cry for you? Small children always do, and then I'll be helpless."

"You'll have to look out for that!" Deta retorted. "When the little baby was left in my hands a few years ago, I had to find out how to care for the little innocent myself and nobody told me anything. I already had mother on my hands and there was plenty for me to do. You can't blame me if I want to earn some money now. If you can't keep the child, you can do with her whatever you please. If she comes to harm you are responsible and I am sure you do not want to burden your conscience any further."

Deta had said more in her excitement than she had intended, just because her conscience was not quite clear. The uncle had risen during her last words and now he gave her such a look that she retreated a few steps. Stretching out his arm in a commanding gesture, he said to her: "Away with you! Begone! Stay wherever you came from and don't venture soon again into my sight!"

Deta did not have to be told twice. She said "Good-bye" to Heidi and "Farewell" to the uncle, and started down the mountain. Like steam her excitement seemed to drive her forward, and she ran down at a tremendous rate. The people in the village called to her now more than they had on her way up, because they all were wondering where she had left the child. They were well acquainted with both and knew their history. When she heard from door and windows: "Where is the child?" "Where have you left her, Deta?" and so forth, she answered more and more reluctantly: "Up with the Alm-Uncle, – with the Alm-Uncle!" She became much provoked because the women called to her from every side: "How could you do it?" "The poor little creature!" "The idea of leaving such a helpless child up there!" and, over and over again: "The poor little dear!" Deta ran as quickly as she could and was glad when she heard no more calls, because, to tell the truth, she herself was uneasy. Her mother had asked her on her deathbed to care for Heidi. But she consoled herself with the thought that she would be able to do more for the child if she could earn some money. She was very glad to go away from people who interfered in her affairs, and looked forward with great delight to her new place.

CHAPTER 2

With the Grandfather

After Deta had disappeared, the Uncle sat down again on the bench, blowing big clouds of smoke out of his pipe. He did not speak, but kept his eyes fastened on the ground. In the meantime Heidi looked about her, and discovering the goat-shed, peeped in. Nothing could be seen inside. Searching for some more interesting thing, she saw the three old fir-trees behind the hut. Here the wind was roaring through the branches and the tree-tops were swaying to and fro. Heidi stood still to listen. After the wind had ceased somewhat, she walked round the hut back to her grandfather. She found him in exactly the same position, and planting herself in front of the old man, with arms folded behind her back, she gazed at him. The grandfather, looking up, saw the child standing motionless before him. "What do you want to do now?" he asked her.

"I want to see what's in the hut," replied Heidi.

"Come then," and with that the grandfather got up and entered the cottage.

"Take your things along," he commanded.

"I do not want them any more," answered Heidi.

The old man, turning about, threw a penetrating glance at her. The child's black eyes were sparkling in expectation of all the things to come. "She is not lacking in intelligence," he muttered to himself. Aloud he added: "Why don't you need them any more?"

"I want to go about like the light-footed goats!"

"All right, you can; but fetch the things and we'll put them in the cupboard." The child obeyed the command. The old man now opened the door, and Heidi followed him into a fairly spacious room, which took in the entire expanse of the hut. In one corner stood a table and a chair, and in another the grandfather's bed. Across the room a large kettle was suspended over the hearth, and opposite to it a large door was sunk into the wall. This the grandfather opened. It was the cupboard, in which all his clothes were kept. In one shelf were a few shirts, socks and towels; on another a few plates, cups and glasses; and on the top shelf Heidi could see a round loaf of bread, some bacon and cheese. In this cupboard the grandfather kept everything that he needed for his subsistence. When he opened it, Heidi pushed her things as far behind the grandfather's clothes as she could reach. She did not want them found again in a hurry. After looking around attentively in the room, she asked, "Where am I going to sleep, grandfather?"

"Wherever you want to," he replied. That suited Heidi exactly. She peeped into all the corners of the room and looked at every little nook to find a cosy place to sleep. Beside the old man's bed she saw a ladder. Climbing up, she arrived at a hayloft, which was filled with fresh and fragrant hay. Through a tiny round window she could look far down into the valley.

"I want to sleep up here," Heidi called down. "Oh, it is lovely here. Please come up, grandfather, and see it for yourself."

"I know it," sounded from below.

"I am making the bed now," the little girl called out again, while she ran busily to and fro. "Oh, do come up and bring a sheet, grandfather, for every bed must have a sheet."

"Is that so?" said the old man. After a while he opened

the cupboard and rummaged around in it. At last he pulled out a long coarse cloth from under the shirts. It somewhat resembled a sheet, and with this he climbed up to the loft. Here a neat little bed was already prepared. On top the hay was heaped up high so that the head of the occupant would lie exactly opposite the window.

The grandfather was well pleased with the arrangement. To prevent the hard floor from being felt, he made the couch twice as thick. Then he and Heidi together put the heavy sheet on, tucking the ends in well. Heidi looked thoughtfully at her fresh, new bed and said, "Grandfather, we have forgotten something."

"What?" he asked.

"I have no cover. When I go to bed I always creep in between the sheet and the cover."

"What shall we do if I haven't any?" asked the grandfather.

"Never mind, I'll just take some more hay to cover me," Heidi reassured him, and was just going to the heap of hay when the old man stopped her.

"Just wait one minute," he said, and went down to his own bed. From it he took a large, heavy linen bag and brought it to the child.

"Isn't this better than hay?" he asked.

Heidi pulled the sack to and fro with all her might, but she could not unfold it, for it was too heavy for her little arms. The grandfather put the thick cover on the bed while Heidi watched him. After it was all done, she said: "What a nice bed I have now, and what a splendid cover! I only wish the evening was here, that I might go to sleep in it."

"I think we might eat something first," said the grandfather. "Don't you think so?"

Heidi had forgotten everything else in her interest for the bed; but when she was reminded of her dinner, she noticed how terribly hungry she really was. She had had only a piece of bread and a cup of thin coffee very early in the morning, before her long journey. Heidi said approvingly: "I think we might, grandfather!"

"Let's go down then, if we agree," said the old man, and followed close behind her. Going up to the fireplace, he pushed the big kettle aside and reached for a smaller one that was suspended on a chain. Then sitting down on a three-legged stool, he kindled a bright fire. When the kettle was boiling, the old man put a large piece of cheese on a long iron fork, and held it over the fire, turning it to and fro, till it was golden-brown on all sides. Heidi had watched him eagerly. Suddenly she ran to the cupboard. When her grandfather brought a pot and the toasted cheese to the table, he found it already nicely set with two plates and two knives and the bread in the middle. Heidi had seen the things in the cupboard and knew that they would be needed for the meal.

"I am glad to see that you can think for yourself," said the grandfather, while he put the cheese on top of the bread, "but something is missing yet."

Heidi saw the steaming pot and ran back to the cupboard in all haste. A single little bowl was on the shelf. That did not perplex Heidi though, for she saw two glasses standing behind. With those three things she returned to the table.

"You certainly can help yourself! Where shall you sit, though?" asked the grandfather, who occupied the only chair himself, Heidi flew to the hearth, and bringing back the little stool, sat down on it.

"Now you have a seat, but it is much too low. In fact, you are too little to reach the table from my chair. Now you shall have something to eat at last!" and with that the grandfather filled the little bowl with milk. Putting it on his chair, he pushed it as near to the stool as was possible, and in that way Heidi had a table before her. He commanded her to eat the large piece of bread and the slice of golden cheese. He sat down himself on a corner of the table and started his own dinner. Heidi drank without stopping, for she felt exceedingly thirsty after her long journey. Taking a long breath, she put down her little bowl.

"How do you like the milk?" the grandfather asked her.

"I never tasted better," answered Heidi.

"Then you shall have more," and with that the grandfather filled the little bowl again. The little girl ate and drank with the greatest enjoyment. After she was through, both went out into the goat-shed. Here the old man busied himself, and Heidi watched him attentively while he was sweeping and putting down fresh straw for the goats to sleep on. Then he went to the little shop alongside and fashioned a high chair for Heidi, to the little girl's greatest amazement.

"What is this?" asked the grandfather.

"This is a chair for me. I am sure of it because it is so high. How quickly it was made!" said the child, full of admiration and wonder.

"She knows what is what and has her eyes on the right place," the grandfather said to himself, while he walked around the hut, fastening a nail or a loose board here and there. He wandered about with his hammer and nails, repairing whatever was in need of fixing. Heidi followed him at every step and watched the performance with great enjoyment and attention.

At last the evening came. The old fir-trees were rustling and a mighty wind was roaring and howling through the tree-tops. Those sounds thrilled Heidi's heart and filled it with happiness and joy. She danced and jumped about under the trees, for those sounds made her feel as if a wonderful thing had happened to her. The grandfather stood under the door, watching her, when suddenly a shrill whistle was heard. Heidi stood still and the grandfather joined her outside. Down from the heights came one goat after another, with Peter in their midst. Uttering a cry of joy, Heidi ran into the middle of the flock, greeting her old friends. When they had all reached the hut, they stopped on their way and two beautiful slender goats came out of the herd, one of them white and the other brown. They came up to the grandfather, who held out some salt in his hands to them, as he did every night. Heidi tenderly caressed first one and then the other, seeming beside herself with joy.

"Are they ours, grandfather? Do they both belong to us? Are they going to the stable? Are they going to stay with us?" Heidi kept on asking in her excitement. The grandfather hardly could put in a "yes, yes, surely" between her numerous questions. When the goats had licked up all the salt, the old man said, "Go in, Heidi, and fetch your bowl and the bread."

Heidi obeyed and returned instantly. The grandfather milked a full bowl from the white goat, cut a piece of bread for the child, and told her to eat. "Afterwards you can go to bed. If you need some shirts and other linen, you will find them in the bottom of the cupboard. Aunt Deta has left a bundle for you. Now good-night, I have to look after the goats and lock them up for the night."

"Good-night, grandfather! Oh, please tell me what their names are," called Heidi after him.

"The white one's name is Schwänli and the brown one I call Bärli," was his answer.

"Good-night, Schwänli! Good-night, Bärli," the little girl called loudly, for they were just disappearing in the shed. Heidi now sat down on the bench and took her supper. The strong wind nearly blew her from her seat, so she hurried with her meal, to be able to go inside and up to her bed. She slept in it as well as a prince on his royal couch.

Very soon after Heidi had gone up, before it was quite dark, the old man also sought his bed. He was always up in the morning with the sun, which rose early over the mountainside in those summer days. It was a wild, stormy night; the hut was shaking in the gusts and all the boards were creaking.

The wind howled through the chimney and the old fir-trees shook so strongly that many a dry branch came crashing down. In the middle of the night the grandfather got up, saying to himself: "I am sure she is afraid." Climbing up the ladder, he went up to Heidi's bed. The first moment everything lay in darkness, when all of a sudden the moon came out behind the clouds and sent his brilliant light across Heidi's bed. Her cheeks were burning red and she lay peacefully on her round and chubby arms. She must have had a happy dream, for she was smiling in her sleep. The grandfather stood and watched her till a cloud flew over the moon and left everything in total darkness. Then he went down to seek his bed again.

CHAPTER 3

On the Pasture

Heidi was awakened early next morning by a loud whistle. Opening her eyes, she saw her little bed and the hay beside her bathed in golden sunlight. For a short while she did not know where she was, but when she heard her grandfather's deep voice outside, she recollected everything. She remembered how she had come up the mountain the day before and left old Ursula, who was always shivering with cold and sat near the stove all day. While Heidi lived with Ursula, she had always been obliged to keep in the house, where the old woman could see her. Being deaf, Ursula was afraid to let Heidi go outdoors, and the child had often fretted in the narrow room and had longed to run outside. She was therefore delighted to find herself in her new home and hardly could wait to see the goats again. Jumping out of bed, she put on her few things and in a short time went down the ladder and ran outside. Peter was already there with his flock, waiting for Schwänli and Bärli, whom the grandfather was just bringing to join the other goats.

"Do you want to go with him to the pasture?" asked the grandfather.

"Yes," cried Heidi, clapping her hands.

"Go now, and wash yourself first, for the sun will laugh at you if he sees how dirty you are. Everything is ready there for you," he added, pointing to a large tub of water that stood in the sun. Heidi did as she was told, and washed and rubbed herself till her cheeks were glowing. In the meanwhile the grandfather called to Peter to come into the hut and bring his bag along. The boy followed the old man, who commanded him to open the bag in which he carried his scanty dinner. The grandfather put into the bag a piece of bread and a slice of cheese, that were easily twice as large as those the boy had in the bag himself.

"The little bowl goes in, too," said the Uncle, "for the child does not know how to drink straight from the goat, the way you do. She is going to stay with you all day, therefore milk two bowls full for her dinner. Look out that she does not fall over the rocks! Do you hear?"

Just then Heidi came running in. "Grandfather, can the sun still laugh at me?" she asked. The child had rubbed herself so violently with the coarse towel which the grandfather had put beside the tub that her face, neck and arms were as red as a lobster. With a smile the grandfather said: "No, he can't laugh any more now; but when you come home to-night you must go into the tub like a fish. When one goes about like the goats, one gets dirty feet. Be off!"

They started merrily up the Alp. A cloudless, deep-blue sky looked down on them, for the wind had driven away every little cloud in the night. The fresh green mountain-side was bathed in brilliant sunlight, and many blue and yellow flowers had opened. Heidi was wild with joy and ran from side to side. In one place she saw big patches of fine red primroses, on another spot blue gentians sparkled in the grass, and every-where the golden rock-roses were nodding to her. In her transport at finding such treasures, Heidi even forgot Peter and his goats. She ran far ahead of him and then strayed away off to one side, for the sparkling flowers tempted her here and there. Picking whole bunches of them to take home with her, she put them all into her little apron.

Peter, whose round eyes could only move about slowly, had a hard time looking out for her. The goats were even worse, and only by shouting and whistling, especially by swinging his rod, could he drive them together.

"Heidi, where are you now?" he called quite angrily.

"Here," it sounded from somewhere. Peter could not see her, for she was sitting on the ground behind a little mound, which was covered with fragrant flowers. The whole air was filled with their perfume, and the child drew it in, in long breaths.

"Follow me now!" Peter called out. "The grandfather has told me to look out for you, and you must not fall over the rocks."

"Where are they?" asked Heidi without even stirring.

"Way up there, and we have still far to go. If you come quickly, we may see the eagle there and hear him shriek."

That tempted Heidi, and she came running to Peter, with her apron full of flowers.

"You have enough now," he declared. "If you pick them all to-day, there won't be any left to-morrow." Heidi admitted that, besides which she had her apron already full. From now on she stayed at Peter's side. The goats, scenting the pungent herbs, also hurried up without delay.

Peter generally took his quarters for the day at the foot of a high cliff, which seemed to reach far up into the sky. Overhanging rocks on one side made it dangerous, so that the grandfather was wise to warn Peter.

After they had reached their destination, the boy took off his bag, putting it in a little hollow in the ground. The wind often blew in violent gusts up there, and Peter did not want to lose his precious load. Then he lay down in the sunny grass, for he was very tired.

Heidi, taking off her apron, rolled it tightly together and

put it beside Peter's bag. Then, sitting down beside the boy, she looked about her. Far down she saw the glistening valley; a large field of snow rose high in front of her. Heidi sat a long time without stirring, with Peter asleep by her side and the goats climbing about between the bushes. A light breeze fanned her cheek and those big mountains about her made her feel happy as never before. She looked up at the mountain-tops till they all seemed to have faces, and soon they were familiar to her, like old friends. Suddenly she heard a loud, sharp scream, and looking up she beheld the largest bird she had ever seen, flying above her. With outspread wings he flew in large circles over Heidi's head.

"Wake up, Peter!" Heidi called. "Look up, Peter, and see the eagle there!"

Peter got wide wake, and then they both watched the bird breathlessly. It rose higher and higher into the azure, till it disappeared at last behind the mountain-peak.

"Where has it gone?" Heidi asked.

"Home to its nest," was Peter's answer.

"Oh, does it really live way up there? How wonderful that must be! But tell me why it screams so loud?" Heidi inquired.

"Because it has to," Peter replied.

"Oh, let's climb up there and see its nest!" implored Heidi, but Peter, expressing decided disapproval in his voice, answered: "Oh dear, Oh dear, not even goats could climb up there! Grandfather has told me not to let you fall down the rocks, so we can't go!"

Peter now began to call loudly and to whistle, and soon all the goats were assembled on the green field. Heidi ran into their midst, for she loved to see them leaping and playing about.

Peter in the meantime was preparing dinner for Heidi and himself, by putting her large pieces on one side and his own small ones on the other. Then he milked Bärli and put the full bowl in the middle. When he was ready, he called to the little girl. But it took some time before she obeyed his call.

"Stop jumping, now," said Peter, "and sit down; your dinner is ready."

"Is this milk for me?" she inquired.

"Yes it is; those large pieces also belong to you. When you are through with the milk, I'll get you some more. After that I'll get mine."

"What milk do you get?" Heidi inquired.

"I get it from my own goat, that speckled one over there. But go ahead and eat!" Peter commanded again. Heidi obeyed, and when the bowl was empty, he filled it again. Breaking off a piece of bread for herself, she gave Peter the rest, which was still bigger than his own portion had been. She handed him also the whole slice of cheese, saying: "You can eat that, I have had enough!"

Peter was speechless with surprise, for it would have been impossible for him ever to give up any of his share. Not taking Heidi in earnest, he hesitated till she put the things on his knees. Then he saw she really meant it, and he seized his prize. Nodding his thanks to her, he ate the most luxurious meal he had ever had in all his life. Heidi was watching the goats in the meantime, and asked Peter for their names.

The boy could tell them all to her, for their names were about the only thing he had to carry in his head. She soon knew them, too, for she had listened attentively. One of them was the Big Turk, who tried to stick his big horns into all the others. Most of the goats ran away from their rough comrade. The bold Thistlefinch alone was not afraid, and running his horns three or four times into the other, so astonished the Turk with his great daring that he stood still and gave up fighting, for the Thistlefinch had sharp horns and met him in the most warlike attitude. A small, white goat, called Snowhopper, kept up bleating in the most piteous way, which induced Heidi to console it several times. Heidi at last went to the little thing again, and throwing her arms around its head, she asked, "What is the matter with you, Snowhopper? Why do you always cry for help?" The little goat pressed close to Heidi's side and became perfectly quiet. Peter was still eating, but between the swallows he called to Heidi: "She is so unhappy, because the old goat has left us. She was sold to somebody in Mayenfeld two days ago."

"Who was the old goat?"

"Her mother, of course."

"Where is her grandmother?"

"She hasn't any."

"And her grandfather?"

"Hasn't any either."

"Poor little Snowhopper!" said Heidi, drawing the little creature tenderly to her. "Don't grieve any more; see, I am coming up with you every day now, and if there is anything the matter, you can come to me."

Snowhopper rubbed her head against Heidi's shoulder and stopped bleating. When Peter had finally finished his dinner, he joined Heidi.

The little girl had just been observing that Schwänli and Bärli were by far the cleanest and prettiest of the goats. They evaded the obtrusive Turk with a sort of contempt and always managed to find the greenest bushes for themselves. She mentioned it to Peter, who replied: "I know! Of course they are the prettiest, because the uncle washes them and gives them salt. He has the best stable by far."

All of a sudden Peter, who had been lying on the ground, jumped up and bounded after the goats. Heidi, knowing that something must have happened, followed him. She saw him running to a dangerous abyss on the side. Peter had noticed how the rash Thistlefinch had gone nearer and nearer to the dangerous spot. Peter only just came in time to prevent the goat from falling down over the very edge. Unfortunately

Peter had stumbled over a stone in his hurry and was only able to catch the goat by one leg. The Thistlefinch, being enraged to find himself stopped in his charming ramble, bleated furiously. Not being able to get up, Peter loudly called for help. Heidi immediately saw that Peter was nearly pulling off the animal's leg. She quickly picked some fragrant herbs and holding them under the animal's nose, she said soothingly: "Come, come, Thistlefinch, and be sensible. You might fall down there and break your leg. That would hurt you horribly."

The goat turned about and devoured the herbs Heidi held in her hand. When Peter got to his feet, he led back the runaway with Heidi's help. When he had the goat in safety, he raised his rod to beat it for punishment. The goat retreated shyly, for it knew what was coming. Heidi screamed loudly: "Peter, no, do not beat him! look how scared he is."

"He well deserves it," snarled Peter, ready to strike. But Heidi, seizing his arm, shouted, full of indignation: "You mustn't hurt him! Let him go!"

Heidi's eyes were sparkling, and when he saw her with her commanding mien, he desisted and dropped his rope. "I'll let him go, if you give me a piece of your cheese again to-morrow," he said, for he wanted a compensation for his fright.

"You may have it all to-morrow and every day, because I don't need it," Heidi assured him. "I shall also give you a big piece of bread, if you promise never to beat any of the goats."

"I don't care," growled Peter, and in that way he gave his promise.

Thus the day had passed, and the sun was already sinking down behind the mountains. Sitting on the grass, Heidi looked at the bluebells and the wild roses that were shining in the last rays of the sun. The peaks also started to glow, and Heidi suddenly called to the boy: "Oh, Peter, look! everything is on fire. The mountains are burning and the sky, too. Oh, look! the moon over there is on fire, too. Do you see the mountains all in a glow? Oh, how beautiful the snow looks! Peter, the eagle's nest is surely on fire, too. Oh, look at the fir-trees over there!"

Peter was quietly peeling his rod, and looking up, said to Heidi: "This is no fire; it always looks like that."

"But what is it then?" asked Heidi eagerly, gazing about her everywhere.

"It gets that way of itself," explained Peter.

"Oh look! Everything is all rosy now! Oh, look at this mountain over there with the snow and the sharp peaks. What is its name?"

"Mountains have no names," he answered.

"Oh, see, how beautiful! It looks as if many, many roses were growing on those cliffs. Oh, now they are getting grey. Oh dear! the fire has gone out and it is all over. What a terrible shame!" said Heidi quite despondently.

"It will be the same again tomorrow," Peter reassured her. "Come now, we have to go home."

When Peter had called the goats together, they started downwards.

"Will it be like that every day when we are up?" asked Heidi, eagerly.

"It usually is," was the reply.

"What about tomorrow?" she inquired.

"Tomorrow it will be like that, I am sure," Peter affirmed.

That made Heidi feel happy again. She walked quietly by Peter's side, thinking over all the new things she had seen. At last, reaching the hut, they found the grandfather waiting for them on a bench under the fir-trees. Heidi ran up to him and the two goats followed, for they knew their master. Peter called to her: "Come again tomorrow! Good-night!"

Heidi gave him her hand, assuring him that she would

come, and finding herself surrounded by the goats, she hugged Snowhopper a last time.

When Peter had disappeared, Heidi returned to her grandfather. "Oh grandfather! it was so beautiful! I saw the fire and the roses on the rocks! And see the many, many flowers I am bringing you!" With that Heidi shook them out of her apron. But oh, how miserable they looked! Heidi did not even know them any more.

"What is the matter with them, grandfather? They looked so different!" Heidi exclaimed in her fright.

"They are made to bloom in the sun and not to be shut up in an apron," said the grandfather.

"Then I shall never pick them any more! Please, grandfather, tell me why the eagle screeches so loudly," asked Heidi.

"First go and take a bath, while I go into the shed to get your milk. Afterwards we'll go inside together and I'll tell you all about it during supper-time."

They did as was proposed, and when Heidi sat on her high chair before her milk, she asked the same question as before.

"Because he is sneering at the people down below, who sit in the villages and make each other angry. He calls down to them: – 'If you would go apart to live up on the heights like me, you would feel much better!'" The grandfather said these last words with such a wild voice, that it reminded Heidi of the eagle's screech.

"Why do the mountains have no names, grandfather?" asked Heidi.

"They all have names, and if you tell me their shape I can name them for you."

Heidi described several and the old man could name them all. The child told him now about all the happenings of the day, and especially about the wonderful fire. She asked how it came about.

"The sun does it," he exclaimed. "Saying good-night

to the mountains, he throws his most beautiful rays to them, that they may not forget him till the morning."

Heidi was so much pleased with this explanation, that she could hardly wait to see the sun's good-night greetings repeated. It was time now to go to bed, and Heidi slept soundly all night. She dreamt that the little Snowhopper was bounding happily about on the glowing mountains with many glistening roses blooming round her.

CHAPTER 4

In the Grandmother's Hut

Next morning Peter came again with his goats, and Heidi went up to the pasture with them. This happened day after day, and in this healthy life Heidi grew stronger, and more sunburnt every day. Soon the autumn came and when the wind was blowing across the mountainside, the grandfather would say: "You must stay home to-day, Heidi; for the wind can blow such a little thing as you down into the valley with a single gust."

It always made Peter unhappy when Heidi did not come along, for he saw nothing but misfortunes ahead of him; he hardly knew how to pass his time, and besides, he was deprived of his abundant dinner. The goats were so accustomed to Heidi by this time, that they did not follow Peter when she was not with him.

Heidi herself did not mind staying at home, for she loved nothing better than to watch her grandfather with his saw and hammer. Sometimes the grandfather would make small round cheeses on those days, and there was no greater pleasure for Heidi than to see him stir the butter with his bare arms. When the wind would howl through the fir-trees on those stormy days, Heidi would run out to the grove, thrilled and happy by the wondrous roaring in the branches. The sun had lost its vigor, and the child had to put on her shoes and stockings and her little dress.

The weather got colder and colder, and when Peter came up in the morning, he would blow into his hands, he was so frozen. At last even Peter could not come any more, for a deep snow had fallen over night. Heidi stood at the window, watching the snow falling down. It kept on snowing till it reached the windows; still it did not stop, and soon the windows could not be opened, and they were all shut in. When it had lasted for several days, Heidi thought that it would soon cover up the cottage. It finally stopped, and the grandfather went out to shovel the snow away from the door and windows, piling it up high here and there. In the afternoon the two were sitting near the fire when noisy steps were heard outside and the door was pushed open. It was Peter, who had come up to see Heidi. Muttering, "Good-evening," he went up to the fire. His face was beaming, and Heidi had to laugh when she saw little waterfalls trickling down from his person, for all the ice and snow had melted in the great heat.

The grandfather now asked Peter how he got along in school. Heidi was so interested that she asked him a hundred questions. Poor Peter, who was not an easy talker, found himself in great difficulty answering the little girl's inquiries, but at least it gave him leisure to dry his clothes.

During this conversation the grandfather's eyes had been twinkling, and at last he said to the boy: "Now that you have been under fire, general, you need some strengthening. Come and join us at supper."

With that the old man prepared a meal which amply satisfied Peter's appetite. It had begun to get dark, and Peter knew that it was time to go. He had said good-bye and thank you, when turning to Heidi he remarked:

"I'll come next Sunday, if I may. By the way, Heidi, grandmother asked me to tell you that she would love to see you."

Heidi immediately approved of this idea, and her first word next morning was: "Grandfather, I must go down to grandmother. She is expecting me."

Four days later the sun was shining and the tight-packed frozen snow was crackling under every step. Heidi was sitting at the dinner-table, imploring the old man to let her make the visit then, when he got up, and fetching down her heavy cover, told her to follow him. They went out into the glistening snow; no sound was heard and the snow-laden fir-trees shone and glittered in the sun. Heidi in her transport was running to and fro: "Grandfather, come out! Oh, look at the trees! They are all covered with silver and gold," she called to the grandfather, who had just come out of his workshop with a wide sled. Wrapping the child up in her cover, he put her on the sled, holding her fast. Off they started at such a pace that Heidi shouted for joy, for she seemed to be flying like a bird. The sled had stopped in front of Peter's hut, and grandfather said: "Go in. When it gets dark, start on your way home." When he had unwrapped her, he turned homewards with his sled.

Opening the door, Heidi found herself in a tiny, dark kitchen, and going through another door, she entered a narrow chamber. Near a table a woman was seated, busy with mending Peter's coat, which Heidi had recognized immediately. A bent old woman was sitting in a corner, and Heidi, approaching her at once, said: "How do you do, grandmother? I have come now, and I hope I haven't kept you waiting too long!"

Lifting her head, the grandmother sought for Heidi's hand. Feeling it thoughtfully, she said: "Are you the little girl who lives up with the uncle? Is your name Heidi?"

"Yes," Heidi replied. "The grandfather just brought me down in the sled."

"How is it possible? Your hands are as warm as toast! Brigida, did the uncle really come down with the child?"

Brigida, Peter's mother, had gotten up to look at the

child. She said: "I don't know if he did, but I don't think so. She probably doesn't know."

Heidi, looking up, said quite decidedly: "I know that grandfather wrapped me up in a cover when we coasted down together."

"Peter was right after all," said the grandmother. "We never thought the child would live more than three weeks with him. Brigida, tell me what she looks like."

"She has Adelheid's fine limbs and black eyes, and curly hair like Tobias and the old man. I think she looks like both of them."

While the women were talking, Heidi had been taking in everything. Then she said: "Grandmother, look at the shutter over there. It is hanging loose. If grandfather were here, he would fasten it. It will break the window-pane! Just look at it."

"What a sweet child you are," said the grandmother tenderly. "I can hear it, but I cannot see it, child. This cottage rattles and creaks, and when the wind blows, it comes in through every chink. Some day the whole house will break to pieces and fall on top of us. If only Peter knew how to mend it! We have no one else."

"Why, grandmother, can't you see the shutter?" asked Heidi.

"Child, I cannot see anything," lamented the old woman.

"Can you see it when I open the shutter to let in the light?"

"No, no, not even then. Nobody can ever show me the light again."

"But you can see when you go out into the snow, where everything is bright. Come with me, grandmother, I'll show you!" and Heidi, taking the old woman by the hand, tried to lead her out. Heidi was frightened and got more anxious all the time.

"Just let me stay here, child. Everything is dark for

me, and my poor eyes can neither see the snow nor the light."

"But grandmother, does it not get light in the summer, when the sun shines down on the mountains to say good-night, setting them all aflame?"

"No, child, I can never see the fiery mountains any more. I have to live in darkness, always."

Heidi burst out crying now and sobbed aloud. "Can nobody make it light for you? Is there nobody who can do it, grandmother? Nobody?"

The grandmother tried all possible means to comfort the child; it wrung her heart to see her terrible distress. It was awfully hard for Heidi to stop crying when she had once begun, for she cried so seldom. The grandmother said: "Heidi, let me tell you something. People who cannot see love to listen to friendly words. Sit down beside me and tell me all about yourself. Talk to me about your grandfather, for it has been long since I have heard anything about him. I used to know him very well."

Heidi suddenly wiped away her tears, for she had had a cheering thought. "Grandmother, I shall tell grandfather about it, and I am sure he can make it light for you. He can mend your little house and stop the rattling."

The old woman remained silent, and Heidi, with the greatest vivacity, began to describe her life with the grandfather. Listening attentively, the two women would say to each other sometimes: "Do you hear what she says about the uncle? Did you listen?"

Heidi's tale was interrupted suddenly by a great thumping on the door; and who should come in but Peter. No sooner had he seen Heidi, than he smiled, opening his round eyes as wide as possible. Heidi called, "Good-evening, Peter!"

"Is it really time for him to come home!" exclaimed Peter's grandmother. "How quickly the time has flown. Good-evening, little Peter; how is your reading going?"

"Just the same," the boy replied.

"Oh, dear, I was hoping for a change at last. You are nearly twelve years old, my boy."

"Why should there be a change?" inquired Heidi with greatest interest.

"I am afraid he'll never learn it after all. On the shelf over there is an old prayer-book with beautiful songs. I have forgotten them all, for I do not hear them any more. I longed that Peter should read them to me some day, but he will never be able to!"

Peter's mother got up from her work now, saying, "I must make a light. The afternoon has passed and now it's getting dark."

When Heidi heard those words, she started, and holding out her hand to all, she said: "Good-night. I have to go, for it is getting dark." But the anxious grandmother called out: "Wait, child, don't go up alone! Go with her, Peter, and take care that she does not fall. Don't let her get cold, do you hear? Has Heidi a shawl?"

"I haven't, but I won't be cold," Heidi called back, for she had already escaped through the door. She ran so fast that Peter could hardly follow her. The old woman frettingly called out: "Brigida, run after her. Get a warm shawl, she'll freeze in this cold night. Hurry up!" Brigida obeyed. The children had hardly climbed any distance, when they saw the old man coming and with a few vigorous steps he stood beside them.

"I am glad you kept you word, Heidi," he said; and packing her into her cover, he started up the hill, carrying the child in his arms. Brigida had come in time to see it, and told the grandmother what she had witnessed.

"Thank God, thank God!" the old woman said. "I hope she'll come again; she has done me so much good! What a soft heart she has, the darling, and how nicely she can talk." All evening the grandmother said to herself, "If only he lets her come again! I have something to look forward to in this world now, thank God!"

Heidi could hardly wait before they reached the cottage. She had tried to talk on the way, but no sound could be heard through the heavy cover. As soon as they were inside the hut she began: "Grandfather, we must take some nails and a hammer down tomorrow; a shutter is loose in grandmother's house and many other places shake. Everything rattles in her house."

"Is that so? Who says we must?"

"Nobody told me, but I know," Heidi replied. "Everything is loose in the house, and poor grandmother told me she was afraid that the house might tumble down. And grandfather, she cannot see the light. Can you help her and make it light for her? How terrible it must be to be afraid in the dark and nobody there to help you! Oh, please, grandfather, do something to help her! I know you can."

Heidi had been clinging to her grandfather and looking up to him with trusting eyes. At last he said, glancing down: "All right, child, we'll see that it won't rattle any more. We can do it tomorrow."

Heidi was so overjoyed at these words that she danced around the room shouting: "We'll do it tomorrow! We can do it tomorrow!"

The grandfather, keeping his word, took Heidi down the following day with the same instructions as before. After Heidi had disappeared, he went around the house inspecting it.

The grandmother, in her joy at seeing the child again, had stopped the wheel and called: "Here is the child again! She has come again!" Heidi, grasping her outstretched hands, sat herself on a low stool at the old woman's feet and began to chat. Suddenly violent blows were heard outside; the grandmother in her fright nearly upset the spinning-wheel and screamed: "Oh, God, it has come at last. The hut is tumbling down!"

"Grandmother, don't be frightened," said the child,

while she put her arms around her. "Grandfather is just fastening the shutter and fixing everything for you."

"Is it possible? Has God not forgotten us after all? Brigida, have you heard it? Surely that is a hammer. Ask him to come in a moment, if it is he, for I must thank him."

When Brigida went out, she found the old man busy with putting a new beam along the wall. Approaching him, she said: "Mother and I wish you a good-afternoon. We are very much obliged to you for doing us such a service, and mother would like to see you. There are few that would have done it, uncle, and how can we thank you?"

"That will do," he interrupted. "I know what your opinion about me is. Go in, for I can find what needs mending myself."

Brigida obeyed, for the uncle had a way that nobody could oppose. All afternoon the uncle hammered around; he even climbed up on the roof, where much was missing. At last he had to stop, for the last nail was gone from his pocket. The darkness had come in the meantime, and Heidi was ready to go up with him, packed warmly in his arms.

Thus the winter passed. Sunshine had come again into the blind woman's life, and made her days less dark and dreary. Early every morning she would begin to listen for Heidi's footsteps, and when the door was opened and the child ran in, the grandmother exclaimed every time more joyfully: "Thank God, she has come again!"

Heidi would talk about her life, and make the grandmother smile and laugh, and in that way the hours flew by. In former times the old woman had always sighed: "Brigida, is the day not over yet?" but now she always exclaimed after Heidi's departure: "How quickly the afternoon has gone by. Don't you think so, too, Brigida?" Her daughter had to assent, for Heidi had long ago won her heart. "If only God will spare us the child!" the grandmother would often say. "I hope the uncle will always be kind, as he is now."—"Does Heidi look well, Brigida?" was a frequent question, which always got a reassuring answer.

Heidi also became very fond of the old grandmother, and when the weather was fair, she visited her every day that winter. Whenever the child remembered that the grandmother was blind, she would get very sad; her only comfort was that her coming brought such happiness. The grandfather soon had mended the cottage; often he would take down big loads of timber, which he used to good purpose. The grandmother vowed that no rattling could be heard any more, and that, thanks to the uncle's kindness, she slept better that winter than she had done for many a year.

CHAPTER 5

Two Visitors

Two winters had nearly passed. Heidi was happy, for the spring was coming again, with the soft delicious wind that made the fir-trees roar. Soon she would be able to go up to the pasture, where blue and yellow flowers greeted her at every step. She was nearly eight years old, and had learned to take care of the goats, who ran after her like little dogs. Several times the village teacher had sent word by Peter that the child was wanted in school, but the old man had not paid any attention to the message and had kept her with him as before. It was a beautiful morning in March. The snow had melted on the slopes, and was going fast. Snowdrops were peeping through the ground, which seemed to be getting ready for spring. Heidi was running to and fro before the door, when she suddenly saw an old gentleman, dressed in black, standing beside her. As she appeared frightened, he said kindly: "You must not be afraid of me, for I love children. Give me your hand, Heidi, and tell me where your grandfather is."

"He is inside, making round wooden spoons," the child replied, opening the door while she spoke.

It was the old pastor of the village, who had known the grandfather years ago. After entering, he approached the old man, saying: "Good-morning, neighbor."

The old man got up, surprised, and offering a seat to the visitor, said: "Good-morning, Mr. Parson. Here is a wooden chair, if it is good enough."

Sitting down, the parson said: "It is long since I have seen you, neighbor. I have come to-day to talk over a matter with you. I am sure you can guess what it is about."

The clergyman here looked at Heidi, who was standing near the door.

"Heidi, run out to see the goats," said the grandfather, "and bring them some salt; you can stay till I come."

Heidi disappeared on the spot. "The child should have come to school a year ago," the parson went on to say. "Didn't you get the teacher's warning? What do you intend to do with the child?"

"I do not want her to go to school," said the old man, unrelentingly.

"What do you want the child to be?"

"I want her to be free and happy as a bird!"

"But she is human, and it is high time for her to learn something. I have come now to tell you about it, so that you can make your plans. She must come to school next winter, remember that."

"I shan't do it, pastor!" was the reply.

"Do you think there is no way?" the clergyman replied, a little hotly. "You know the world, for you have travelled far. What little sense you show!"

"You think I am going to send this delicate child to school in every storm and weather!" the old man said excitedly. "It is a two hours' walk, and I shall not let her go; for the wind often howls so that it chokes me if I venture out. Did you know Adelheid, her mother? She was a sleep-walker, and had fainting-fits. Nobody shall compel me to let her go; I will gladly fight it out in court."

"You are perfectly right," said the clergyman kindly. "You could not send her to school from here. Why don't you come down to live among us again? You are leading a strange life here; I wonder how you can keep the child warm in winter."

"She has young blood and a good cover. I know where to find good wood, and all winter I keep a fire going. I couldn't live in the village, for the people there and I despise each other; we had better keep apart."

"You are mistaken, I assure you! Make your peace with God, and then you'll see how happy you will be."

The clergyman had risen, and holding out his hand, he said cordially: "I shall count on you next winter, neighbor. We shall receive you gladly, reconciled with God and man."

But the uncle replied firmly, while he shook his visitor by the hand: "Thank you for your kindness, but you will have to wait in vain."

"God be with you," said the parson, and left him sadly.

The old man was out of humor that day, and when Heidi begged to go to the grandmother, he only growled: "Not to-day." Next day they had hardly finished their dinner, when another visitor arrived. It was Heidi's aunt Deta; she wore a hat with feathers and a dress with such a train that it swept up everything that lay on the cottage floor. While the uncle looked at her silently, Deta began to praise him and the child's red cheeks. She told him that it had not been her intention to leave Heidi with him long, for she knew she must be in his way. She had tried to provide for the child elsewhere, and at last she had found a splendid chance for her. Very rich relations of her lady, who owned the largest house in Frankfurt, had a lame daughter. This poor little girl was confined to her rolling-chair and needed a companion at her lessons. Deta had heard from her lady that a sweet, quaint child was wanted as playmate and schoolmate for the invalid. She had gone to the housekeeper and told her all about Heidi. The lady, delighted with the idea, had told her to fetch the child at once. She had come now, and it was a lucky chance for Heidi, "for one never knew what might happen in such a case, and who could tell—"

"Have you finished?" the old man interrupted her at last.

"Why, one might think I was telling you the silliest things. There is not a man in Prätiggan who would not thank God for such news."

"Bring them to somebody else, but not to me," said the uncle, coldly.

Deta, flaming up, replied: "Do you want to hear what I think? Don't I know how old she is; eight years old and ignorant of everything. They have told me that you refuse to send her to church and to school. She is my only sister's child, and I shall not bear it, for I am responsible. You do not care for her, how else could you be indifferent to such luck. You had better give way or I shall get the people to back me. If I were you, I would not have it brought to court; some things might be warmed up that you would not care to hear about."

"Be quiet!" the uncle thundered with flaming eyes. "Take her and ruin her, but do not bring her before my sight again. I do not want to see her with feathers in her hat and wicked words like yours."

With long strides he went out.

"You have made him angry!" said Heidi with a furious look.

"He won't be cross long. But come now, where are your things?" asked Deta.

"I won't come," Heidi replied.

"What?" Deta said passionately. But changing her tone, she continued in a more friendly manner: "Come now; you don't understand me. I am taking you to the most beautiful place you have ever seen." After packing up Heidi's clothes she said again, "Come, child, and take your hat. It is not very nice, but we can't help it."

"I shall not come," was the reply.

"Don't be stupid and obstinate, like a goat. Listen to me. Grandfather is sending us away and we must do what he commands, or he will get more angry still. You'll see how fine it is in Frankfurt. If you do not like it, you can come home again and by that time grandfather will have forgiven us."

"Can I come home again to-night?" asked Heidi.

"Come now, I told you you could come back. If we get to Mayenfeld today, we can take the train to-morrow. That will make you fly home again in the shortest time!"

Holding the bundle, Deta led the child down the mountain. On their way they met Peter, who had not gone to school that day. The boy thought it was a more useful occupation to look for hazel-rods than to learn to read, for he always needed the rods. He had had a most successful day, for he carried an enormous bundle on his shoulder. When he caught sight of Heidi and Deta, he asked them where they were going.

"I am going to Frankfurt with Aunt Deta," Heidi replied; "but first I must see grandmother, for she is waiting."

"Oh no, it is too late. You can see her when you come back, but not now," said Deta, pulling Heidi along with her, for she was afraid that the old woman might detain the child.

Peter ran into the cottage and hit the table with his rods. The grandmother jumped up in her fright and asked him what that meant.

"They have taken Heidi away," Peter said with a groan.

"Who has, Peter? Where has she gone?" the unhappy grandmother asked. Brigida had seen Deta walking up the footpath a short while ago and soon they guessed what had happened. With a trembling hand the old woman opened a window and called out as loudly as she could: "Deta, Deta, don't take the child away. Don't take her from us."

When Heidi heard that she struggled to get free, and said: "I must go to grandmother; she is calling me."

But Deta would not let her go. She urged her on by saying that she might return soon again. She also suggested that Heidi might bring a lovely present to the grandmother when she came back.

Heidi liked this prospect and followed Deta without more ado. After a while she asked: "What shall I bring to the grandmother?"

"You might bring her some soft white rolls, Heidi. I think the black bread is too hard for poor grandmother to eat."

"Yes, I know, aunt, she always gives it to Peter," Heidi confirmed her. "We must go quickly now; we might get to Frankfurt today and then I can be back tomorrow with the rolls."

Heidi was running now, and Deta had to follow. She was glad enough to escape the questions that people might ask her in the village. People could see that Heidi was pulling her along, so she said: "I can't stop. Don't you see how the child is hurrying? We have still far to go," whenever she heard from all sides: "Are you taking her with you?" "Is she running away from the uncle?" "What a wonder she is still alive!" "What red cheeks she has," and so on. Soon they had escaped and had left the village far behind them.

From that time on the uncle looked more angry than ever when he came to the village. Everybody was afraid of him, and the women would warn their children to keep out of his sight.

He came down but seldom, and then only to sell his cheese and buy his provisions. Often people remarked how lucky it was that Heidi had left him. They had seen her hurrying away, so they thought that she had been glad to go.

The old grandmother alone stuck to him faithfully. Whenever anybody came up to her, she would tell them what good care the old man had taken of Heidi. She also told them that he had mended her little house. These reports reached the village, of course, but people only half believed them, for the grandmother was infirm and old. She began her days with sighing again. "All happiness has left us with the child. The days are so long and dreary, and I have no joy left. If only I could hear Heidi's voice before I die," the poor old woman would exclaim, day after day.

CHAPTER 6

A New Chapter with New Things

In a beautiful house in Frankfurt lived a sick child by the name of Clara Sesemann. She was sitting in a comfortable rolling-chair, which could be pushed from room to room. Clara spent most of her time in the study, where long rows of bookcases lined the walls. This room was used as a living-room, and here she was also given her lessons.

Clara had a pale, thin face with soft blue eyes, which at that moment were watching the clock impatiently. At last she said: "Oh Miss Rottenmeier, isn't it time yet?"

The lady so addressed was the housekeeper, who had lived with Clara since Mrs. Sesemann's death. Miss Rottenmeier wore a peculiar uniform with a long cape, and a high cap on her head. Clara's father, who was away from home a great deal, left the entire management of the house to this lady, on the condition that his daughter's wishes should always be considered.

While Clara was waiting, Deta had arrived at the front door with Heidi. She was asking the coachman who had brought her if she could go upstairs.

"That's not my business," grumbled the coachman; "you must ring for the butler."

Sebastian, the butler, a man with large brass buttons on his coat, soon stood before her.

"May I see Miss Rottenmeier?" Deta asked.

"That's not my business," the butler announced. "Ring for Tinette, the maid." With that, he disappeared.

Deta, ringing again, saw a girl with a brilliant white cap on her head, coming down the stairway. The maid stopped half-way down and asked scornfully: "What do you want?"

Deta repeated her wish again. Tinette told her to wait while she went upstairs, but it did not take long before the two were asked to come up.

Following the maid, they found themselves in the study. Deta held on to Heidi's hand and stayed near the door.

Miss Rottenmeier, slowly getting up, approached the newcomers. She did not seem pleased with Heidi, who wore her hat and shawl and was looking up at the lady's headdress with innocent wonder.

"What is your name?" the lady asked.

"Heidi," was the child's clear answer.

"What? Is that a Christian name? What name did you receive in baptism?" inquired the lady again.

"I don't remember that any more," the child replied.

"What an answer! What does that mean?" said the house-keeper, shaking her head. "Is the child ignorant or pert, Miss Deta?"

"I shall speak for the child, if I may, madam," Deta said, after giving Heidi a little blow for her unbecoming answer. "The child has never been in such a fine house and does not know how to behave. I hope the lady will forgive her manners. She is called Adelheid after her mother, who was my sister."

"Oh well, that is better. But Miss Deta, the child seems peculiar for her age. I thought I told you that Miss Clara's companion would have to be twelve years old like her, to be able to share her studies. How old is Adelheid?"

"I am sorry, but I am afraid she is somewhat younger than I thought. I think she is about ten years old."

"Grandfather said that I was eight years old," said Heidi

now. Deta gave her another blow, but as the child had no idea why, she did not get embarrassed.

"What, only eight years old!" Miss Rottenmeier exclaimed indignantly. "How can we get along? What have you learned? What books have you studied?"

"None," said Heidi.

"But how did you learn to read?"

"I can't read and Peter can't do it either," Heidi retorted.

"For mercy's sake! you cannot read?" cried the lady in her surprise. "How is it possible? What else have you studied?"

"Nothing," replied Heidi, truthfully.

"Miss Deta, how could you bring this child?" said the housekeeper, when she was more composed.

Deta, however, was not easily intimidated, and said: "I am sorry, but I thought this child would suit you. She *is* small, but older children are often spoilt and not like her. I must go now, for my mistress is waiting. As soon as I can, I'll come to see how the child is getting along." With a bow she was outside and with a few quick steps hurried down-stairs.

Miss Rottenmeier followed her and tried to call her back, for she wanted to ask Deta a number of questions.

Heidi was still standing on the same spot. Clara had watched the scene, and called to the child now to come to her.

Heidi approached the rolling-chair.

"Do you want to be called Heidi or Adelheid?" asked Clara.

"My name is Heidi and nothing else," was the child's answer.

"I'll call you Heidi then, for I like it very much," said Clara. "I have never heard the name before. What curly hair you have! Was it always like that?"

"I think so."

"Did you like to come to Frankfurt?" asked Clara again.

"Oh, no, but then I am going home again to-morrow,

and shall bring grandmother some soft white rolls," Heidi explained.

"What a curious child you are," said Clara. "You have come to Frankfurt to stay with me, don't you know that? We shall have our lessons together, and I think it will be great fun when you learn to read. Generally the morning seems to have no end, for Mr. Candidate comes at ten and stays till two. That is a long time, and he has to yawn himself, he gets so tired. Miss Rottenmeier and he both yawn together behind their books, but when I do it, Miss Rottenmeier makes me take cod-liver oil and says that I am ill. So I must swallow my yawns, for I hate the oil. What fun it will be now, when you learn to read!"

Heidi shook her head doubtfully at these prospects.

"Everybody must learn to read, Heidi. Mr. Candidate is very patient and will explain it all to you. You won't know what he means at first, for it is difficult to understand him. It won't take long to learn, though, and then you will know what he means."

When Miss Rottenmeier found that she was unable to recall Deta, she came back to the children. She was in a very excited mood, for she felt responsible for Heidi's coming and did not know how to cancel this unfortunate step. She soon got up again to go to the dining-room, criticising the butler and giving orders to the maid. Sebastian, not daring to show his rage otherwise, noisily opened the folding doors. When he went up to Clara's chair, he saw Heidi watching him intently. At last she said: "You look like Peter."

Miss Rottenmeier was horrified with this remark, and sent them all into the dining-room. After Clara was lifted on to her chair, the housekeeper sat down beside her. Heidi was motioned to sit opposite the lady. In that way they were placed at the enormous table. When Heidi saw a roll on her plate, she turned to Sebastian, and pointing at it, asked, "Can I have this?" Heidi had already great confidence in the butler, especially on account of the resemblance she had discovered. The butler nodded, and when he saw Heidi put the bread in her pocket, could hardly keep from laughing. He came to Heidi now with a dish of small baked fishes. For a long time the child did not move; then turning her eyes to the butler, she said: "Must I eat that?" Sebastian nodded, but another pause ensued. "Why don't you give it to me?" the child quietly asked, looking at her plate. The butler, hardly able to keep his countenance, was told to place the dish on the table and leave the room.

When he was gone, Miss Rottenmeier explained to Heidi with many signs how to help herself at table. She also told her never to speak to Sebastian unless it was important. After that the child was told how to accost the servants and the governess. When the question came up of how to call Clara, the older girl said, "Of course you shall call me Clara."

A great many rules followed now about behavior at all times, about the shutting of doors and about going to bed, and a hundred other things. Poor Heidi's eyes were closing, for she had risen at five that morning, and leaning against her chair she fell asleep. When Miss Rottenmeier had finished instructions, she said: "I hope you will remember everything, Adelheid. Did you understand me?"

"Heidi went to sleep a long time ago," said Clara, highly amused.

"It is atrocious what I have to bear with this child," exclaimed Miss Rottenmeier, ringing the bell with all her might. When the two servants arrived, they were hardly able to rouse Heidi enough to show her to her bed-room.

CHAPTER 7

Miss Rottenmeier Has an
Uncomfortable Day

When Heidi opened her eyes next morning, she did not know where she was. She found herself on a high white bed in a spacious room. Looking around she observed long white curtains before the windows, several chairs, and a sofa covered with cretonne; in a corner she saw a wash-stand with many curious things standing on it.

Suddenly Heidi remembered all the happenings of the previous day. Jumping out of bed, she dressed in a great hurry. She was eager to look at the sky and the ground below, as she had always done at home. What was her disappointment when she found that the windows were too high for her to see anything except the walls and windows opposite. Trying to open them, she turned from one to the other, but in vain. The poor child felt like a little bird that is placed in a glittering cage for the first time. At last she had to resign herself, and sat down on a low stool, thinking of the melting snow on the slopes and the first flowers of spring that she had hailed with such delight.

Suddenly Tinette opened the door and said curtly: "Breakfast's ready."

Heidi did not take this for a summons, for the maid's

face was scornful and forbidding. She was waiting patiently for what would happen next, when Miss Rottenmeier burst into the room, saying: "What is the matter, Adelheid? Didn't you understand? Come to breakfast!"

Heidi immediately followed the lady into the dining-room, where Clara greeted her with a smile. She looked much happier than usual, for she expected new things to happen that day. When breakfast had passed without disturbance, the two children were allowed to go into the library together and were soon left alone.

"How can I see down to the ground?" Heidi asked.

"Open a window and peep out," replied Clara, amused at the question.

"But it is impossible to open them," Heidi said, sadly.

"Oh no. You can't do it and I can't help you, either, but if you ask Sebastian he'll do it for you."

Heidi was relieved. The poor child had felt like a prisoner in her room. Clara now asked Heidi what her home had been like, and Heidi told her gladly about her life in the hut.

The tutor had arrived in the meantime, but he was not asked to go to the study as usual. Miss Rottenmeier was very much excited about Heidi's coming and all the complications that arose therefrom. She was really responsible for it, having arranged everything herself. She presented the unfortunate case before the teacher, for she wanted him to help her to get rid of the child. Mr. Candidate, however, was always careful of his judgments, and not afraid of teaching beginners.

When the lady saw that he would not side with her, she let him enter the study alone, for the A,B,C held great horrors for her. While she considered many problems, a frightful noise as of something falling was heard in the adjoining room, followed by a cry to Sebastian for help. Running in, she beheld a pile of books and papers on the floor, with the table-cover on top. A black stream of ink flowed across the length of the room. Heidi had disappeared.

"There," Miss Rottenmeier exclaimed, wringing her hands. "Everything drenched with ink. Did such a thing ever happen before? This child brings nothing but misfortunes on us."

The teacher was standing up, looking at the devastation, but Clara was highly entertained by these events, and said: "Heidi has not done it on purpose and must not be punished. In her hurry to get away she caught on the table-cover and pulled it down. I think she must never have seen a coach in all her life, for when she heard a carriage rumbling by, she rushed out like mad."

"Didn't I tell you, Mr. Candidate, that she has no idea whatever about behavior? She does not even know that she has to sit quiet at her lessons. But where has she gone? What would Mr. Sesemann say if she should run away?"

When Miss Rottenmeier went down-stairs to look for the child, she saw her standing at the open door, looking down the street.

"What are you doing here? How can you run away like that?" scolded Miss Rottenmeier.

"I heard the fir-trees rustle, but I can't see them and do not hear them any more," replied Heidi, looking in great perplexity down the street. The noise of the passing carriage had reminded her of the roaring of the south-wind on the Alp.

"Fir-trees? What nonsense! We are not in a wood. Come with me now to see what you have done." When Heidi saw the devastation that she had caused, she was greatly surprised, for she had not noticed it in her hurry.

"This must never happen again," said the lady sternly. "You must sit quiet at your lessons; if you get up again I shall tie you to your chair. Do you hear me?"

Heidi understood, and gave a promise to sit quietly during her lessons from that time on. After the servants had straightened the room, it was late, and there was no more time for studies. Nobody had time to yawn that morning.

In the afternoon, while Clara was resting, Heidi was left to herself. She planted herself in the hall and waited for the butler to come up-stairs with the silver things. When he reached the head of the stairs, she said to him: "I want to ask you something." She saw that the butler seemed angry, so she reassured him by saying that she did not mean any harm.

"All right, Miss, what is it?"

"My name is not Miss, why don't you call me Heidi?"

"Miss Rottenmeier told me to call you Miss."

"Did she? Well then, it must be so. I have three names already," sighed the child.

"What can I do for you?" asked Sebastian now.

"Can you open a window for me?"

"Certainly," he replied.

Sebastian got a stool for Heidi, for the window-sill was too high for her to see over. In great disappointment, Heidi turned her head away.

"I don't see anything but a street of stone. Is it the same way on the other side of the house?"

"Yes."

"Where do you go to look far down on everything?"

"On a church-tower. Do you see that one over there with the golden dome? From there you can overlook everything."

Heidi immediately stepped down from the stool and ran down-stairs. Opening the door, she found herself in the street, but she could not see the tower any more. She wandered on from street to street, not daring to accost any of the busy people. Passing a corner, she saw a boy who had a barrel-organ on his back and a curious animal on his arm. Heidi ran to him and asked: "Where is the tower with the golden dome?"

"Don't know," was the reply.

"Who can tell me?"

"Don't know."

"Can you show me another church with a tower?"

"Of course I can."

"Then come and show me."

"What are you going to give me for it?" said the boy, holding out his hand. Heidi had nothing in her pocket but a little flower-picture. Clara had only given it to her this morning, so she was loath to part with it. The temptation to look far down into the valley was too great for her, though, and she offered him the gift. The boy shook his head, to Heidi's satisfaction.

"What else do you want?"

"Money."

"I have none, but Clara has some. How much must I give you?"

"Twenty pennies."

"All right, but come."

While they were wandering down the street, Heidi found out what a barrel-organ was, for she had never seen one. When they arrived before an old church with a tower, Heidi was puzzled what to do next, but having discovered a bell, she pulled it with all her might. The boy agreed to wait for Heidi and show her the way home if she gave him a double fee.

The lock creaked now from inside, and an old man opened the door. In an angry voice, he said: "How do you dare to ring for me? Can't you see that it is only for those who want to see the tower?"

"But I do," said Heidi.

"What do you want to see? Did anybody send you?" asked the man.

"No; but I want to look down from up there."

"Get home and don't try it again." With that the tower-keeper was going to shut the door, but Heidi held his coat-tails and pleaded with him to let her come. The tower-keeper looked at the child's eyes, which were nearly full of tears.

"All right, come along, if you care so much," he said, taking her by the hand. The two climbed up now many, many steps, which got narrower all the time. When they had arrived on top, the old man lifted Heidi up to the open window.

Heidi saw nothing but a sea of chimneys, roofs and towers, and her heart sank. "Oh, dear, it's different from the way I thought it would be," she said.

"There! what could such a little girl know about a view? We'll go down now and you must promise never to ring at my tower any more."

On their way they passed an attic, where a large grey cat guarded her new family in a basket. This cat caught half-a-dozen mice every day for herself, for the old tower was full of rats and mice. Heidi gazed at her in surprise, and was delighted when the old man opened the basket.

"What charming kittens, what cunning little creatures!" she exclaimed in her delight, when she saw them crawling about, jumping and tumbling.

"Would you like to have one?" the old man asked.

"For me? to keep?" Heidi asked, for she could not believe her ears.

"Yes, of course. You can have several if you have room for them," the old man said, glad to find a good home for the kittens.

How happy Heidi was! Of course there was enough room in the huge house, and Clara would be delighted when she saw the cunning things.

"How can I take them with me?" the child asked, after she had tried in vain to catch one.

"I can bring them to your house, if you tell me where you live," said Heidi's new friend, while he caressed the old cat, who had lived with him many years.

"Bring them to Mr. Sesemann's house; there is a golden dog on the door, with a ring in his mouth."

The old man had lived in the tower a long time and knew everybody; Sebastian also was a special friend of his.

"I know," he said. "But to whom shall I send them? Do you belong to Mr. Sesemann?"

"No. Please send them to Clara; she will like them, I am sure."

Heidi could hardly tear herself away from the pretty things, so the old man put one kitten in each of her pockets to console her. After that she went away.

The boy was waiting patiently for her, and when she had taken leave of the tower-keeper, she asked the boy: "Do you know where Mr. Sesemann's house is?"

"No," was the reply.

She described it as well as she could, till the boy remembered it. Off they started, and soon Heidi found herself pulling the door-bell. When Sebastian arrived he said: "Hurry up." Heidi went in, and the boy was left outside, for Sebastian had not even seen him.

"Come up quickly, little Miss," he urged. "They are all waiting for you in the dining-room. Miss Rottenmeier looks like a loaded cannon. How could you run away like that?"

Heidi sat down quietly on her chair. Nobody said a word, and there was an uncomfortable silence. At last Miss Rottenmeier began with a severe and solemn voice: "I shall speak with you later, Adelheid. How can you leave the house without a word? Your behavior was very remiss. The idea of walking about till so late!"

"Meow!" was the reply.

"I didn't," Heidi began—"Meow!"

Sebastian nearly flung the dish on the table, and disappeared.

"This is enough," Miss Rottenmeier tried to say, but her voice was hoarse with fury. "Get up and leave the room."

Heidi got up. She began again. "I made—" "Meow! meow! meow!—"

"Heidi," said Clara now, "why do you always say 'meow' again, if you see that Miss Rottenmeier is angry?"

"I am not doing it, it's the kittens," she explained.

"What? Cats? Kittens?" screamed the housekeeper. "Sebastian, Tinette, take the horrible things away!" With that she ran into the study, locking herself in, for she feared kittens beyond anything on earth. When Sebastian had finished his laugh, he came into the room. He had foreseen the excitement, having caught sight of the kittens when Heidi came in. The scene was a very peaceful one now; Clara held the little kittens in her lap, and Heidi was kneeling beside her. They both played happily with the two graceful creatures. The butler promised to look after the new-comers and prepared a bed for them in a basket.

A long time afterwards, when it was time to go to bed, Miss Rottenmeier cautiously opened the door. "Are they away?" she asked. "Yes," replied the butler, quickly seizing the kittens and taking them away.

The lecture that Miss Rottenmeier was going to give Heidi was postponed to the following day, for the lady was too much exhausted after her fright. They all went quietly to bed, and the children were happy in the thought that their kittens had a comfortable bed.

CHAPTER 8

Great Disturbances in the Sesemann House

A short time after the tutor had arrived next morning, the door-bell rang so violently that Sebastian thought it must be Mr. Sesemann himself. What was his surprise when a dirty street-boy, with a barrel-organ on his back, stood before him!

"What do you mean by pulling the bell like that?" the butler said.

"I want to see Clara."

"Can't you at least say 'Miss Clara', you ragged urchin?" said Sebastian harshly.

"She owes me forty pennies," said the boy.

"You are crazy! How do you know Miss Clara lives here?"

"I showed her the way yesterday and she promised to give me forty pennies."

"What nonsense! Miss Clara never goes out. You had better take yourself off, before I send you!"

The boy, however, did not even budge, and said: "I saw her. She has curly hair, black eyes and talks in a funny way."

"Oh," Sebastian chuckled to himself, "that was the little Miss."

Pulling the boy into the house, he said: "All right, you can follow me. Wait at the door till I call you, and then you can play something for Miss Clara."

Knocking at the study-door, Sebastian said, when he had entered: "A boy is here who wants to see Miss Clara."

Clara, delighted at his interruption, said: "Can't he come right up, Mr. Candidate?"

But the boy was already inside, and started to play. Miss Rottenmeier was in the adjoining room when she heard the sounds. Where did they come from? Hurrying into the study, she saw the street-boy playing to the eager children.

"Stop! stop!" she called, but in vain, for the music drowned her voice. Suddenly she made a big jump, for there, between her feet, crawled a black turtle. Only when she shrieked for Sebastian could her voice be heard. The butler came straight in, for he had seen everything behind the door, and a great scene it had been! Glued to a chair in her fright, Miss Rottenmeier called: "Send the boy away! Take them away!"

Sebastian obediently pulled the boy after him; then he said: "Here are forty pennies from Miss Clara and forty more for playing. It was well done, my boy."

With that he closed the door behind him. Miss Rottenmeier found it wiser now to stay in the study to prevent further disturbances. Suddenly there was another knock at the door. Sebastian appeared with a large basket, which had been brought for Clara.

"We had better have our lesson before we inspect it," said Miss Rottenmeier. But Clara, turning to the tutor, asked: "Oh, please, Mr. Candidate, can't we just peep in, to see what it is?"

"I am afraid that you will think of nothing else," the teacher began. Just then something in the basket, which had been only lightly fastened, moved, and one, two, three and still more little kittens jumped out, scampering around the room with the utmost speed. They bounded over the tutor's boots and bit his trousers; they climbed up on Miss Rottenmeier's dress and crawled around her feet. Mewing and running, they caused a frightful confusion. Clara called out in delight: "Oh, look at the cunning creatures; look how they jump! Heidi, look at that one, and oh, see the one over there?"

Heidi followed them about, while the teacher shook them off. When the housekeeper had collected her wits after the great fright, she called for the servants. They soon arrived and stored the little kittens safely in the new bed.

No time had been found for yawning that day, either!

When Miss Rottenmeier, who had found out the culprit, was alone with the children in the evening, she began severely:

"Adelheid, there is only one punishment for you. I am going to send you to the cellar, to think over your dreadful misdeeds, in company with the rats."

A cellar held no terrors for Heidi, for in her grandfather's cellar fresh milk and the good cheese had been kept, and no rats had lodged there.

But Clara shrieked: "Oh, Miss Rottenmeier, you must wait till Papa comes home, and then he can punish Heidi."

The lady unwillingly replied: "All right, Clara, but I shall also speak a few words to Mr. Sesemann." With those words she left the room. Since the child's arrival everything had been upset, and the lady often felt discouraged, though nothing remarkable happened for a few days.

Clara, on the contrary, enjoyed her companion's society, for she always did funny things. In her lesson she could never get her letters straight. They meant absolutely nothing to her, except that they would remind her of goats and eagles. The girls always spent their evenings together, and Heidi would entertain her friend with tales of her former life, till her longing grew so great that she added: "I have to go home now. I must go tomorrow."

Clara's soothing words and the prospect of more rolls for the grandmother kept the child. Every day after dinner she was left alone in her room for some hours. Thinking of the green fields at home, of the sparkling flowers on the mountains, she would sit in a corner till her desire for all those things became too great to bear. Her aunt had clearly told her that she might return, if she wished to do so, so one day she resolved to leave for the Alm-hut. In a great hurry she packed the bread in the red shawl, and putting on her old straw hat, started off. The poor child did not get very far. At the door she encountered Miss Rottenmeier, who stared at Heidi in mute surprise.

"What are you up to?" she exploded. "Haven't I forbidden you to run away? You look like a vagabond!"

"I was only going home," whispered the frightened child.

"What, you want to run away from this house? What would Mr. Sesemann say? What is it that does not suit you here? Don't you get better treatment than you deserve? Have you ever before had such food, service and such a room? Answer!"

"No," was the reply.

"Don't I know that?" the furious lady proceeded. "What a thankless child you are, just idle and good-for-nothing!"

But Heidi could not bear it any longer. She loudly wailed: "Oh, I want to go home. What will poor Snowhopper do without me? Grandmother is waiting for me every day. Poor Thistlefinch gets blows if Peter gets no cheese, and I must see the sun again when he says good-night to the mountains. How the eagle would screech if he saw all the people here in Frankfurt!"

"For mercy's sake, the child is crazy!" exclaimed Miss Rottenmeier, running up the stairs. In her hurry she had bumped into Sebastian, who was just then coming down.

"Bring the unlucky child up!" she called to him, rubbing her head.

"All right, many thanks," answered the butler, rubbing his head, too, for he had encountered something far harder than she had.

When the butler came down, he saw Heidi standing near the door with flaming eyes, trembling all over. Cheerfully he asked: "What has happened, little one? Do not take it to heart, and cheer up. She nearly made a hole in my head just now, but we must not get discouraged. Oh, no! – Come, up with you; she said so!"

Heidi walked up-stairs very slowly. Seeing her so changed, Sebastian said:

"Don't give in! Don't be so sad! You have been so courageous till now; I have never heard you cry yet. Come up now, and when the lady's away we'll go and look at the kittens. They are running round like wild!"

Nodding cheerlessly, the child disappeared in her room.

That night at supper Miss Rottenmeier watched Heidi constantly, but nothing happened. The child sat as quiet as a mouse, hardly touching her food, except the little roll.

Talking with the tutor next morning, Miss Rottenmeier told him her fears about Heidi's mind. But the teacher had more serious troubles still, for Heidi had not even learned her A,B,C in all this time.

Heidi was sorely in need of some clothes, so Clara had given her some. Miss Rottenmeier was just busy arranging the child's wardrobe, when she suddenly returned.

"Adelheid," she said contemptuously, "what do I find? A big pile of bread in your wardrobe! I never heard the like. Yes, Clara, it is true." Then, calling Tinette, she ordered her to take away the bread and the old straw hat she had found.

"No, don't! I must keep my hat! The bread is for grandmother," cried Heidi in despair.

"You stay here, while we take the rubbish away," said the lady sternly.

Heidi threw herself down now on Clara's chair and sobbed as if her heart would break.

"Now I can't bring grandmother any rolls! Oh, they were for grandmother!" she lamented.

"Heidi, don't cry any more," Clara begged. "Listen! When you go home some day, I am going to give you as many rolls as you had, and more. They will be much softer and better than those stale ones you have kept. Those were not fit to eat, Heidi. Stop now, please, and don't cry any more!"

Only after a long, long time did Heidi become quiet. When she had heard Clara's promise, she cried: "Are you really going to give me as many as I had?"

At supper, Heidi's eyes were swollen and it was still hard for her to keep from crying. Sebastian made strange signs to her that she did not understand. What did he mean?

Later, though, when she climbed into her high bed, she found her old beloved straw hat hidden under her cover. So Sebastian had saved it for her and had tried to tell her! She crushed it for joy, and wrapping it in a handkerchief, she hid it in the furthest corner of her wardrobe.

CHAPTER 9

The Master of the House Hears of Strange Doings

A few days afterwards there was great excitement in the Sesemann residence, for the master of the house had just arrived. The servants were taking upstairs one load after another, for Mr. Sesemann always brought many lovely things home with him.

When he entered his daughter's room, Heidi shyly retreated into a corner. He greeted Clara affectionately, and she was equally delighted to see him, for she loved her father dearly. Then he called to Heidi: "Oh, there is our little Swiss girl. Come and give me your hand! That's right. Are you good friends, my girls, tell me now? You don't fight together, what?"

"Oh, no, Clara is always kind to me," Heidi replied.

"Heidi has never even tried to fight, Papa," Clara quickly remarked.

"That's good, I like to hear that," said the father rising. "I must get my dinner now, for I am hungry. I shall come back soon and show you what I have brought home with me."

In the dining-room he found Miss Rottenmeier surveying the table with a most tragic face. "You do not look very happy at my arrival, Miss Rottenmeier. What is the matter? Clara seems well enough," he said to her.

"Oh, Mr. Sesemann, we have been terribly disappointed," said the lady.

"How do you mean?" asked Mr. Sesemann, calmly sipping his wine.

"We had decided, as you know, to have a companion for Clara. Knowing as I did that you would wish me to get a noble, pure child, I thought of this Swiss child, hoping she would go through life like a breath of pure air, hardly touching the earth."

"I think that even Swiss children are made to touch the earth, otherwise they would have to have wings."

"I think you understand what I mean. I have been terribly disappointed, for this child has brought the most frightful animals into the house. Mr. Candidate can tell you!"

"The child does not look very terrible. But what do you mean?"

"I cannot explain it, because she does not seem in her right mind at times."

Mr. Sesemann was getting worried at last, when the tutor entered.

"Oh, Mr. Candidate, I hope you will explain. Please take a cup of coffee with me and tell me about my daughter's companion. Make it short, if you please!"

But this was impossible for Mr. Candidate, who had to greet Mr. Sesemann first. Then he began to reassure his host about the child, pointing out to him that her education had been neglected till then, and so on. But poor Mr. Sesemann, unfortunately, did not get his answer, and had to listen to very long-winded explanations of the child's character. At last Mr. Sesemann got up, saying: "Excuse me, Mr. Candidate, but I must go over to Clara now."

He found the children in the study. Turning to Heidi, who had risen at his approach, he said: "Come, little one, get me – get me a glass of water."

"Fresh water?"

"Of course, fresh water," he replied. When Heidi had gone, he sat down near Clara, holding her hand. "Tell me, little Clara," he asked, "please tell me clearly what animals Heidi has brought into the house; is she really not right in her mind?"

Clara now began to relate to her father all the incidents with the kittens and the turtle, and explained Heidi's speeches that had so frightened the lady. Mr. Sesemann laughed heartily and asked Clara if she wished Heidi to remain.

"Of course, Papa. Since she is here, something amusing happens every day; it used to be so dull, but now Heidi keeps me company."

"Very good, very good, Clara; Oh! Here is your friend back again. Did you get nice fresh water?" asked Mr. Sesemann.

Heidi handed him the glass and said: "Yes, fresh from the fountain."

"You did not go to the fountain yourself, Heidi?" said Clara.

"Certainly, but I had to get it from far, there were so many people at the first and at the second fountain. I had to go down another street and there I got it. A gentleman with white hair sends his regards to you, Mr. Sesemann."

Clara's father laughed and asked: "Who was the gentleman?"

"When he passed by the fountain and saw me there with a glass, he stood still and said: 'Please give me to drink, for you have a glass; to whom are you bringing the water?' Then I said: 'I am bringing it to Mr. Sesemann.' When he heard that he laughed very loud and gave me his regards for you, with the wish that you would enjoy your drink."

"I wonder who it was? What did the gentleman look like?"

"He has a friendly laugh and wears a gold pendant with a red stone on his thick gold chain; there is a horsehead on his cane."

"Oh, that was the doctor—" "That was my old doctor," exclaimed father and daughter at the same time.

In the evening, Mr. Sesemann told Miss Rottenmeier that Heidi was going to remain, for the children were very fond of each other and he found Heidi normal and very sweet. "I want the child to be treated kindly," Mr. Sesemann added decidedly. "Her peculiarities must not be punished. My mother is coming very soon to stay here, and she will help you to manage the child, for there is nobody in this world that my mother could not get along with, as you know, Miss Rottenmeier."

"Of course, I know that, Mr. Sesemann," replied the lady, but she was not very much pleased at the prospect.

Mr. Sesemann only stayed two weeks, for his business called him back to Paris. He consoled his daughter by telling her that his mother was coming in a very few days. Mr. Sesemann had hardly left, when the grandmother's visit was announced for the following day.

Clara was looking forward to this visit, and told Heidi so much about her dear grandmama that Heidi also began to call her by that name, to Miss Rottenmeier's disapproval, who thought that the child was not entitled to this intimacy.

CHAPTER 10

A Grandmama

The following evening great expectation reigned in the house. Tinette had put on a new cap, Sebastian was placing footstools in front of nearly every armchair, and Miss Rottenmeier walked with great dignity about the house, inspecting everything.

When the carriage at last drove up, the servants flew downstairs, followed by Miss Rottenmeier in more measured step. Heidi had been sent to her room to await further orders, but it was not long before Tinette opened the door and said brusquely: "Go into the study!"

The grandmama, with her kind and loving way, immediately befriended the child and made her feel as if she had known her always. To the housekeeper's great mortification, she called the child Heidi, remarking to Miss Rottenmeier: "If somebody's name is Heidi, I call her so."

The housekeeper soon found that she had to respect the grandmother's ways and opinions. Mrs. Sesemann always knew what was going on in the house the minute she entered it. On the following afternoon Clara was resting and the old lady had shut her eyes for five minutes, when she got up again and went into the dining-room. With a suspicion that the housekeeper was probably asleep, she went to this lady's room, knocking loudly on the door. After a while somebody stirred inside, and with a bewildered face Miss Rottenmeier appeared, staring at the unexpected visitor.

"Rottenmeier, where is the child? How does she pass her time? I want to know," said Mrs. Sesemann.

"She just sits in her room, not moving a finger; she has not the slightest desire to do something useful, and that is why she thinks of such absurd things that one can hardly mention them in polite society."

"I should do exactly the same thing, if I were left alone like that. Please bring her to my room now, I want to show her some pretty books I have brought with me."

"That is just the trouble. What should she do with books? In all this time she has not even learned the A,B,C for it is impossible to instil any knowledge into this being. If Mr. Candidate was not as patient as an angel, he would have given up teaching her long ago."

"How strange! The child does not look to me like one who cannot learn the A,B,C," said Mrs. Sesemann. "Please fetch her now; we can look at the pictures anyway."

The housekeeper was going to say more, but the old lady had turned already and gone to her room. She was thinking over what she had heard about Heidi, making up her mind to look into the matter.

Heidi had come and was looking with wondering eyes at the splendid pictures in the large books, that Grandmama was showing her. Suddenly she screamed aloud, for there on the picture she saw a peaceful flock grazing on a green pasture. In the middle a shepherd was standing, leaning on his crook. The setting sun was shedding a golden light over everything. With glowing eyes Heidi devoured the scene; but suddenly she began to sob violently.

The grandmama took her little hand in hers and said in the most soothing voice: "Come, child, you must not cry. Did this remind you of something? Now stop, and I'll tell you the story to-night. There are lovely stories in this book, that people can read and tell. Dry your tears now, darling, I must ask you something. Stand up now and look at me! Now we are merry again!"

Heidi did not stop at once, but the kind lady gave her ample time to compose herself, saying from time to time: "Now it's all over. Now we'll be merry again."

When the child was quiet at last, she said: "Tell me now how your lessons are going. What have you learnt, child, tell me?"

"Nothing," Heidi sighed; "but I knew that I never could learn it."

"What is it that you can't learn?"

"I can't learn to read; it is too hard."

"What next? Who gave you this information?"

"Peter told me, and he tried over and over again, but he could not do it, for it is too hard."

"Well, what kind of boy is he? Heidi, you must not believe what Peter tells you, but try for yourself. I am sure you had your thoughts elsewhere when Mr. Candidate showed you the letters."

"It's no use," Heidi said with such a tone as if she was resigned to her fate.

"I am going to tell you something, Heidi," said the kind lady now. "You have not learnt to read because you have believed what Peter said. You shall believe me now, and I prophesy that you will learn it in a very short time, as a great many other children do that are like you and not like Peter. When you can read, I am going to give you this book. You have seen the shepherd on the green pasture, and then you'll be able to find out all the strange things that happen to him. Yes, you can hear the whole story, and what he does with his sheep and his goats. You would like to know, wouldn't you, Heidi?"

Heidi had listened attentively, and said now with sparkling eyes: "If I could only read already!"

"It won't be long, I can see that. Come now and let us go to Clara." With that they both went over to the study.

Since the day of Heidi's attempted flight a great change had come over the child. She had realized that it would hurt her kind friends if she tried to go home again. She knew now that she could not leave, as her Aunt Deta had promised, for they all, especially Clara and her father and the old lady, would think her ungrateful. But the burden grew heavier in her heart and she lost her appetite, and got paler and paler. She could not get to sleep at night from longing to see the mountains with the flowers and the sunshine, and only in her dreams she would be happy. When she woke up in the morning, she always found herself on her high white bed, far away from home. Burying her head in her pillow, she would often weep a long, long time.

Mrs. Sesemann had noticed the child's unhappiness, but let a few days pass by, hoping for a change. But the change never came, and often Heidi's eyes were red even in the early morning. So she called the child to her room one day and said, with great sympathy in her voice: "Tell me, Heidi, what is the matter with you? What is making you so sad?"

But as Heidi did not want to appear thankless, she replied sadly: "I can't tell you."

"No? Can't you tell Clara perhaps?"

"Oh, no, I can't tell anyone," Heidi said, looking so unhappy that the old lady's heart was filled with pity.

"I tell you something, little girl," she continued. "If you have a sorrow that you cannot tell to anyone, you can go to Our Father in Heaven. You can tell Him everything that troubles you, and if we ask Him He can help us and take our suffering away. Do you understand me, child? Don't you pray every night? Don't you thank Him for all His gifts and ask Him to protect you from evil?"

"Oh no, I never do that," replied the child.

"Have you never prayed, Heidi? Do you know what I mean?"

"I only prayed with my first grandmother, but it is so long ago, that I have forgotten."

"See, Heidi, I understand now why you are so unhappy. We all need somebody to help us, and just think how wonderful it is, to be able to go to the Lord, when something distresses us and causes us pain. We can tell Him everything and ask Him to comfort us, when nobody else can do it. He can give us happiness and joy."

Heidi was gladdened by these tidings, and asked: "Can we tell Him everything, everything?"

"Yes, Heidi, everything."

The child, withdrawing her hand from the grandmama, said hurriedly, "Can I go now?"

"Yes, of course," was the reply, and with this Heidi ran to her room. Sitting down on a stool she folded her hands and poured out her heart to God, imploring Him to help her and let her go home to her grandfather.

About a week later, Mr. Candidate asked to see Mrs. Sesemann, to tell her of something unusual that had occurred. Being called to the lady's room, he began: "Mrs. Sesemann, something has happened that I never expected," and with many more words the happy grandmama was told that Heidi had suddenly learned to read with the utmost correctness, most rare with beginners.

"Many strange things happen in this world," Mrs. Sesemann remarked, while they went over to the study to witness Heidi's new accomplishment. Heidi was sitting close to Clara, reading her a story; she seemed amazed at the strange, new world that had opened up before her. At supper Heidi found the large book with the beautiful pictures on her plate, and looking doubtfully at grandmama, she saw the old lady nod. "Now it belongs to you, Heidi," she said.

"Forever? Also when I am going home?" Heidi inquired, confused with joy.

"Certainly, forever!" the grandmama assured her. "Tomorrow we shall begin to read it."

"But Heidi, you must not go home; no, not for many years," Clara exclaimed, "especially when grandmama goes away. You must stay with me."

Heidi still looked at her book before going to bed that night, and this book became her dearest treasure. She would look at the beautiful pictures and read all the stories aloud to Clara. Grandmama would quietly listen and explain something here and there, making it more beautiful than before. Heidi loved the pictures with the shepherd best of all; they told the story of the prodigal son, and the child would read and re-read it till she nearly knew it all by heart. Since Heidi had learned to read and possessed the book, the days seemed to fly, and the time had come near that the grandmama had fixed for her departure.

CHAPTER 11

Heidi Gains in Some Respects and
Loses in Others

The grandmama sent for Heidi every day after dinner, while
Clara was resting and Miss Rottenmeier disappeared into her
room. She talked to Heidi and amused her in various ways,
showing her how to make clothes for pretty little dolls that
she had brought. Unconsciously Heidi had learned to sew,
and made now the sweetest dresses and coats for the little
people out of lovely materials the grandmama would give her.
Often Heidi would read to the old lady, for the oftener she
read over the stories the dearer they became to her. The child
lived everything through with the people in the tales and was
always happy to be with them again. But she never looked
really cheerful and her eyes never sparkled merrily as before.

In the last week of Mrs. Sesemann's stay, Heidi was
called again to the old lady's room. The child entered with
her beloved book under her arm. Mrs. Sesemann drew Heidi
close to her, and laying the book aside, she said: "Come, child,
and tell me why you are so sad. Do you still have the same
sorrow?"

"Yes," Heidi replied.

"Did you confide it to Our Lord?"

"Yes."

"Do you pray to Him every day that He may make you happy again and take your affliction away?"

"Oh no, I don't pray any more."

"What do I hear, Heidi? Why don't you pray?"

"It does not help, for God has not listened. I don't wonder," she added, "for if all the people in Frankfurt pray every night, He cannot listen to them all. I am sure He has not heard me."

"Really? Why are you so sure?"

"Because I have prayed for the same thing many, many weeks and God has not done what I have asked Him to."

"That is not the way, Heidi. You see, God in heaven is a good Father to all of us, who knows what we need better than we do. When something we ask for is not very good for us, He gives us something much better, if we confide in Him and do not lose confidence in His love. I am sure what you asked for was not very good for you just now; He has heard you, for He can hear the prayers of all the people in the world at the same time, because He is God Almighty and not a mortal like us. He heard your prayers and said to Himself: 'Yes, Heidi shall get what she is praying for in time.' Now, while God was looking down on you to hear your prayers, you lost confidence and went away from Him. If God does not hear your prayers any more, He will forget you also and let you go. Don't you want to go back to Him, Heidi, and ask His forgiveness? Pray to Him every day, and hope in Him, that He may bring cheer and happiness to you."

Heidi had listened attentively; she had unbounded confidence in the old lady, whose words had made a deep impression on her. Full of repentance, she said: "I shall go at once and ask Our Father to pardon me. I shall never forget Him any more!"

"That's right, Heidi; I am sure He will help you in time, if you only trust in Him," the grandmother consoled her. Heidi went to her room now and prayed earnestly to God that He would forgive her and fulfill her wish.

The day of departure had come, but Mrs. Sesemann arranged everything in such a way that the children hardly realized she was actually going. Still everything was empty and quiet when she had gone, and the children hardly knew how to pass their time.

Next day, Heidi came to Clara in the afternoon and said: "Can I always, always read to you now, Clara?"

Clara assented, and Heidi began. But she did not get very far, for the story she was reading told of a grandmother's death. Suddenly she cried aloud: "Oh, now grandmother is dead!" and wept in the most pitiful fashion. Whatever Heidi read always seemed real to her, and now she thought it was her own grandmother at home. Louder and louder she sobbed: "Now poor grandmother is dead and I can never see her any more; and she never got one single roll!"

Clara attempted to explain the mistake, but Heidi was too much upset. She pictured to herself how terrible it would be if her dear old grandfather would die too while she was far away. How quiet and empty it would be in the hut, and how lonely she would be!

Miss Rottenmeier had overheard the scene, and approaching the sobbing child she said impatiently: "Adelheid, now you have screamed enough. If I hear you again giving way to yourself in such a noisy fashion, I shall take your book away forever!"

Heidi turned pale at that, for the book was her greatest treasure. Quickly drying her tears, she choked down her sobs. After that Heidi never cried again; often she could hardly repress her sobs and was obliged to make the strangest faces to keep herself from crying out. Clara often looked at her, full of surprise, but Miss Rottenmeier did not notice them and found no occasion to carry out her threat. However, the poor child got more cheerless every day, and looked so thin and pale that Sebastian became worried. He tried to encourage her at table to help herself to all the good dishes, but listlessly she would let them pass and hardly touch them. In the evening she would cry quietly, her heart bursting with longing to go home.

Thus the time passed by. Heidi never knew if it was summer or winter, for the walls opposite never changed. They drove out very seldom, for Clara was only able to go a short distance. They never saw anything else than streets, houses and busy people; no grass, no fir-trees and no mountains. Heidi struggled constantly against her sorrow, but in vain. Autumn and winter had passed, and Heidi knew that the time was coming when Peter would go up the Alp with his goats, where the flowers were glistening in the sunshine and the mountains were all afire. She would sit down in a corner of her room and put both hands before her eyes, not to see the glaring sunshine on the opposite wall. There she would remain, eating her heart away with longing, till Clara would call for her to come.

CHAPTER 12

The Sesemann House is Haunted

For several days Miss Rottenmeier had been wandering silently about the house. When she went from room to room or along the corridors, she would often glance back as if she were afraid that somebody was following her. If she had to go to the upper floor, where the gorgeous guest-rooms were, or to the lower story, where the big ball-room was situated, she always told Tinette to come with her. The strange thing was, that none of the servants dared to go anywhere alone and always found an excuse to ask each other's company, which requests were always granted. The cook, who had been in the house for many years, would often shake her head and mutter: "That I should live to see this!"

Something strange and weird was happening in the house. Every morning, when the servants came down-stairs, they found the front door wide open. At first everybody had thought that the house must have been robbed, but nothing was missing. Every morning it was the same, despite the double locks that were put on the door. At last John and Sebastian, taking courage, prepared themselves to watch through a night to see who was the ghost. Armed and provided with some strengthening liquor, they repaired to a room down-stairs. First they talked, but soon, getting sleepy, they leaned silently back in their chairs. When the clock from the old church tower struck one, Sebastian awoke and roused his comrade, which was no easy matter. At last, however, John was wide awake, and together they went out into the hall. The same moment a strong wind put out the light that John held in his hand. Rushing back, he nearly upset Sebastian, who stood behind him, and pulling the butler back into the room, he locked the door in furious haste. When the light was lit again, Sebastian noticed that John was deadly pale and trembling like an aspen leaf. Sebastian, not having seen anything, asked anxiously: "What is the matter? What did you see?"

"The door was open and a white form was on the stairs; it went up and was gone in a moment," gasped John. Cold shivers ran down the butler's back. They sat without moving till the morning came, and then, shutting the door, they went upstairs to report to the housekeeper what they had seen. The lady, who was waiting eagerly, heard the tale and immediately sat down to write to Mr. Sesemann. She told him that fright had paralyzed her fingers and that terrible things were happening in the house. Then followed a tale of the appearance of the ghost. Mr. Sesemann replied that he could not leave his business, and advised Miss Rottenmeier to ask his mother to come to stay with them, for Mrs. Sesemann would easily despatch the ghost. Miss Rottenmeier was offended with the tone of the letter, which did not seem to take her account seriously. Mrs. Sesemann also replied that she could not come, so the housekeeper decided to tell the children all about it. Clara, at the uncanny tale, immediately exclaimed that she would not stay alone another moment and that she wished her father to come home. The housekeeper arranged to sleep with the frightened child, while Heidi, who did not know what ghosts were, was perfectly unmoved. Another letter was despatched to Mr. Sesemann, telling him that the excitement might have serious effects on his daughter's delicate constitution, and mentioning several misfortunes that might probably happen if he did not relieve the household from this terror.

This brought Mr. Sesemann. Going to his daughter's room after his arrival, he was overjoyed to see her as well as ever. Clara was also delighted to see her father.

"What new tricks has the ghost played on you, Miss Rottenmeier?" asked Mr. Sesemann with a twinkle in his eye.

"It is no joke, Mr. Sesemann," replied the lady seriously. "I am sure you will not laugh tomorrow. Those strange events indicate that something secret and horrible has happened in this house in days gone by."

"Is that so? this is new to me," remarked Mr. Sesemann. "But will you please not suspect my venerable ancestors? Please call Sebastian; I want to speak to him alone."

Mr. Sesemann knew that the two were not on good terms, so he said to the butler:

"Come here, Sebastian, and tell me honestly, if you have played the ghost for Miss Rottenmeier's pastime?"

"No, upon my word, master; you must not think that," replied Sebastian frankly. "I do not like it quite myself."

"Well, I'll show you and John what ghosts look like by day. You ought to be ashamed of yourselves, strong young men like you! Now go at once to my old friend, Dr. Classen, and tell him to come to me at nine o'clock to-night. Tell him that I came from Paris especially to consult him, and that I want him to sit up all night with me. Do you understand me, Sebastian?"

"Yes indeed! I shall do as you say, Mr. Sesemann." Mr. Sesemann then went up to Clara's room to quiet and comfort her.

Punctually at nine o'clock the doctor arrived. Though his hair was grey, his face was still fresh, and his eyes were lively and kind. When he saw his friend, he laughed aloud and said: "Well, well, you look pretty healthy for one who needs to be watched all night."

"Have patience, my old friend," replied Mr. Sesemann. "I am afraid the person we have to sit up for will look worse, but first we must catch him."

"What? Then somebody *is* sick in this house? What do you mean?"

"Far worse, doctor, far worse. A ghost is in the house. My house is haunted."

When the doctor laughed, Mr. Sesemann continued: "I call that sympathy; I wish my friend Miss Rottenmeier could hear you. She is convinced that an old Sesemann is wandering about, expiating some dreadful deed."

"How did she make his acquaintance?" asked the doctor, much amused.

Mr. Sesemann then explained the circumstances. He said that the matter was either a bad joke which an acquaintance of the servants was playing in his absence, or it was a gang of thieves, who, after intimidating the people, would surely rob his house by and by.

With these explanations they entered the room where the two servants had watched before. A few bottles of wine stood on the table and two bright candelabra shed a brilliant light. Two revolvers were ready for emergencies.

They left the door only partly open, for too much light might drive the ghost away. Then, sitting down comfortably, the two men passed their time by chatting, taking a sip now and then.

"The ghost seems to have spied us and probably won't come to-day," said the doctor.

"We must have patience. It is supposed to come at one," replied his friend.

So they talked till one o'clock. Everything was quiet, and not a sound came from the street. Suddenly the doctor raised his finger.

"Sh! Sesemann, don't you hear something?"

While they both listened, the bar was unfastened, the key was turned, and the door flew open. Mr. Sesemann seized his revolver.

"You are not afraid, I hope?" said the doctor, getting up.

"Better be cautious!" whispered Mr. Sesemann, seizing the candelabrum in the other hand. The doctor followed with his revolver and the light, and so they went out into the hall.

On the threshhold stood a motionless white form, lighted up by the moon.

"Who is there?" thundered the doctor, approaching the figure. It turned and uttered a low shriek. There stood Heidi, with bare feet and in her white night-gown, looking bewildered at the bright light and the weapons. She was shaking with fear, while the two men were looking at her in amazement.

"Sesemann, this seems to be your little water carrier," said the doctor.

"Child, what does this mean?" asked Mr. Sesemann. "What did you want to do? Why have you come down here?"

Pale from fright, Heidi said: "I do not know."

The doctor came forward now. "Sesemann, this case belongs to my field. Please go and sit down while I take her to bed."

Putting his revolver aside, he led the trembling child up-stairs.

"Don't be afraid; just be quiet! Everything is all right; don't be frightened."

When they had arrived in Heidi's room, the doctor put the little girl to bed, covering her up carefully. Drawing a chair near the couch, he waited till Heidi had calmed down and had stopped trembling. Then taking her hand in his, he said kindly: "Now everything is all right again. Tell me where you wanted to go?"

"I did not want to go anywhere," Heidi assured him; "I did not go myself, only I was there all of a sudden."

"Really! Tell me, what did you dream?"

"Oh, I have the same dream every night. I always think I am with my grandfather again and can hear the fir-trees roar. I always think how beautiful the stars must be, and then I open the door of the hut, and oh, it is so wonderful! But when I wake up I am always in Frankfurt." Heidi had to fight the sobs that were rising in her throat.

"Does your back or your head hurt you, child?"

"No, but I feel as if a big stone was pressing me here."

"As if you had eaten something that disagreed with you?"

"Oh no, but as if I wanted to cry hard."

"So, and then you cry out, don't you?"

"Oh no, I must never do that, for Miss Rottenmeier has forbidden it."

"Then you swallow it down? Yes? Do you like to be here?"

"Oh yes," was the faint, uncertain reply.

"Where did you live with your grandfather?"

"Up on the Alp."

"But wasn't it a little lonely there?"

"Oh no, it was so beautiful!" – But Heidi could say no more. The recollection, the excitement of the night and all the restrained sorrow overpowered the child. The tears rushed violently from her eyes and she broke out into loud sobs.

The doctor rose, and soothing her, said: "It won't hurt to cry; you'll go to sleep afterward, and when you wake up everything will come right." Then he left the room.

Joining his anxious friend down-stairs, he said: "Sesemann, the little girl is a sleep-walker, and has unconsciously scared your whole household. Besides, she is so home-sick that her little body has wasted away. We shall have to act quickly. The only remedy for her is to be restored to her native mountain air. This is my prescription, and she must go tomorrow."

"What, sick, a sleep-walker, and wasted away in my house! Nobody even suspected it! You think I should send this child back in this condition, when she has come in good health? No, doctor, ask everything but that. Take her in hand and prescribe for her, but let her get well before I send her back."

"Sesemann," the doctor replied seriously, "just think what you are doing. We cannot cure her with powders and pills. The child has not a strong constitution, and if you keep her here, she might never get well again. If you restore her to the bracing mountain air to which she is accustomed, she probably will get perfectly well again."

When Mr. Sesemann heard this he said, "If that is your advice, we must act at once; this is the only way then." With these words Mr. Sesemann took his friend's arm and walked about with him to talk the matter over. When everything was settled, the doctor took his leave, for the morning had already come and the sun was shining in through the door.

CHAPTER 13

Up the Alp on a Summer Evening

Mr. Sesemann, going upstairs in great agitation, knocked at the housekeeper's door. He asked her to hurry, for preparations for a journey had to be made. Miss Rottenmeier obeyed the summons with the greatest indignation, for it was only half-past four in the morning. She dressed in haste, though with great difficulty, being nervous and excited. All the other servants were summoned likewise, and one and all thought that the master of the house had been seized by the ghost and that he was ringing for help. When they had all come down with terrified looks, they were most surprised to see Mr. Sesemann fresh and cheerful, giving orders. John was sent to get the horses ready and Tinette was told to prepare Heidi for her departure while Sebastian was commissioned to fetch Heidi's aunt. Mr. Sesemann instructed the housekeeper to pack a trunk in all haste for Heidi.

Miss Rottenmeier experienced an extreme disappointment, for she had hoped for an explanation of the great mystery. But Mr. Sesemann, evidently not in the mood to converse further, went to his daughter's room. Clara had been wakened by the unusual noises and was listening eagerly. Her father told her of what had happened and how the doctor had ordered Heidi back to her home, because her condition was serious and might get worse. She might even climb the roof, or be exposed to similar dangers, if she was not cured at once.

Clara was painfully surprised and tried to prevent her father from carrying out his plan. He remained firm, however, promising to take her to Switzerland himself the following summer, if she was good and sensible now. So the child, resigning herself, begged to have Heidi's trunk packed in her room. Mr. Sesemann encouraged her to get together a good outfit for her little friend.

Heidi's aunt had arrived in the meantime. Being told to take her niece home with her, she found no end of excuses, which plainly showed that she did not want to do it; for Deta well remembered the uncle's parting words. Mr. Sesemann dismissed her and summoned Sebastian. The butler was told to get ready for travelling with the child. He was to go to Basle that day and spend the night at a good hotel which his master named. The next day the child was to be brought to her home.

"Listen, Sebastian," Mr. Sesemann said, "and do exactly as I tell you. I know the Hotel in Basle, and if you show my card they will give you good accommodations. Go to the child's room and barricade the windows, so that they can only be opened by the greatest force. When Heidi has gone to bed, lock the door from outside, for the child walks in her sleep and might come to harm in the strange hotel. She might get up and open the door; do you understand?"

"Oh! – Oh! – So it was she?" exclaimed the butler.

"Yes, it was! You are a coward, and you can tell John he is the same. Such foolish men, to be afraid!" With that Mr. Sesemann went to his room to write a letter to Heidi's grandfather.

Sebastian, feeling ashamed, said to himself that he ought to have resisted John and found out alone.

Heidi was dressed in her Sunday frock and stood waiting for further commands.

Mr. Sesemann called her now. "Good-morning, Mr. Sesemann," Heidi said when she entered.

"What do you think about it, little one?" he asked her. Heidi looked up to him in amazement.

"You don't seem to know anything about it," laughed Mr. Sesemann. Tinette had not even told the child, for she thought it beneath her dignity to speak to the vulgar Heidi.

"You are going home to-day."

"Home?" Heidi repeated in a low voice. She had to gasp, so great was her surprise.

"Wouldn't you like to hear something about it?" asked Mr. Sesemann smiling.

"Oh yes, I should like to," said the blushing child.

"Good, good," said the kind gentleman. "Sit down and eat a big breakfast now, for you are going away right afterwards."

The child could not even swallow a morsel, though she tried to eat out of obedience. It seemed to her as if it was only a dream.

"Go to Clara, Heidi, till the carriage comes," Mr. Sesemann said kindly.

Heidi had been wishing to go, and now she ran to Clara's room, where a huge trunk was standing.

"Heidi, look at the things I had packed for you. Do you like them?" Clara asked.

There were a great many lovely things in it, but Heidi jumped for joy when she discovered a little basket with twelve round white rolls for the grandmother. The children had forgotten that the moment for parting had come, when the carriage was announced. Heidi had to get all her own treasures from her room yet. The grandmama's book was carefully packed, and the red shawl that Miss Rottenmeier had purposely left behind. Then putting on her pretty hat, she left her room to say good-bye to Clara. There was not much time left to do so, for Mr. Sesemann was waiting to put Heidi in the carriage. When Miss Rottenmeier, who was standing on the stairs to bid farewell to her pupil, saw the red bundle in Heidi's hand, she seized it and threw it on the ground. Heidi looked imploringly at her kind protector, and Mr. Sesemann, seeing how much she treasured it, gave it back to her. The happy child at parting thanked him for all his goodness. She also sent a message of thanks to the good old doctor, whom she suspected to be the real cause of her going.

While Heidi was being lifted into the carriage, Mr. Sesemann assured her that Clara and he would never forget her. Sebastian followed with Heidi's basket and a large bag with provisions. Mr. Sesemann called out: "Happy journey!" and the carriage rolled away.

Only when Heidi was sitting in the train did she become conscious of where she was going. She knew now that she would really see her grandfather and the grandmother again, also Peter and the goats. Her only fear was that the poor blind grandmother might have died while she was away.

The thing she looked forward to most was giving the soft white rolls to the grandmother. While she was musing over all these things, she fell asleep. In Basle she was roused by Sebastian, for there they were to spend the night.

The next morning they started off again, and it took them many hours before they reached Mayenfeld. When Sebastian stood on the platform of the station, he wished he could have travelled further in the train rather than have to climb a mountain. The last part of the trip might be dangerous, for everything seemed half-wild in this country. Looking round, he discovered a small wagon with a lean horse. A broad-shouldered man was just loading up large bags, which had come by the train. Sebastian, approaching the man, asked some information concerning the least dangerous ascent to the Alp. After a while it was settled that the man should take Heidi and her trunk to the village and see to it that somebody would go up with her from there.

Not a word had escaped Heidi, until she now said, "I can go up alone from the village. I know the road." Sebastian felt relieved, and calling Heidi to him, presented her with a heavy roll of bills and a letter for the grandfather. These precious things were put at the bottom of the basket, under the rolls, so that they could not possibly get lost.

Heidi promised to be careful of them, and was lifted up to the cart. The two old friends shook hands and parted, and Sebastian, with a slightly bad conscience for having deserted the child so soon, sat down on the station to wait for a returning train.

The driver was no other than the village baker, who had never seen Heidi but had heard a great deal about her. He had known her parents and immediately guessed she was the child who had lived with the Alm-Uncle. Curious to know why she came home again, he began a conversation.

"Are you Heidi, the child who lived with the Alm-Uncle?"

"Yes."

"Why are you coming home again? Did you get on badly?"

"Oh no; nobody could have got on better than I did in Frankfurt."

"Then why are you coming back?"

"Because Mr. Sesemann let me come."

"Pooh! why didn't you stay?"

"Because I would rather be with my grandfather on the Alp than anywhere on earth."

"You may think differently when you get there," muttered the baker. "It is strange though, for she must know," he said to himself.

They conversed no more, and Heidi began to tremble with excitement when she recognized all the trees on the road and the lofty peaks of the mountains. Sometimes she felt as if she could not sit still any longer, but had to jump down and run with all her might. They arrived at the village at the stroke of five. Immediately a large group of women and children surrounded the cart, for the trunk and the little passenger had attracted everybody's notice. When Heidi had been lifted down, she found herself held and questioned on all sides. But when they saw how frightened she was, they let her go at last. The baker had to tell of Heidi's arrival with the strange gentleman, and assured all the people that Heidi loved her grandfather with all her heart, let the people say what they would about him.

Heidi, in the meantime, was running up the path; from time to time she was obliged to stop, for her basket was heavy and she lost her breath. Her one idea was: "If only grandmother still sits in her corner by her spinning wheel! – Oh, if she should have died!" When the child caught sight of the hut at last, her heart began to beat. The quicker she ran, the more it beat, but at last she tremblingly opened the door. She ran into the middle of the room, unable to utter one tone, she was so out of breath.

"Oh God," it sounded from one corner, "our Heidi used to come in like that. Oh, if I just could have her again with me before I die. Who has come?"

"Here I am! grandmother, here I am!" shouted the child, throwing herself on her knees before the old woman. She seized her hands and arms and snuggling up to her did not for joy utter one more word. The grandmother had been so surprised that she could only silently caress the child's curly hair over and over again. "Yes, yes," she said at last, "this is Heidi's hair, and her beloved voice. Oh my God, I thank Thee for this happiness." Out of her blind eyes big tears of joy fell down on Heidi's hand. "Is it really you, Heidi? Have you really come again?"

"Yes, yes, grandmother," the child replied. "You must not cry, for I have come and will never leave you any more. Now you won't have to eat hard black bread any more for a little while. Look what I have brought you."

Heidi put one roll after another into the grandmother's lap.

"Ah, child, what a blessing you bring to me!" the old woman cried. "But you are my greatest blessing yourself, Heidi!" Then, caressing the child's hair and flushed cheeks, she entreated: "Just say one more word, that I may hear your voice."

While Heidi was talking, Peter's mother arrived, and exclaimed in her amazement: "Surely, this is Heidi. But how can that be?"

The child rose to shake hands with Brigida, who could not get over Heidi's splendid frock and hat.

"You can have my hat, I don't want it any more; I have my old one still," Heidi said, pulling out her old crushed straw hat. Heidi had remembered her grandfather's words to Deta about her feather hat; that was why she had kept her old hat so carefully. Brigida at last accepted the gift after a great many remonstrances. Suddenly Heidi took off her pretty dress and tied her old shawl about her. Taking the grandmother's hand, she said: "Good-bye, I must go home to grandfather now, but I shall come again tomorrow. Good-night, grandmother."

"Oh, please come again to-morrow, Heidi," implored the old woman, while she held her fast.

"Why did you take your pretty dress off?" asked Brigida.

"I'd rather go to grandfather that way, or else he might not know me any more, the way you did."

Brigida accompanied the child outside and said mysteriously: "He would have known you in your frock; you ought to have kept it on. Please be careful, child, for Peter tells us that the uncle never says a word to anyone and always seems so angry." But Heidi was unconcerned, and saying good-night, climbed up the path with the basket on her arm. The evening sun was shining down on the grass before her. Every few minutes Heidi stood still to look at the mountains behind her.

Suddenly she looked back and beheld such glory as she had not even seen in her most vivid dream. The rocky peaks were flaming in the brilliant light, the snow-fields glowed and rosy clouds were floating overhead. The grass was like an expanse of gold, and below her the valley swam in golden mist. The child stood still, and in her joy and transport tears ran down her cheeks. She folded her hands, and looking up to heaven, thanked the Lord that He had brought her home again. She thanked Him for restoring her to her beloved mountains, – in her happiness she could hardly find words to pray. Only when the glow had subsided, was Heidi able to follow the path again.

She climbed so fast that she could soon discover, first the tree-tops, then the roof, finally the hut. Now she could see her grandfather sitting on his bench, smoking a pipe. Above the cottage the fir-trees gently swayed and rustled in the evening breeze. At last she had reached the hut, and throwing herself in her grandfather's arms, she hugged him and held him tight. She could say nothing but "Grandfather! grandfather! grandfather!" in her agitation.

The old man said nothing either, but his eyes were moist, and loosening Heidi's arms at last, he sat her on his knee. When he had looked at her a while, he said: "So you have come home again, Heidi? Why? You certainly do not look very cityfied! Did they send you away?"

"Oh no, you must not think that, grandfather. They all were so good to me; Clara, Mr. Sesemann and grandmama. But grandfather, sometimes I felt as if I could not bear it any longer to be away from you! I thought I should choke; I could not tell any one, for that would have been ungrateful. Suddenly, one morning Mr. Sesemann called me very early, I think it was the doctor's fault and – but I think it is probably written in this letter;" with that Heidi brought the letter and the bank-roll from her basket, putting them on her grandfather's lap.

"This belongs to you," he said, laying the roll beside him. Having read the letter, he put it in his pocket.

"Do you think you can still drink milk with me, Heidi?" he asked, while he stepped into the cottage. "Take your money with you, you can buy a bed for it and clothes for many years."

"I don't need it at all, grandfather," Heidi assured him; "I have a bed and Clara has given me so many dresses that I shan't need any more all my life."

"Take it and put it in the cupboard, for you will need it some day."

Heidi obeyed, and danced around the hut in her delight to see all the beloved things again. Running up to the loft, she exclaimed in great disappointment: "Oh grandfather, my bed is gone."

"It will come again," the grandfather called up from below; "how could I know that you were coming back? Get your milk now!"

Heidi, coming down, took her old seat. She seized her bowl and emptied it eagerly, as if it was the most wonderful thing she had ever tasted. "Grandfather, our milk is the best in all the world."

Suddenly Heidi, hearing a shrill whistle, rushed outside, as Peter and all his goats came racing down. Heidi greeted the boy, who stopped, rooted to the spot, staring at her. Then she ran into the midst of her beloved friends, who had not forgotten her either. Schwänli and Bärli bleated for joy, and all her other favorites pressed near to her. Heidi was beside herself with joy, and caressed little Snowhopper and patted Thistlefinch, till she felt herself pushed to and fro among them.

"Peter, why don't you come down and say good-night to me?" Heidi called to the boy.

"Have you come again?" he exclaimed at last. Then he took Heidi's proffered hand and asked her, as if she had been always there: "Are you coming up with me to-morrow?"

"No, to-morrow I must go to grandmother, but perhaps the day after."

Peter had a hard time with his goats that day, for they would not follow him. Over and over again they came back to Heidi, till she entered the shed with Bärli and Schwänli and shut the door.

When Heidi went up to her loft to sleep, she found a fresh, fragrant bed waiting for her; and she slept better that night than she had for many, many months, for her great and burning longing had been satisfied. About ten times that night the grandfather rose from his couch to listen to Heidi's quiet breathing. The window was filled up with hay, for from now on the moon was not allowed to shine on Heidi any more. But Heidi slept quietly, for she had seen the flaming mountains and had heard the fir-trees roar.

CHAPTER 14

On Sunday When the Church Bells Ring

Heidi was standing under the swaying fir-trees, waiting for her grandfather to join her. He had promised to bring up her trunk from the village while she went in to visit the grandmother. The child was longing to see the blind woman again and to hear how she had liked the rolls. It was Saturday, and the grandfather had been cleaning the cottage. Soon he was ready to start. When they had descended and Heidi entered Peter's hut, the grandmother called lovingly to her: "Have you come again, child?"

She took hold of Heidi's hand and held it tight. Grandmother then told the little visitor how good the rolls had tasted, and how much stronger she felt already. Brigida related further that the grandmother had only eaten a single roll, being so afraid to finish them too soon. Heidi had listened attentively, and said now: "Grandmother, I know what I shall do. I am going to write to Clara and she'll surely send me a whole lot more."

But Brigida remarked: "That is meant well, but they get hard so soon. If I only had a few extra pennies, I could buy some from our baker. He makes them too, but I am hardly able to pay for the black bread."

Heidi's face suddenly shone. "Oh, grandmother, I have

an awful lot of money," she cried. "Now I know what I'll do with it. Every day you must have a fresh roll and two on Sundays. Peter can bring them up from the village."

"No, no, child," the grandmother implored. "That must not be. You must give it to grandfather and he'll tell you what to do with it."

But Heidi did not listen but jumped gaily about the little room, calling over and over again: "Now grandmother can have a roll every day. She'll get well and strong, and," she called with fresh delight, "maybe your eyes will see again, too, when you are strong and well."

The grandmother remained silent, not to mar the happiness of the child. Seeing the old hymn-book on the shelf, Heidi said:

"Grandmother, shall I read you a song from your book now? I can read quite nicely!" she added after a pause.

"Oh yes, I wish you would, child. Can you really read?"

Heidi, climbing on a chair, took down the dusty book from a shelf. After she had carefully wiped it off, she sat down on a stool.

"What shall I read, grandmother?"

"Whatever you want to," was the reply. Turning the pages, Heidi found a song about the sun, and decided to read that aloud. More and more eagerly she read, while the grandmother, with folded arms, sat in her chair. An expression of indescribable happiness shone in her countenance, though tears were rolling down her cheeks. When Heidi had repeated the end of the song a number of times, the old woman exclaimed: "Oh, Heidi, everything seems bright to me again and my heart is light. Thank you, child, you have done me so much good."

Heidi looked enraptured at the grandmother's face, which had changed from an old, sorrowful expression to a joyous one.

She seemed to look up gratefully, as if she could already behold the lovely, celestial gardens told of in the hymn.

Soon the grandfather knocked on the window, for it was time to go. Heidi followed quickly, assuring the grandmother that she would visit her every day now; on the days she went up to the pasture with Peter, she would return in the early afternoon, for she did not want to miss the chance to make the grandmother's heart joyful and light. Brigida urged Heidi to take her dress along, and with it on her arm the child joined the old man and immediately told him what had happened.

On hearing of her plan to purchase rolls for the grandmother every day, the grandfather reluctantly consented.

At this the child gave a bound, shouting: "Oh grandfather, now grandmother won't ever have to eat hard, black bread any more. Oh, everything is so wonderful now! If God Our Father had done immediately what I prayed for, I should have come home at once and could not have brought half as many rolls to grandmother. I should not have been able to read either. Grandmama told me that God would make everything much better than I could ever dream. I shall always pray from now on, the way grandmama taught me. When God does not give me something I pray for, I shall always remember how everything has worked out for the best this time. We'll pray every day, grandfather, won't we, for otherwise God might forget us."

"And if somebody should forget to do it?" murmured the old man.

"Oh, he'll get on badly, for God will forget him, too. If he is unhappy and wretched, people don't pity him, for they will say: 'he went away from God, and now the Lord, who alone can help him, has no pity on him'."

"Is that true, Heidi? Who told you so?"

"Grandmama explained it all to me."

After a pause the grandfather said: "Yes, but if it has happened, then there is no help; nobody can come back to the Lord, when God has once forgotten him."

"But grandfather, everybody can come back to Him;

grandmama told me that, and besides there is the beautiful story in my book. Oh, grandfather, you don't know it yet, and I shall read it to you as soon as we get home."

The grandfather had brought a big basket with him, in which he carried half the contents of Heidi's trunk; it had been too large to be conveyed up the steep ascent. Arriving at the hut and setting down his load, he had to sit beside Heidi, who was ready to begin the tale. With great animation Heidi read the story of the prodigal son, who was happy at home with his father's cows and sheep. The picture showed him leaning on his staff, watching the sunset. "Suddenly he wanted to have his own inheritance, and be able to be his own master. Demanding the money from his father, he went away and squandered all. When he had nothing in the world left, he had to go as servant to a peasant, who did not own fine cattle like his father, but only swine; his clothes were rags, and for food he only got the husks on which the pigs were fed. Often he would think what a good home he had left, and when he remembered how good his father had been to him and his own ungratefulness, he would cry from repentance and longing. Then he said to himself: 'I shall go to my father and ask his forgiveness.' When he approached his former home, his father came out to meet him—"

"What do you think will happen now?" Heidi asked. "You think that the father is angry and will say: 'Didn't I tell you?' But just listen: 'And his father saw him and had compassion and ran and fell on his neck. And the son said: Father, I have sinned against Heaven and in Thy sight, and am no more worthy to be called Thy son. But the father said to his servants: Bring forth the best robe and put it on him; and put a ring on his hand and shoes on his feet; and bring hither the fatted calf and kill it; and let us eat and be merry: For this my son was dead and is alive again; he was lost, and is found.' And they began to be merry."

"Isn't it a beautiful story, grandfather?" asked Heidi, when he sat silently beside her.

"Yes, Heidi, it is," said the grandfather, but so seriously that Heidi quietly looked at the pictures. "Look how happy he is," she said, pointing to it.

A few hours later, when Heidi was sleeping soundly, the old man climbed up the ladder. Placing a little lamp beside the sleeping child, he watched her a long, long time. Her little hands were folded and her rosy face looked confident and peaceful. The old man now folded his hands and said in a low voice, while big tears rolled down his cheeks: "Father, I have sinned against Heaven and Thee, and am no more worthy to be Thy son!"

The next morning found the uncle standing before the door, looking about him over valley and mountain. A few early bells sounded from below and the birds sang their morning anthems.

Re-entering the house, he called: "Heidi, get up! The sun is shining! Put on a pretty dress, for we are going to church!"

That was a new call, and Heidi obeyed quickly. When the child came downstairs in her smart little frock, she opened her eyes wide. "Oh, grandfather!" she exclaimed, "I have never seen you in your Sunday coat with the silver buttons. Oh, how fine you look!"

The old man, turning to the child, said with a smile: "You look nice, too; come now!" With Heidi's hand in his they wandered down together. The nearer they came to the village, the louder and richer the bells resounded. "Oh grandfather, do you hear it? It seems like a big, high feast," said Heidi.

When they entered the church, all the people were singing. Though they sat down on the last bench behind, the people had noticed their presence and whispered it from ear to ear. When the pastor began to preach, his words were a loud thanksgiving that moved all his hearers. After the service the old man and the child walked to the parsonage. The clergyman had opened the door and received them with friendly words. "I have come to ask your forgiveness for my harsh words," said the uncle. "I want to follow your advice to spend the winter here among you. If the people look at me askance, I can't expect any better. I am sure, Mr. Pastor, you will not do so."

The pastor's friendly eyes sparkled, and with many a kind word he commended the uncle for this change, and putting his hand on Heidi's curly hair, ushered them out. Thus the people, who had been all talking together about this great event, could see that their clergyman shook hands with the old man. The door of the parsonage was hardly shut, when the whole assembly came forward with outstretched hands and friendly greetings. Great seemed to be their joy at the old man's resolution; some of the people even accompanied him on his homeward way. When they had parted at last, the uncle looked after them with his face shining as with an inward light. Heidi looked up to him and said: "Grandfather, you have never looked so beautiful!"

"Do you think so, child?" he said with a smile. "You see, Heidi, I am more happy than I deserve; to be at peace with God and men makes one's heart feel light. God has been good to me, to send you back."

When they arrived at Peter's hut, the grandfather opened the door and entered. "How do you do, grandmother," he called out. "I think we must start to mend again, before the fall wind comes."

"Oh my God, the uncle!" exclaimed the grandmother in joyous surprise. "How happy I am to be able to thank you for what you have done, uncle! Thank you, God bless you for it."

With trembling joy the grandmother shook hands with her old friend. "There is something else I want to say to you, uncle," she continued. "If I have ever hurt you in any way, do not punish me. Do not let Heidi go away again before I die. I cannot tell you what Heidi means to me!" So saying, she held the clinging child to her.

"No danger of that, grandmother, I hope we shall all stay together now for many years to come."

Brigida now showed Heidi's feather hat to the old man and asked him to take it back. But the uncle asked her to keep it, since Heidi had given it to her.

"What blessings this child has brought from Frankfurt," Brigida said. "I often wondered if I should not send our little Peter too. What do you think, uncle?"

The uncle's eyes sparkled with fun, when he replied: "I am sure it would not hurt Peter; nevertheless I should wait for a fitting occasion before I sent him."

The next moment Peter himself arrived in great haste. He had a letter for Heidi, which had been given to him in the village. What an event, a letter for Heidi! They all sat down at the table while the child read it aloud. The letter was from Clara Sesemann, who wrote that everything had got so dull since Heidi left. She said that she could not stand it very long, and therefore her father had promised to take her to Ragatz this coming fall. She announced that Grandmama was coming too, for she wanted to see Heidi and her grandfather. Grandmama, having heard about the rolls, was sending some coffee, too, so that the grandmother would not have to eat them dry. Grandmama also insisted on being taken to the grandmother herself when she came on her visit.

Great was the delight caused by this news, and what with all the questions and plans that followed, the grandfather himself forgot how late it was. This happy day, which had united them all, caused the old woman to say at parting: "The most beautiful thing of all, though, is to be able to shake hands again with an old friend, as in days gone by; it is a great comfort to find again, what we have treasured. I hope you'll come soon again, uncle. I am counting on the child for tomorrow."

This promise was given. While Heidi and her grandfather were on their homeward path, the peaceful sound of evening bells accompanied them. At last they reached the cottage, which seemed to glow in the evening light.

PART TWO

Heidi Makes Use of Her Experience

CHAPTER 15

Preparations for a Journey

The kind doctor who had sent Heidi home to her beloved mountains was approaching the Sesemann residence on a sunny day in September. Everything about him was bright and cheerful, but the doctor did not even raise his eyes from the pavement to the blue sky above. His face was sad and his hair had turned very gray since spring. A few months ago the doctor had lost his only daughter, who had lived with him since his wife's early death. The blooming girl had been his only joy, and since she had gone from him the ever-cheerful doctor was bowed down with grief.

When Sebastian opened the door to the physician he bowed very low, for the doctor made friends wherever he went.

"I am glad you have come doctor," Mr. Sesemann called to his friend as he entered. "Please let us talk over this trip to Switzerland again. Do you still give the same advice, now that Clara is so much better?"

"What must I think of you, Sesemann?" replied the doctor, sitting down. "I wish your mother was here. Everything is clear to her and things go smoothly then. This is the third time to-day that you have called me, and always for the same thing!"

"It is true, it must make you impatient," said Mr. Sesemann. Laying his hand on his friend's shoulder, he continued: "I cannot say how hard it is for me to refuse Clara this trip. Haven't I promised it to her and hasn't she looked forward to it for months? She has borne all her suffering so patiently, just because she had hoped to be able to visit her little friend on the Alp. I hate to rob her of this pleasure. The poor child has so many trials and so little change."

"But, Sesemann, you must do it," was the doctor's answer. When his friend remained silent, he continued: "Just think what a hard summer Clara has had! She never was more ill and we could not attempt this journey without risking the worst consequences. Remember, we are in September now, and though the weather may still be fine on the Alp, it is sure to be very cool. The days are getting short, and she could only spend a few hours up there, if she had to return for the night. It would take several hours to have her carried up from Ragatz. You see yourself how impossible it is! I shall come in with you, though, to talk to Clara, and you'll find her sensible. I'll tell you of my plan for next May. First she can go to Ragatz to take the baths. When it gets warm on the mountain, she can be carried up from time to time. She'll be stronger then and much more able to enjoy those excursions than she is now. If we hope for an improvement in her condition, we must be extremely cautious and careful, remember that!"

Mr. Sesemann, who had been listening with the utmost submission, now said anxiously: "Doctor, please tell me honestly if you still have hope left for any change?"

With shrugging shoulders the doctor replied: "Not very much. But think of me, Sesemann! Have you not a child, who loves you and always welcomes you? You don't have to come back to a lonely house and sit down alone at your table. Your child is well taken care of, and if she has many privations, she also has many advantages. Sesemann, you do not need to be pitied! Just think of my lonely home!"

Mr. Sesemann had gotten up and was walking round the room, as he always did when something occupied his thoughts. Suddenly he stood before his friend and said: "Doctor, I have an idea. I cannot see you sad any longer. You must get away. You shall undertake this trip and visit Heidi in our stead."

The doctor had been surprised by this proposal, and tried to object. But Mr. Sesemann was so full of his new project that he pulled his friend with him into his daughter's room, not leaving him time for any remonstrances. Clara loved the doctor, who had always tried to cheer her up on his visits by bright and funny tales. She was sorry for the change that had come over him and would have given much to see him happy again. When he had shaken hands with her, both men pulled up their chairs to Clara's bedside. Mr. Sesemann began to speak of their journey and how sorry he was to give it up. Then he quickly began to talk of his new plan.

Clara's eyes had filled with tears. But she knew that her father did not like to see her cry, and besides she was sure that her papa would only forbid her this pleasure because it was absolutely necessary to do so.

So she bravely fought her tears, and caressing the doctor's hand, said:

"Oh please, doctor, do go to Heidi; then you can tell me all about her, and can describe her grandfather to me, and Peter, with his goats, – I seem to know them all so well. Then you can take all the things to her that I had planned to take myself. Oh, please doctor, go, and then I'll be good and take as much cod-liver oil as ever you want me to."

Who can tell if this promise decided the doctor? At any rate he answered with a smile: "Then I surely must go, Clara, for you will get fat and strong, as we both want to see you. Have you settled yet when I must go?"

"Oh, you had better go tomorrow morning, doctor," Clara urged.

"She is right," the father assented; "the sun is shining and you must not lose any more glorious days on the Alp."

The doctor had to laugh. "Why don't you chide me for being here still? I shall go as quickly as I can, Sesemann."

Clara gave many messages to him for Heidi. She also told him to be sure to observe everything closely, so that he would be able to tell her all about it when he came back. The things for Heidi were to be sent to him later, for Miss Rottenmeier, who had to pack them, was out on one of her lengthy wanderings about town.

The doctor promised to comply with all Clara's wishes and to start the following day.

Clara rang for the maid and said to her, when she arrived: "Please, Tinette, pack a lot of fresh, soft coffee-cake in this box." A box had been ready for this purpose many days. When the maid was leaving the room she murmured: "That's a silly bother!"

Sebastian, who had happened to overhear some remarks, asked the physician when he was leaving to take his regards to the little Miss, as he called Heidi.

With a promise to deliver this message the doctor was just hastening out, when he encountered an obstacle. Miss Rottenmeier, who had been obliged to return from her walk on account of the strong wind, was just coming in. She wore a large cape, which the wind was blowing about her like two full sails. Both had retreated politely to give way to each other. Suddenly the wind seemed to carry the housekeeper straight towards the doctor, who had barely time to avoid her. This little incident, which had ruffled Miss Rottenmeier's temper very much, gave the doctor occasion to soothe her, as she liked to be soothed by this man, whom she respected more than anybody in the world. Telling her of his intended visit, he entreated her to pack the things for Heidi as only she knew how.

Clara had expected some resistance from Miss Rottenmeier

about the packing of her presents. What was her surprise when this lady showed herself most obliging, and immediately, on being told, brought together all the articles! First came a heavy coat for Heidi, with a hood, which Clara meant her to use on visits to the grandmother in the winter. Then came a thick warm shawl and a large box with coffee-cake for the grandmother. An enormous sausage for Peter's mother followed, and a little sack of tobacco for the grandfather. At last a lot of mysterious little parcels and boxes were packed, things that Clara had gathered together for Heidi. When the tidy pack lay ready on the ground, Clara's heart filled with pleasure at the thought of her little friend's delight.

Sebastian now entered, and putting the pack on his shoulder, carried it to the doctor's house without delay.

CHAPTER 16

A Guest on the Alp

The early dawn was tinging the mountains and a fresh morning-breeze rocked the old fir-trees to and fro. Heidi opened her eyes, for the rustling of the wind had awakened her. These sounds always thrilled her heart, and now they drew her out of bed. Rising hurriedly, she soon was neatly dressed and combed.

Coming down the little ladder and finding the grandfather's bed empty, she ran outside. The old man was looking up at the sky to see what the weather was going to be like that day. Rosy clouds were passing overhead, but gradually the sky grew more blue and deep, and soon a golden light passed over the heights, for the sun was rising in all his glory.

"Oh, how lovely! Good-morning, grandfather," Heidi exclaimed.

"Are your eyes bright already?" the grandfather retorted, holding out his hand.

Heidi then ran over to her beloved fir-trees and danced about, while the wind was howling in the branches.

After the old man had washed and milked the goats, he brought them out of the shed. When Heidi saw her friends again, she caressed them tenderly, and they in their turn nearly crushed her between them. Sometimes when Bärli got too wild, Heidi would say: "But Bärli, you push me like the Big Turk," and that was enough to quiet the goat.

Soon Peter arrived with the whole herd, the jolly Thistlefinch ahead of all the others. Heidi, being soon in the mist of them, was pushed about among them. Peter was anxious to say a word to the little girl, so he gave a shrill whistle, urging the goats to climb ahead. When he was near her he said reproachfully: "You really might come with me to-day!"

"No, I can't, Peter," said Heidi. "They might come from Frankfurt any time. I must be home when they come."

"How often you have said that," grumbled the boy.

"But I mean it," replied Heidi. "Do you really think I want to be away when they come from Frankfurt? Do you really think that, Peter?"

"They could come to uncle," Peter growled.

Then the grandfather's strong voice was heard: "Why doesn't the army go forward? Is it the field-marshal's fault, or the fault of the troop?"

Peter immediately turned about and led his goats up the mountain without more ado.

Since Heidi had come home again to her grandfather she did many things that had never occurred to her before. For instance, she would make her bed every morning, and run about the hut, tidying and dusting. With an old rag she would rub the chairs and table till they all shone, and the grandfather would exclaim: "It is always Sunday with us now; Heidi has not been away in vain."

On this day after breakfast, when Heidi began her self-imposed task, it took her longer than usual, for the weather was too glorious to stay within. Over and over again a bright sunbeam would tempt the busy child outside. How could she stay indoors, when the glistening sunshine was pouring down and all the mountains seemed to glow? She had to sit down on the dry, hard ground and look down into the valley and all about her. Then, suddenly remembering her little duties, she would hasten back. It was not long, though, till the roaring fir-trees tempted her again. The grandfather had been busy in his little shop, merely glancing over at the child from time to time. Suddenly he heard her call: "Oh grandfather, come!"

He was frightened and came out quickly He saw her running down the hill crying: "They are coming, they are coming. Oh, the doctor is coming first."

When Heidi at last reached her old friend, he held out his hand, which Heidi immediately seized. In the full joy of her heart, she exclaimed: "How do you do, doctor? And I thank you a thousand times!"

"How are you, Heidi? But what are you thanking me for already?" the doctor asked, with a smile.

"Because you let me come home again," the child explained.

The gentleman's face lit up like sunshine. He had certainly not counted on such a reception on the Alp. On the contrary! Not even noticing all the beauty around him, he had climbed up sadly, for he was sure that Heidi probably would not know him any more. He thought that he would be far from welcome, being obliged to cause her a great disappointment. Instead, he beheld Heidi's bright eyes looking up at him in gratefulness and love. She was still holding his arm, when he said: "Come now, Heidi, and take me to your grandfather, for I want to see where you live."

Like a kind father he had taken her hand, but Heidi stood still and looked down the mountain-side.

"But where are Clara and grandmama?" she asked.

"Child, I must tell you something now which will grieve you as much as it grieves me," replied the doctor. "I had to come alone, for Clara has been very ill and could not travel. Of course grandmama has not come either; but the spring will soon be here, and when the days get long and warm, they will surely visit you."

Heidi was perfectly amazed; she could not understand how all those things that she had pictured to herself so clearly would not happen after all. She was standing perfectly motionless, confused by the blow.

It was some time before Heidi remembered that, after all, she had come down to meet the doctor. Looking up at her friend, she was struck by his sad and cheerless face. How changed he was since she had seen him! She did not like to see people unhappy, least of all the good, kind doctor. He must be sad because Clara and grandmama had not come, and to console him she said: "Oh, it won't last long till spring comes again; then they will come for sure; they'll be able to stay much longer then, and that will please Clara. Now we'll go to grandfather."

Hand in hand she climbed up with her old friend. All the way she tried to cheer him up by telling him again and again of the coming summer days. After they had reached the cottage, she called out to her grandfather quite happily:

"They are not here yet, but it won't be very long before they are coming!"

The grandfather warmly welcomed his guest, who did not seem at all a stranger, for had not Heidi told him many things about the doctor? They all three sat down on the bench before the door, and the doctor told of the object of his visit. He whispered to the child that something was coming up the mountain very soon which would bring her more pleasure than his visit. What could it be?

The uncle advised the doctor to spend the splendid days of autumn on the Alp, if possible, and to take a little room in the village instead of in Ragatz; then he could easily walk up every day to the hut, and from there the uncle could take him all around the mountains. This plan was accepted.

The sun was in its zenith and the wind had ceased. Only a soft delicious breeze fanned the cheeks of all.

The uncle now got up and went into the hut, returning soon with a table and their dinner.

"Go in, Heidi, and set the table here. I hope you will excuse our simple meal," he said, turning to his guest.

"I shall gladly accept this delightful invitation; I am sure that dinner will taste good up here," said the guest, looking down over the sun-bathed valley.

Heidi was running to and fro, for it gave her great joy to be able to wait on her kind protector. Soon the uncle appeared with the steaming milk, the toasted cheese, and the finely-sliced, rosy meat that had been dried in the pure air. The doctor enjoyed his dinner better than any he had ever tasted.

"Yes, we must send Clara up here. How she could gather strength!" he said; "If she would have an appetite like mine to-day, she couldn't help getting nice and fat."

At this moment a man could be seen walking up with a large sack on his shoulders. Arriving on top, he threw down his load, breathing in the pure, fresh air.

Opening the cover, the doctor said: "This has come for you from Frankfurt, Heidi. Come and look what is in it."

Heidi timidly watched the heap, and only when the gentleman opened the box with the cakes for the grandmother she said joyfully: "Oh, now grandmother can eat this lovely cake." She was taking the box and the beautiful shawl on her arm and was going to race down to deliver the gifts, when the men persuaded her to stay and unpack the rest. What was her delight at finding the tobacco and all the other things. The men had been talking together, when the child suddenly planted herself in front of them and said: "These things have not given me as much pleasure as the dear doctor's coming." Both men smiled.

When it was near sunset, the doctor rose to start on his way down. The grandfather, carrying the box, the shawl and the sausage, and the guest holding the little girl by the hand, they wandered down the mountain-side. When they reached Peter's hut, Heidi was told to go inside and wait for her grandfather there. At parting she asked: "Would you like to come with me up to the pasture to-morrow, doctor?"

"With pleasure. Good-bye, Heidi," was the reply. The grandfather had deposited all the presents before the door, and it took Heidi long to carry in the huge box and the sausage. The shawl she put on the grandmother's knee.

Brigida had silently watched the proceedings, and could not open her eyes wide enough when she saw the enormous sausage. Never in her life had she seen the like, and now she really possessed it and could cut it herself.

"Oh grandmother, don't the cakes please you awfully? Just look how soft they are!" the child exclaimed. What was her amazement when she saw the grandmother more pleased with the shawl, which would keep her warm in winter.

"Grandmother, Clara has sent you that," Heidi said.

"Oh, what kind good people they are to think of a poor old woman like me! I never thought I should ever own such a splendid wrap."

At this moment Peter came stumbling in.

"The uncle is coming up behind me, and Heidi must—" that was as far as he got, for his eyes had fastened on the sausage. Heidi, however, had already said good-bye, for she knew what he had meant. Though her uncle never went by the hut any more without stepping in, she knew it was too late to-day. "Heidi, come, you must get your sleep," he called through the open door. Bidding them all good-night, he took Heidi by the hand and under the glistening stars they wandered home to their peaceful cottage.

CHAPTER 17

Retaliation

Early the next morning the doctor climbed up the mountain in company with Peter and his goats. The friendly gentleman made several attempts to start a conversation with the boy, but as answer to his questions he got nothing more than monosyllables. When they arrived on top, they found Heidi already waiting, fresh and rosy as the early dawn.

"Are you coming?" asked Peter as usual.

"Of course I shall, if the doctor comes with us," replied the child.

The grandfather, coming out of the hut, greeted the newcomer with great respect. Then he went up to Peter, and hung on his shoulder the sack, which seemed to contain more than usual that day.

When they had started on their way, Heidi kept urging forward the goats, which were crowding about her. When at last she was walking peacefully by the doctor's side, she began to relate to him many things about the goats and all their strange pranks, and about the flowers, rocks and birds they saw. When they arrived at their destination, time seemed to have flown. Peter all the time was sending many an angry glance at the unconscious doctor, who never even noticed it.

Heidi now took the doctor to her favorite spot. From there

they could hear the peaceful-sounding bells of the grazing cattle below. The sky was deep blue, and above their heads the eagle was circling with outstretched wings. Everything was luminous and bright about them, but the doctor had been silent. Suddenly looking up, he beheld Heidi's radiant eyes.

"Heidi, it is beautiful up here," he said. "But how can anybody with a heavy heart enjoy the beauty? Tell me!"

"Oh," exclaimed Heidi, "one never has a sad heart here. One only gets unhappy in Frankfurt."

A faint smile passed over the doctor's face. Then he began: "But if somebody has brought his sorrow away with him, how would you comfort him?"

"God in Heaven alone can help him."

"That is true, child," remarked the doctor. "But what can we do when God Himself has sent us the affliction?"

After meditating a moment, Heidi replied: "One must wait patiently, for God knows how to turn the saddest things to something happy in the end. God will show us what He has meant to do for us. But He will only do so if we pray to Him patiently."

"I hope you will always keep this beautiful belief, Heidi," said the doctor. Then looking up at the mighty cliffs above, he continued: "Think how sad it would make us not to be able to see all these beautiful things. Wouldn't that make us doubly sad? Can you understand me, child?"

A great pain shot through Heidi's breast. She had to think of the poor grandmother. Her blindness was always a great sorrow to the child, and she had been struck with it anew. Seriously she replied:

"Oh yes, I can understand it. But then we can read grandmother's songs; they make us happy and bright again."

"Which songs, Heidi?"

"Oh, those of the sun, and of the beautiful garden, and then the last verses of the long one. Grandmother loves them so that I always have to read them over three times," said Heidi.

"I wish you would say them to me, child, for I should like to hear them," said the doctor.

Heidi, folding her hands, began the consoling verses. She stopped suddenly, however, for the doctor did not seem to listen. He was sitting motionless, holding his hand before his eyes. Thinking that he had fallen asleep, she remained silent. But the verses had recalled his childhood days; he seemed to hear his mother and see her loving eyes, for when he was a little boy she had sung this song to him. A long time he sat there, till he discovered that Heidi was watching him.

"Heidi, your song was lovely," he said with a more joyful voice. "We must come here another day and then you can recite it to me again."

During all this time Peter had been boiling with anger. Now that Heidi had come again to the pasture with him, she did nothing but talk to the old gentleman. It made him very cross that he was not even able to get near her. Standing a little distance behind Heidi's friend, he shook his fist at him, and soon afterwards both fists, finally raising them up to the sky, as Heidi and the doctor remained together.

When the sun stood in its zenith and Peter knew that it was noon, he called over to them with all his might: "Time to eat."

When Heidi was getting up to fetch their dinner, the doctor just asked for a glass of milk, which was all he wanted. The child also decided to make the milk her sole repast, running over to Peter and informing him of their resolution.

When the boy found that the whole contents of the bag was his, he hurried with his task as never in his life before. But he felt guilty on account of his former anger at the kind gentleman. To show his repentance he held his hands up flat to the sky, indicating by his action that his fists did not mean anything any more. Only after that did he start with his feast.

Heidi and the doctor had wandered about the pasture till the gentleman had found it time to go. He wanted Heidi to remain where she was, but she insisted on accompanying him. All the way down she showed him many places where the pretty mountain flowers grew, all of whose names she could tell him. When they parted at last, Heidi waved to him. From time to time he turned about, and seeing the child still standing there, he had to think of his own little daughter who used to wave to him like that when he went away from home.

The weather was warm and sunny that month. Every morning the doctor came up to the Alp, spending his day very often with the old man. Many a climb they had together that took them far up, to the bare cliffs near the eagle's haunt. The uncle would show his guest all the herbs that grew on hidden places and were strengthening and healing. He could tell many strange things of the beasts that lived in holes in rock or earth, or in the high tops of trees.

In the evening they would part, and the doctor would exclaim: "My dear friend, I never leave you without having learned something."

But most of his days he spent with Heidi. Then the two would sit together on the child's favorite spot, and Peter, quite subdued, behind them. Heidi had to recite the verses, as she had done the first day, and entertain him with all the things she knew.

At last the beautiful month of September was over. One morning the doctor came up with a sadder face than usual. The time had come for him to go back to Frankfurt, and great was the uncle's sadness at that news. Heidi herself could hardly realize that her loving friend, whom she had been seeing every day, was really leaving. The doctor himself was loath to go, for the Alp had become as a home to him. But it was necessary for him to go, and shaking hands with the grandfather, he said good-bye, Heidi going along with him a little way.

Hand in hand they wandered down, till the doctor stood

still. Then caressing Heidi's curly hair, he said: "Now I must go, Heidi! I wish I could take you along with me to Frankfurt; then I could keep you."

At those words, all the rows and rows of houses and streets, Miss Rottenmeier and Tinette rose before Heidi's eyes. Hesitating a little, she said: "I should like it better if you would come to see us again."

"I believe that will be better. Now farewell!" said the friendly gentleman. When they shook hands his eyes filled with tears. Turning quickly he hurried off.

Heidi, standing on the same spot, looked after him. What kind eyes he had! But they had been full of tears. All of a sudden she began to cry bitterly, and ran after her friend, calling with all her might, but interrupted by her sobs:

"Oh doctor, doctor!"

Looking round he stood still and waited till the child had reached him. Her tears came rolling down her cheeks while she sobbed: "I'll come with you to Frankfurt and I'll stay as long as ever you want me to. But first I must see grandfather."

"No, no, dear child," he said affectionately, "not at once. You must remain here, I don't want you to get ill again. But if I should get sick and lonely and ask you to come to me, would you come and stay with me? Can I go away and think that somebody in this world still cares for me and loves me?"

"Yes, I shall come to you the same day, for I really love you as much as grandfather," Heidi assured him, crying all the time.

Shaking hands again, they parted. Heidi stayed on the same spot, waving her hand and looking after her departing friend till he seemed no bigger than a little dot. Then he looked back a last time at Heidi and the sunny Alp, muttering to himself: "It is beautiful up there. Body and soul get strengthened in that place and life seems worth living again."

CHAPTER 18

Winter in the Village

The snow lay so deep around the Alm-hut that the windows seemed to stand level with the ground and the house-door had entirely disappeared. Round Peter's hut it was the same. When the boy went out to shovel the snow, he had to creep through the window; then he would sink deep into the soft snow and kick with arms and legs to get free. Taking a broom, the boy would have to clear away the snow from the door to prevent its falling into the hut.

The uncle had kept his word; when the first snow had fallen, he had moved down to the village with Heidi and his goats. Near the church and the parish house lay an old ruin that once had been a spacious building. A brave soldier had lived there in days gone by; he had fought in the Spanish war, and coming back with many riches, had built himself a splendid house. But having lived too long in the noisy world to be able to stand the monotonous life in the little town, he soon went away, never to come back. After his death, many years later, though the house was already beginning to decay, a distant relation of his took possession of it. The new proprietor did not want to build it up again, so poor people moved in. They had to pay little rent for the house, which was gradually crumbling and falling to pieces. Years ago, when the uncle had come to the village with Tobias, he had lived there. Most of the time it had been empty, for the winter lasted long, and cold winds would blow through the chinks in the walls. When poor people lived there, their candles would be blown out and they would shiver with cold in the dark. But the uncle, had known how to help himself. In the fall, as soon as he had resolved to live in the village, he came down frequently, fitting up the place as best he could.

On approaching the house from the back, one entered an open room, where nearly all the walls lay in ruins. On one side the remains of a chapel could be seen, now covered with the thickest ivy. A large hall came next, with a beautiful stone floor and grass growing in the crevices. Most of the walls were gone and part of the ceiling also. If a few thick pillars had not been left supporting the rest, it would undoubtedly have tumbled down. The uncle had made a wooden partition here for the goats, and covered the floor with straw. Several corridors, most of them half decayed, led finally to a chamber with a heavy iron door. This room was still in good condition and had dark wood panelling on the four firm walls. In one corner was an enormous stove, which nearly reached up to the ceiling. On the white tiles were painted blue pictures of old towers surrounded by high trees, and of hunters with their hounds. There also was a scene with a quiet lake, where, under shady oak-trees, a fisherman was sitting. Around the stove a bench was placed. Heidi loved to sit there, and as soon as she had entered their new abode, she began to examine the pictures. Arriving at the end of the bench, she discovered a bed, which was placed between the wall and the stove. "Oh grandfather, I have found my bed-room," exclaimed the little girl. "Oh, how fine it is! Where are you going to sleep?"

"Your bed must be near the stove, to keep you warm," said the old man. "Now come and look at mine."

With that the grandfather led her into his bed-room. From there a door led into the hugest kitchen Heidi had ever seen. With a great deal of trouble the grandfather had fitted up this place. Many boards were nailed across the walls and the door had been fastened with heavy wires, for beyond, the building lay in ruins. Thick underbrush was growing there, sheltering thousands of insects and lizards. Heidi was delighted with her new home, and when Peter arrived next day, she did not rest till he had seen every nook and corner of the curious dwelling-place.

Heidi slept very well in her chimney corner, but it took her many days to get accustomed to it. When she woke up in the morning and could not hear the fir-trees roar, she would wonder where she was. Was the snow too heavy on the branches? Was she away from home? But as soon as she heard her grandfather's voice outside, she remembered everything and would jump merrily out of bed.

After four days had gone by, Heidi said to her grand-father: "I must go to grandmother now, she has been alone so many days."

But the grandfather shook his head and said: "You can't go yet, child. The snow is fathoms deep up there and is still falling. Peter can hardly get through. A little girl like you would be snowed up and lost in no time. Wait a while till it freezes and then you can walk on top of the crust."

Heidi was very sorry, but she was so busy now that the days flew by. Every morning and afternoon she went to school, eagerly learning whatever was taught her. She hardly ever saw Peter there, for he did not come very often. The mild teacher would only say from time to time: "It seems to me, Peter is not here again! School would do him good, but I guess there is too much snow for him to get through." But when Heidi came home towards evening, Peter generally paid her a visit.

After a few days the sun came out for a short time at

noon, and the next morning the whole Alp glistened and shone like crystal. When Peter was jumping as usual into the snow that morning, he fell against something hard, and before he could stop himself he flew a little way down the mountain. When he had gained his feet at last, he stamped upon the ground with all his might. It really was frozen as hard as stone. Peter could hardly believe it, and quickly running up and swallowing his milk, and putting his bread in his pocket, he announced: "I must go to school to-day!"

"Yes, go and learn nicely," answered his mother.

Then, sitting down on his sled, the boy coasted down the mountain like a shot. Not being able to stop his course when he reached the village, he coasted down further and further, till he arrived in the plain, where the sled stopped of itself. It was already late for school, so the boy took his time and only arrived in the village when Heidi came home for dinner.

"We've got it!" announced the boy, on entering.

"What, general?" asked the uncle.

"The snow," Peter replied.

"Oh, now I can go up to grandmother!" Heidi rejoiced. "But Peter, why didn't you come to school? You could coast down to-day," she continued reproachfully.

"I went too far on my sled and then it was too late," Peter replied.

"I call that deserting!" said the uncle. "People who do that must have their ears pulled; do you hear?"

The boy was frightened, for there was no one in the world whom he respected more than the uncle.

"A general like you ought to be doubly ashamed to do so," the uncle went on. "What would you do with the goats if they did not obey you any more?"

"Beat them," was the reply.

"If you knew of a boy that was behaving like a disobedient goat and had to get spanked, what would you say?"

"Serves him right."

"So now you know it, goat-general: if you miss school again, when you ought to be there, you can come to me and get your due."

Now at last Peter understood what the uncle had meant. More kindly, the old man then turned to Peter and said, "Come to the table now and eat with us. Then you can go up with Heidi, and when you bring her back at night, you can get your supper here."

This unexpected change delighted Peter. Not losing any time, he soon disposed of his full plate. Heidi, who had given the boy most of her dinner, was already putting on Clara's new coat. Then together they climbed up, Heidi chatting all the time. But Peter did not say a single word. He was preoccupied and had not even listened to Heidi's tales. Before they entered the hut, the boy said stubbornly: "I think I had rather go to school than get a beating from the uncle." Heidi promptly confirmed him in his resolution.

When they went into the room, Peter's mother was alone at the table mending. The grandmother was nowhere to be seen. Brigida now told Heidi that the grandmother was obliged to stay in bed on those cold days, as she did not feel very strong. That was something new for Heidi. Quickly running to the old woman's chamber, she found her lying in a narrow bed, wrapped up in her grey shawl and thin blanket.

"Thank Heaven!" the grandmother exclaimed when she heard her darling's step. All autumn and winter long a secret fear had been gnawing at her heart, that Heidi would be sent for by the strange gentleman of whom Peter had told her so much. Heidi had approached the bed, asking anxiously: "Are you very sick, grandmother?"

"No, no, child," the old woman reassured her, "the frost has gone into my limbs a little."

"Are you going to be well again as soon as the warm weather comes?" inquired Heidi.

"Yes, yes, and if God wills, even sooner. I want to go back to my spinning-wheel and I nearly tried it to-day. I'll get up to-morrow, though," the grandmother said confidently, for she had noticed how frightened Heidi was.

The last speech made the child feel more happy. Then, looking wonderingly at the grandmother, she said: "In Frankfurt people put on a shawl when they go out. Why are you putting it on in bed, grandmother?"

"I put it on to keep me warm, Heidi. I am glad to have it, for my blanket is very thin."

"But, grandmother, your bed is slanting down at your head, where it ought to be high. No bed ought to be like that."

"I know, child, I can feel it well." So saying, the old woman tried to change her position on the pillow that lay under her like a thin board. "My pillow never was very thick, and sleeping on it all these years has made it flat."

"Oh dear, if I had only asked Clara to give me the bed I had in Frankfurt!" Heidi lamented. "It had three big pillows on it; I could hardly sleep because I kept sliding down from them all the time. Could you sleep with them, grandmother?"

"Of course, because that would keep me warm. I could breathe so much easier, too," said the grandmother, trying to find a higher place to lie on. "But I must not talk about it any more, for I have to be thankful for many things. I get the lovely roll every day and have this beautiful warm shawl. I also have you, my child! Heidi, wouldn't you like to read me something to-day?"

Heidi immediately fetched the book and read one song after another. The grandmother in the meantime was lying with folded hands; her face, which had been so sad a short time ago, was lit up with a happy smile.

Suddenly Heidi stopped.

"Are you well again, grandmother?" she asked.

"I feel very much better, Heidi. Please finish the song, will you?"

The child obeyed, and when she came to the last words,

> When mine eyes grow dim and sad,
> Let Thy love more brightly burn,
> That my soul, a wanderer glad,
> Safely homeward may return.

"Safely homeward may return!" she exclaimed: "Oh, grandmother, I know what it is like to come home." After a while she said: "It is getting dark, grandmother, I must go home now. I am glad that you feel better again."

The grandmother, holding the child's hand in hers, said: "Yes, I am happy again, though I have to stay in bed. Nobody knows how hard it is to lie here alone, day after day. I do not hear a word from anybody and cannot see a ray of sunlight. I have very sad thoughts sometimes, and often I feel as if I could not bear it any longer. But when I can hear those blessed songs that you have read to me, it makes me feel as if a light was shining into my heart, giving me the purest joy."

Shaking hands, the child now said good-night, and pulling Peter with her, ran outside. The brilliant moon was shining down on the white snow, light as day. The two children were already flying down the Alp, like birds soaring through the air.

After Heidi had gone to bed that night, she lay awake a little while, thinking over everything the grandmother had said, especially about the joy the songs had given her. If only poor grandmother could hear those comforting words every day! Heidi knew that it might be a week or two again before she could repeat her visit. The child became very sad when she thought how uncomfortable and lonely the old woman would be. Was there no way for help? Suddenly Heidi had an idea, and it thrilled her so that she felt as if she could not wait till morning came to put her plan in execution. But in her excitement she had forgotten her evening prayer, so sitting up in bed, she prayed fervently to God. Then, falling back into the fragrant hay, she soon slept peacefully and soundly still the bright morning came.

CHAPTER 19

Winter Still Continues

Peter arrived punctually at school next day. He had brought his lunch with him in a bag, for all the children that came from far away ate in school, while the others went home. In the evening Peter as usual paid his visit to Heidi.

The minute he opened the door she ran up to him, saying: "Peter, I have to tell you something."

"Say it," he replied.

"You must learn to read now," said the child.

"I have done it already."

"Yes, yes, Peter, but I don't mean it that way," Heidi eagerly proceeded; "you must learn so that you really know how afterwards."

"I can't," Peter remarked.

"Nobody believes you about that any more, and I won't either," Heidi said resolutely. "When I was in Frankfurt, grandmama told me that it wasn't true and that I shouldn't believe you."

Peter's astonishment was great.

"I'll teach you, for I know how; when you have learnt it, you must read one or two songs to grandmother every day."

"I shan't!" grumbled the boy.

This obstinate refusal made Heidi very angry. With

flaming eyes she planted herself before the boy and said: "I'll tell you what will happen, if you don't want to learn. Your mother has often said that she'll send you to Frankfurt. Clara showed me the terrible, large boys' school there, where you'll have to go. You must stay there till you are a man, Peter! You mustn't think that there is only one teacher there, and such a kind one as we have here. No, indeed! There are whole rows of them, and when they are out walking they have high black hats on their heads. I saw them myself, when I was out driving!"

Cold shivers ran down Peter's back.

"Yes, you'll have to go there, and when they find out that you can't read or even spell, they'll laugh at you!"

"I'll do it," said Peter, half angry and half frightened.

"Oh, I am glad. Let us start right away!" said Heidi joyfully, pulling Peter over to the table. Among the things that Clara had sent, Heidi had found a little book with the A,B,C and some rhymes. She had chosen this for the lessons. Peter, having to spell the first rhyme, found great difficulty, so Heidi said, "I'll read it to you, and then you'll be able to do it better. Listen:

> 'If A, B, C you do not know,
> Before the school board you must go.'"

"I won't go," said Peter stubbornly.

"Where?"

"Before the court."

"Hurry up and learn the three letters, then you won't have to!"

Peter, beginning again, repeated the three letters till Heidi said:

"Now you know them."

Having observed the good result of the first rhyme, she began to read again:

"D, E, F you then must read,
Or of misfortune take good heed!
Who over L and M doth stumble,
Must pay a penance and feel humble.
There's trouble coming; if you knew,
You'd quickly learn N, O, P, Q.
If still you halt on R, S, T,
You'll suffer for it speedily."

Heidi, stopping, looked at Peter, who was so frightened by all these threats and mysterious horrors that he sat as still as a mouse. Heidi's tender heart was touched, and she said comfortingly: "Don't be afraid, Peter; if you come to me every day, you'll soon learn all the letters and then those things won't happen. But come every day, even when it snows. Promise!"

Peter did so, and departed. Obeying Heidi's instructions, he came daily to her for his lesson.

Sometimes the grandfather would sit in the room, smoking his pipe; often the corners of his mouth would twitch as if he could hardly keep from laughing.

He generally invited Peter to stay to supper afterwards, which liberally rewarded the boy for all his great exertions.

Thus the days passed by. In all this time Peter had really made some progress, though the rhymes still gave him difficulty.

When they had come to U, Heidi read:

"Whoever mixes U and V,
Will go where he won't want to be!"

and further,

"If W you still ignore,
Look at the rod beside the door."

Often Peter would growl and object to those measures, but nevertheless he kept on learning, and soon had but three letters left.

The next few days the following rhymes, with their threats, made Peter more eager than ever.

> If you the letter X forget
> For you no supper will be set.
> If you still hesitate with Y,
> For shame you'll run away and cry.

When Heidi read the last,

> "And he who makes his Z with blots,
> Must journey to the Hottentots,"

Peter sneered: "Nobody even knows where they are!"

"I am sure grandfather does," Heidi retorted, jumping up. "Just wait one minute and I shall ask him. He is over with the parson," and with that she had opened the door.

"Wait!" shrieked Peter in great alarm, for he saw himself already transported to those dreadful people. "What is the matter with you?" said Heidi, standing still.

"Nothing, but stay here. I'll learn," he blubbered. But Heidi, wanting to know something about the Hottentots herself, could only be kept back by piteous screams from Peter. So at last they settled down again, and before it was time to go, Peter knew the last letter, and had even begun to read syllables. From this day on he progressed more quickly.

It was three weeks since Heidi had paid her last visit to the grandmother, for much snow had fallen since. One evening, Peter, coming home, said triumphantly:

"I can do it!"

"What is it you can do, Peter?" asked his mother, eagerly.

"Read."

"What, is it possible? Did you hear it, grandmother?" exclaimed Brigida.

The grandmother also was curious to learn how this had happened.

"I must read a song now; Heidi told me to," Peter continued. To the women's amazement, Peter began. After every verse his mother would exclaim, "Who would have ever thought it!" while the grandmother remained silent.

One day later, when it happened that it was Peter's turn to read in school, the teacher said:

"Peter, must I pass you by again, as usual? Or do you want to try – I shall not say to read, but to stammer through a line?"

Peter began and read three lines without stopping.

In dumb astonishment, the teacher, putting down his book, looked at the boy.

"What miracle has happened to you?" he exclaimed. "For a long time I tried to teach you with all my patience, and you were not even able to grasp the letters, but now that I had given you up as hopeless, you have not only learnt how to spell, but even to read. How did this happen, Peter?"

"It was Heidi," the boy replied.

In great amazement, the teacher looked at the little girl. Then the kind man continued:

"I have noticed a great change in you, Peter. You used to stay away from school, sometimes more than a week, and lately you have not even missed a day. Who has brought about this change?"

"The uncle."

Every evening now Peter on his return home read one song to his grandmother, but never more. To the frequent praises of Brigida, the old woman once replied: "I am glad he has learnt something, but nevertheless I am longing for the spring to come. Then Heidi can visit me, for when she reads, the verses sound so different. I cannot always follow Peter, and the songs don't thrill me the way they do when Heidi says them!"

And no wonder! For Peter would often leave out long and difficult words, – what did three or four words matter! So it happened sometimes that there were hardly any nouns left in the hymns that Peter read.

CHAPTER 20

News from Distant Friends

May had come. Warm sunshine was bathing the whole Alp in glorious light, and having melted the last snow, had brought the first spring flowers to the surface. A merry spring wind was blowing, drying up the damp places in the shadow. High above in the azure heaven the eagle floated peacefully.

Heidi and her grandfather were back on the Alp. The child was so happy to be home again that she jumped about among the beloved objects. Here she discovered a new spring bud, and there she watched the gay little gnats and beetles that were swarming in the sun.

The grandfather was busy in his little shop, and a sound of hammering and sawing could be heard. Heidi had to go and see what the grandfather was making. There before the door stood a neat new chair, while the old man was busy making a second.

"Oh, I know what they are for," said Heidi gaily. "You are making them for Clara and grandmama. Oh, but we need a third – or do you think that Miss Rottenmeier won't come, perhaps?"

"I really don't know," said grandfather: "but it is safer to have a chair for her, if she should come."

Heidi, thoughtfully looking at the backless chairs,

remarked: "Grandfather, I don't think she would sit down on those."

"Then we must invite her to sit down on the beautiful green lounge of grass," quietly answered the old man.

While Heidi was still wondering what the grandfather had meant, Peter arrived, whistling and calling. As usual, Heidi was soon surrounded by the goats, who also seemed happy to be back on the Alp. Peter, angrily pushing the goats aside, marched up to Heidi, thrusting a letter into her hand.

"Did you get a letter for me on the pasture?" Heidi said, astonished.

"No."

"Where did it come from?"

"From my bag."

The letter had been given to Peter the previous evening; putting it in his lunch-bag, the boy had forgotten it there till he opened the bag for his dinner. Heidi immediately recognized Clara's handwriting, and bounding over to her grandfather, exclaimed: "A letter has come from Clara. Wouldn't you like me to read it to you, grandfather?"

Heidi immediately read to her two listeners, as follows: –

Dear Heidi: –
We are all packed up and shall travel in two or three days. Papa is leaving, too, but not with us, for he has to go to Paris first. The dear doctor visits us now every day, and as soon as he opens the door, he calls, 'Away to the Alp!' for he can hardly wait for us to go. If you only knew how he enjoyed being with you last fall! He came nearly every day this winter to tell us all about you and the grandfather and the mountains and the flowers he saw. He said that it was so quiet in the pure, delicious air, away from towns and streets, that

everybody has to get well there. He is much better himself since his visit, and seems younger and happier. Oh, how I look forward to it all! The doctor's advice is, that I shall go to Ragatz first for about six weeks, then I can go to live in the village, and from there I shall come to see you every fine day. Grandmama, who is coming with me, is looking forward to the trip too. But just think, Miss Rottenmeier does not want to go. When grandmama urges her, she always declines politely. I think Sebastian must have given her such a terrible description of the high rocks and fearful abysses, that she is afraid. I think he told her that it was not safe for anybody, and that only goats could climb such dreadful heights. She used to be so eager to go to Switzerland, but now neither Tinette nor she wants to take the risk. I can hardly wait to see you again!

Good-bye, dear Heidi, with much love from grandmama,

I am your true friend,

Clara.

When Peter heard this, he swung his rod to right and left. Furiously driving the goats before him, he bounded down the hill.

Heidi visited the grandmother next day, for she had to tell her the good news. Sitting up in her corner, the old woman was spinning as usual. Her face looked sad, for Peter had already announced the near visit of Heidi's friends, and she dreaded the result.

After having poured out her full heart, Heidi looked at the old woman. "What is it, grandmother?" said the child. "Are you not glad?"

"Oh yes, Heidi, I am glad, because you are happy."

"But, grandmother, you seem so anxious. Do you still think Miss Rottenmeier is coming?"

"Oh no, it is nothing. Give me your hand, for I want to be sure that you are still here. I suppose it will be for the best, even if I shall not live to see the day!"

"Oh, but then I would not care about this coming," said the child.

The grandmother had hardly slept all night for thinking of Clara's coming. Would they take Heidi away from her, now that she was well and strong? But for the sake of the child she resolved to be brave.

"Heidi," she said, "please read me the song that begins with 'God will see to it.'"

Heidi immediately did as she was told; she knew nearly all the grandmother's favorite hymns by now and always found them quickly.

"That does me good, child," the old woman said. Already the expression of her face seemed happier and less troubled. "Please read it a few times over, child," she entreated.

Thus evening came, and when Heidi wandered homewards, one twinkling star after another appeared in the sky. Heidi stood still every few minutes, looking up to the firmament in wonder. When she arrived home, her grandfather also was looking up to the stars, murmuring to himself: "What a wonderful month! – one day clearer than the other. The herbs will be fine and strong this year."

The blossom month had passed, and June, with the long, long days, had come. Quantities of flowers were blooming everywhere, filling the air with perfume. The month was nearing its end, when one morning Heidi came running out of the hut, where she had already completed her duties. Suddenly she screamed so loud that the grandfather hurriedly came out to see what had happened.

"Grandfather! Come here! Look, look!"

A strange procession was winding up the Alm. First

marched two men, carrying an open sedan chair with a young girl in it, wrapped up in many shawls. Then came a stately lady on horseback, who, talking with a young guide beside her, looked eagerly right and left. Then an empty rolling-chair, carried by a young fellow, was followed by a porter who had so many covers, shawls and furs piled up on his basket that they towered high above his head.

"They are coming! they are coming!" cried Heidi in her joy, and soon the party had arrived at the top. Great was the happiness of the children at seeing each other again. When grandmama had descended from her horse, she tenderly greeted Heidi first, and then turned to the uncle, who had approached the group. The two met like two old friends, they had heard so much about each other.

After the first words were exchanged, the grandmother exclaimed: "My dear uncle, what a wonderful residence you have. Who would have ever thought it! Kings could envy you here! Oh, how well my Heidi is looking, just like a little rose!" she continued, drawing the child closely to her side and patting her cheeks. "What glory everywhere! Clara, what do you say to it all?"

Clara, looking about her rapturously, cried: "Oh, how wonderful, how glorious! I have never dreamt it could be as beautiful as that. Oh grandmama, I wish I could stay here!"

The uncle had busied himself in the meantime with getting Clara's rolling-chair for her. Then, going up to the girl, he gently lifted her into her seat. Putting some covers over her knees, he tucked her feet in warmly. It seemed as if the grandfather had done nothing else all his life than nurse lame people.

"My dear uncle," said the grandmama, surprised, "please tell me where you learned that, for I shall send all the nurses I know here immediately."

The uncle smiled faintly, while he replied: "It comes more from care than study."

His face became sad. Before his eyes had risen bygone

times. For that was the way he used to care for his poor wounded captain, whom he had found in Sicily after a violent battle. He alone had been allowed to nurse him till his death, and now he would take just as good care of poor, lame Clara.

When Clara had looked a long time at the cloudless sky above and all the rocky crags, she said longingly: "I wish I could walk round the hut to the fir-trees. If I only could see all the things you told me so much about!"

Heidi pushed with all her might, and behold! the chair rolled easily over the dry grass. When they had come into the little grove, Clara could not see her fill of those splendid trees that must have stood there so many, many years. Although the people had changed and vanished, they had remained the same, ever looking down into the valley.

When they passed the empty goat-shed, Clara said piti-fully: "Oh grandmama, if I could only wait up here for Schwänli and Bärli! I am afraid I shan't see Peter and his goats, if we have to go away so soon again."

"Dear child, enjoy now what you can," said the grand-mama, who had followed.

"Oh, what wonderful flowers!" exclaimed Clara again; "whole bushes of exquisite, red blossoms. Oh, if I could only pick some of those bluebells!"

Heidi, immediately gathering a large bunch, put them in Clara's lap.

"Clara, this is really nothing in comparison with the many flowers in the pasture. You must come up once and see them. There are so many that the ground seems golden with them. If you ever sit down among them, you will feel as if you could never get up any more, it is so beautiful."

"Oh, grandmama, do you think I can ever go up there?" Clara asked with a wild longing in her eyes. "If I could only walk with you, Heidi, and climb round everywhere!"

"I'll push you!" Heidi said for comfort. To show how easy it was, she pushed the chair at such a rate that it would have tumbled down the mountain, if the grandfather had not stopped it at the last moment.

It was time for dinner now. The table was spread near the bench, and soon everybody sat down. The grandmother was so overcome by the view and the delicious wind that fanned her cheek that she remarked: "What a wondrous place this is! I have never seen its like! But what do I see?" she continued. "I think you are actually eating your second piece of cheese, Clara?"

"Oh grandmama, it tastes better than all the things we get in Ragatz," replied the child, eagerly eating the savory dish.

"Don't stop, our mountain wind helps along where the cooking is faulty!" contentedly said the old man.

During the meal the uncle and the grandmama had soon got into a lively conversation. They seemed to agree on many things, and understood each other like old friends. A little later the grandmama looked over to the west.

"We must soon start, Clara, for the sun is already low; our guides will be here shortly."

Clara's face had become sad, and she entreated: "Oh, please let us stay here another hour or so. We haven't even seen the hut yet. I wish the day were twice as long."

The grandmama assented to Clara's wish to go inside. When the rolling-chair was found too broad for the door, the uncle quietly lifted Clara in his strong arms and carried her in. Grandmama was eagerly looking about her, glad to see everything so neat. Then going up the little ladder to the hay-loft, she discovered Heidi's bed. "Is that your bed, Heidi? What a delicious perfume! It must be a healthy place to sleep," she said, looking out through the window. The grandfather, with Clara, was coming up, too, with Heidi following.

Clara was perfectly entranced. "What a lovely place to sleep! Oh, Heidi, you can look right up to the sky from your bed. What a good smell! You can hear the fir-trees roar here, can't you? Oh, I never saw a more delightful bed-room!"

The uncle, looking at the old lady, said now: "I have an idea that it would give Clara new strength to stay up here with us a little while. Of course, I only mean if you did not object. You have brought so many wraps that we can easily make a soft bed for Clara here. My dear lady, you can easily leave the care to me. I'll undertake it gladly."

The children screamed for joy, and grandmama's face was beaming.

"What a fine man you are!" she burst out. "I was just thinking myself that a stay here would strengthen the child, but then I thought of the care and trouble for you. And now you have offered to do it, as if it was nothing at all. How can I thank you enough, uncle?"

After shaking hands many times, the two prepared Clara's bed, which, thanks to the old lady's precautions, was soon so soft that the hay could not be felt through at all.

The uncle had carried his new patient back to her rolling-chair, and there they found her sitting, with Heidi beside her. They were eagerly talking of their plans for the coming weeks. When they were told that Clara might stay for a month or so, their faces beamed more than ever.

The guide, with the horse, and the carriers of the chair, now appeared, but the last two were not needed any more and could be sent away.

When the grandmother got ready to leave, Clara called gaily to her: "Oh grandmama, it won't be long, for you must often come and see us."

While the uncle was leading the horse down the steep incline, the grandmama told him that she would go back to Ragatz, for the Dörfli was too lonely for her. She also promised to come back from time to time.

Before the grandfather had returned, Peter came racing down to the hut with all his goats. Seeing Heidi, they ran up to her in haste, and so Clara made the acquaintance of Schwänli and Bärli and all the others.

Peter, however, kept away, only sending furious looks at the two girls. When they bade him good-night, he only ran away, beating the air with his stick.

The end of the joyous day had come. The two children were both lying in their beds.

"Oh, Heidi!" Clara exclaimed, "I can see so many glittering stars, and I feel as if we were driving in a high carriage straight into the sky."

"Yes, and do you know why the stars twinkle so merrily?" inquired Heidi.

"No, but tell me."

"Because they know that God in heaven looks after us mortals and we never need to fear. See, they twinkle and show us how to be merry, too. But Clara, we must not forget to pray to God and ask Him to think of us and keep us safe."

Sitting up in bed, they then said their evening prayer. As soon as Heidi lay down, she fell asleep. But Clara could not sleep quite yet, it was too wonderful to see the stars from her bed.

In truth she had never seen them before, because in Frankfurt all the blinds were always down long before the stars came out, and at night she had never been outside the house. She could hardly keep her eyes shut, and had to open them again and again to watch the twinkling, glistening stars, till her eyes closed at last and she saw two big, glittering stars in her dream.

CHAPTER 21

Of Further Events on the Alp

The sun was just rising, and the Alm-Uncle was watching how mountain and dale awoke to the new day, and the clouds above grew brighter.

Next, the old man turned to go back into the hut, and softly climbed the ladder. Clara, having just a moment ago opened her eyes, looked about her in amazement. Bright sunbeams danced on her bed. Where was she? But soon she discovered her sleeping friend, and heard the grandfather's cheery voice:

"How did you sleep? Not tired?"

Clara, feeling fresh and rested, said that she had never slept better in all her life. Heidi was soon awake, too, and lost no time in coming down to join Clara, who was already sitting in the sun.

A cool morning breeze fanned their cheeks, and the spicy fragrance from the fir-trees filled their lungs with every breath. Clara had never experienced such well-being in all her life. She had never breathed such pure, cool morning air and never felt such warm, delicious sunshine on her feet and hands. It surpassed all her expectations.

"Oh, Heidi, I wish I could always stay up here with you!" she said.

"Now you can see that everything is as beautiful as I told you," Heidi replied triumphantly. "Up on the Alp with grandfather is the loveliest spot in all the world."

The grandfather was just coming out of the shed with two full bowls of steaming, snow-white milk. Handing one to each of the children, he said to Clara: "This will do you good, little girl. It comes from Schwänli and will give you strength. To your health! Just drink it!" he said encouragingly, for Clara had hesitated a little. But when she saw that Heidi's bowl was nearly empty already, she also drank without even stopping. Oh, how good it was! It tasted like cinnamon and sugar.

"We'll take two tomorrow," said the grandfather.

After their breakfast, Peter arrived. While the goats were rushing up to Heidi, bleating loudly, the grandfather took the boy aside.

"Just listen, and do what I tell you," he said. "From now on you must let Schwänli go wherever she likes. She knows where to get the richest herbs, and you must follow her, even if she should go higher up than usual. It won't do you any harm to climb a little more, and will do all the others good. I want the goats to give me splendid milk, remember. What are you looking at so furiously?"

Peter was silent, and without more ado started off, still angrily looking back now and then. As Heidi had followed a little way, Peter called to her: "You must come along, Heidi, Schwänli has to be followed everywhere."

"No, but I can't," Heidi called back: "I won't be able to come as long as Clara is with me. Grandfather has promised, though, to let us come up with you once."

With those words Heidi returned to Clara, while the goatherd was hurrying onward, angrily shaking his fists.

The children had promised to write a letter to grandmama every day, so they immediately started on their task. Heidi brought out her own little three-legged stool, her school-books and her papers, and with these on Clara's lap they began to write. Clara stopped after nearly every sentence, for she had to look around. Oh, how peaceful it was with the little gnats dancing in the sun and the rustling of the trees! From time to time they could hear the shouting of a shepherd re-echoed from many rocks.

The morning had passed, they knew not how, and dinner was ready. They again ate outside, for Clara had to be in the open air all day, if possible. The afternoon was spent in the cool shadow of the fir-trees. Clara had many things to relate of Frankfurt and all the people that Heidi knew. It was not long before Peter arrived with his flock, but without even answering the girls' friendly greeting, he disappeared with a grim scowl.

While Schwänli was being milked in the shed, Clara said:

"Oh, Heidi, I feel as if I could not wait for my milk. Isn't it funny? All my life I have only eaten because I had to. Everything always tasted to me like cod-liver oil, and I have often wished that I should never have to eat. And now I am so hungry!"

"Oh yes, I know," Heidi replied. She had to think of the days in Frankfurt when her food seemed to stick in her throat.

When at last the full bowls were brought by the old man, Clara, seizing hers, eagerly drank the contents in one draught and even finished before Heidi.

"Please, may I have a little more?" she asked, holding out the bowl.

Nodding, much pleased, the grandfather soon refilled it. This time he also brought with him a slice of bread and butter for the children. He had gone to Maiensass that afternoon to get the butter, and his trouble was well rewarded: they enjoyed it as if it had been the rarest dish.

This evening Clara fell asleep the moment she lay down. Two or three days passed in this pleasant way. The next brought a surprise. Two strong porters came up the Alp, each carrying on his back a fresh, white bed. They also brought a letter from grandmama, in which she thanked the children for their faithful writing, and told them that the beds were meant for them. When they went to sleep that night, they found their new beds in exactly the same position as their former ones had been.

Clara's rapture in her new life grew greater every day, and she could not write enough of the grandfather's kindly care and of Heidi's entertaining stories. She told her grandmama that her first thought in the morning always was: "Thank God, I am still in the Alm-hut."

Grandmama was highly pleased at those reports, and put her projected visit off a little while, for she had found the ride pretty tiring.

The grandfather took excellent care of his little patient, and no day passed on which he did not climb around to find the most savory herbs for Schwänli. The little goat thrived so that everybody could see it in the way her eyes were flashing.

It was the third week of Clara's stay. Every morning after the grandfather had carried her down, he said to her: "Would my Clara try to stand a little?" Clara always sighed, "Oh, it hurts me so!" but though she would cling to him, he made her stand a little longer every day.

This summer was the finest that had been for years. Day after day the sun shone on a cloudless sky, and at night it would pour its purple, rosy light down on the rocks and snow-fields till everything seemed to glow like fire.

Heidi had told Clara over and over again of all the flowers on the pasture, of the masses of golden roses and the blue-flowers that covered the ground. She had just been telling it again, when a longing seized her, and jumping up she ran over to her grandfather, who was busy carving in the shop.

"Oh, grandfather," she cried from afar, "won't you come with us to the pasture tomorrow? Oh, it's so beautiful up there now."

"All right, I will," he replied; "but tell Clara that she must do something to please me; she must try to stand longer this evening for me."

Heidi merrily came running with her message. Of course, Clara promised, for was it not her greatest wish to go up with Heidi to the pasture! When Peter returned this evening, he heard of the plan for the morrow. But for answer Peter only growled, nearly hitting poor Thistlefinch in his anger.

The children had just resolved to stay awake all night to talk about the coming day, when their conversation suddenly ceased and they were both peacefully slumbering. In her dreams Clara saw before her a field that was thickly strewn with light-blue flowers, while Heidi heard the eagle scream to her from above, "Come, come, come!"

CHAPTER 22

Something Unexpected Happens

The next day dawned cloudless and fair. The grandfather was still with the children, when Peter came climbing up; his goats kept at a good distance from him, to evade the rod, which was striking right and left. The truth was that the boy was terribly embittered and angry by the changes that had come. When he passed the hut in the morning, Heidi was always busy with the strange child, and in the evening it was the same. All summer long Heidi had not been up with him a single time; it was too much! And to-day she was coming at last, but again in company with this hateful stranger.

It was then that Peter noticed the rolling-chair standing near the hut. After carefully glancing about him, he rushed at the hated object and pushed it down the incline. The chair fairly flew away and had soon disappeared.

Peter's conscience smote him now, and he raced up the Alp, not daring to pause till he had reached a blackberry bush. There he could hide, when the uncle might appear. Looking down, he watched his fallen enemy tumbling downwards, downwards.

Sometimes it was thrown high up into the air, to crash down again the next moment harder than ever. Pieces were falling from it right and left, and were blown about. Now the stranger would have to travel home and Heidi would be his again! But Peter had forgotten that a bad deed always brings a punishment.

Heidi just now came out of the hut. The grandfather, with Clara, followed. Heidi at first stood still, and then, running right and left, she returned to the old man.

"What does this mean? Have you rolled the chair away Heidi?" he asked.

"I am just looking for it everywhere, grandfather. You said it was beside the shop door," said the child, still hunting for the missing object. A strong wind was blowing, which at this moment violently closed the shop-door.

"Grandfather, the wind has done it," exclaimed Heidi eagerly. "Oh dear! if it has rolled all the way down to the village, it will be too late to go to-day. It will take us a long time to fetch it."

"If it has rolled down there, we shall never get it any more, for it will be smashed to pieces," said the old man, looking down and measuring the distance from the corner of the hut.

"I don't see how it happened," he remarked.

"What a shame! now I'll never be able to go up to the pasture," lamented Clara. "I am afraid I'll have to go home now. What a pity, what a pity!"

"You can find a way for her to stay, grandfather, can't you?"

"We'll go up to the pasture to-day, as we have planned. Then we shall see what further happens."

The children were delighted, and the grandfather lost no time in getting ready. First he fetched a pile of covers, and seating Clara on a sunny spot on the dry ground, he got their breakfast.

"I wonder why Peter is so late to-day," he said, leading his goats out of the shed. Then, lifting Clara up on one strong arm, he carried the covers on the other.

"Now, march!" he cried. "The goats come with us."

That suited Heidi, and with one arm round Schwänli and the other round Bärli, she wandered up. Her little companions were so pleased at having her with them again that they nearly crushed her with affection.

What was their astonishment when, arriving on top, they saw Peter already lying on the ground, with his peaceful flock about him.

"What did you mean by going by us like that? I'll teach you!" called the uncle to him.

Peter was frightened, for he knew the voice.

"Nobody was up yet," the boy retorted.

"Have you seen the chair?" asked the uncle again.

"Which?" Peter growled.

The uncle said no more. Unfolding the covers, he put Clara down on the dry grass. Then, when he had been assured of Clara's comfort, he got ready to go home. The three were to stay there till his return in the evening. When dinner time had come, Heidi was to prepare the meal and see that Clara got Schwänli's milk.

The sky was a deep blue, and the snow on the peaks was glistening. The eagle was floating above the rocky crags. The children felt wonderfully happy. Now and then one of the goats would come and lie down near them. Tender little Snowhopper came oftener than any and would rub her head against their shoulders.

They had been sitting quietly for a few hours, drinking in the beauty about them, when Heidi suddenly began to long for the spot where so many flowers grew. In the evening it would be too late to see them, for they always shut their little eyes by then.

"Oh, Clara," she said hesitatingly, "would you be angry if I went away from you a minute and left you alone? I want to see the flowers; But wait!—" Jumping away, she brought Clara some bunches of fragrant herbs and put them in her lap. Soon after she returned with little Snowhopper.

"So, now you don't need to be alone," said Heidi. When Clara had assured her that it would give her pleasure to be left alone with the goats, Heidi started on her walk. Clara slowly handed one leaf after another to the little creature; it became more and more confiding, and cuddling close to the child, ate the herbs out of her hand. It was easy to see how happy it was to be away from the boisterous big goats, which often annoyed it. Clara felt a sensation of contentment such as she had never before experienced. She loved to sit there on the mountain-side with the confiding little goat by her. A great desire rose in her heart that hour. She longed to be her own master and be able to help others instead of being helped by them. Many other thoughts and ideas rushed through her mind. How would it be to live up here in continual sunshine? The world seemed so joyous and wonderful all of a sudden. Premonitions of future undreamt-of happiness made her heart beat. Suddenly she threw both arms about the little goat and said: "Oh, little Snowhopper how beautiful it is up here! If I could always stay with you!"

Heidi in the meantime had reached the spot, where, as she had expected, the whole ground was covered with yellow rock-roses. Near together in patches the bluebells were nodding gently in the breeze. But all the perfume that filled the air came from the modest little brown flowers that hid their heads between the golden flower-cups. Heidi stood enraptured, drawing in the perfumed air.

Suddenly she turned and ran back to Clara, shouting to her from far: "Oh, you must come, Clara, it is so lovely there. In the evening it won't be so fine any more. Don't you think I could carry you?"

"But Heidi," Clara said, "of course you can't; you are much smaller than I am. Oh, I wish I could walk!"

Heidi meditated a little. Peter was still lying on the ground. He had been staring down for hours, unable to believe what he saw before him. He had destroyed the chair to get rid of the stranger, and there she was again, sitting right beside his playmate.

Heidi now called to him to come down, but as reply he only grumbled: "Shan't come."

"But you must; come quickly, for I want you to help me. Quickly!" urged the child.

"Don't want to," sounded the reply.

Heidi hurried up the mountain now and shouted angrily to the boy: "Peter, if you don't come this minute, I shall do something that you won't like."

Those words scared Peter, for his conscience was not clear. His deed had rejoiced him till this moment, when Heidi seemed to talk as if she knew it all. What if the grandfather should hear about it! Trembling with fear, Peter obeyed.

"I shall only come if you promise not to do what you said," insisted the boy.

"No, no, I won't. Don't be afraid," said Heidi compassionately: "Just come along; it isn't so hard."

Peter, on approaching Clara, was told to help raise the lame child from the ground on one side, while Heidi helped on the other. This went easily enough, but difficulties soon followed. Clara was not able to stand alone, and how could they get any further?

"You must take me round the neck," said Heidi, who had seen what poor guides they made.

The boy, who had never offered his arm to anybody in his life, had to be shown how first, before further efforts could be made. But it was too hard. Clara tried to set her feet forward, but got discouraged.

"Press your feet on the ground more and I am sure it will hurt you less," suggested Heidi.

"Do you think so?" said Clara, timidly.

But, obeying, she ventured a firmer step and soon another, uttering a little cry as she went.

"Oh, it really has hurt me less," she said joyfully.

"Try it again," Heidi urged her. Clara did, and took another step, and then another, and another still. Suddenly she cried aloud: "Oh, Heidi, I can do it. Oh, I really can. Just look! I can take steps, one after another."

Heidi rapturously exclaimed: "Oh, Clara, can you really? Can you walk? Oh, can you take steps now? Oh, if only grandfather would come! Now you can walk, Clara, now you can walk," she kept on saying joyfully.

Clara held on tight to the children, but with every new step she became more firm.

"Now you can come up here every day," cried Heidi. "Now we can walk wherever we want to and you don't have to be pushed in a chair any more. Now you'll be able to walk all your life. Oh, what joy!"

Clara's greatest wish, to be able to be well like other people, had been fulfilled at last. It was not very far to the flowering field. Soon they reached it and sat down among the wealth of bloom. It was the first time that Clara had ever rested on the dry, warm earth. All about them the flowers nodded and exhaled their perfume. It was a scene of exquisite beauty.

The two children could hardly grasp this happiness that had come to them. It filled their hearts brimming full and made them silent. Peter also lay motionless, for he had gone to sleep.

Thus the hours flew, and the day was long past noon. Suddenly all the goats arrived, for they had been seeking the children. They did not like to graze in the flowers, and were glad when Peter awoke with their loud bleating. The poor boy was mightily bewildered, for he had dreamt that the rolling-chair with the red cushions stood again before his eyes. On awaking, he had still seen the golden nails; but soon he discovered that they were nothing but flowers. Remembering his deed, he obeyed Heidi's instructions willingly.

When they came back to their former place, Heidi lost no time in setting out the dinner. The bag was very full to-day, and Heidi hurried to fulfill her promise to Peter, who with bad conscience had understood her threat differently. She made three heaps of the good things, and when Clara and she were through, there was still a lot left for the boy. It was too bad that all this treat did not give him the usual satisfaction, for something seemed to stick in his throat.

Soon after their belated dinner, the grandfather was seen climbing up the Alp. Heidi ran to meet him, confusedly telling him of the great event. The old man's face shone at this news. Going over to Clara, he said: "So you have risked it? Now we have won."

Then picking her up, he put one arm around her waist, and the other one he stretched out as support, and with his help she marched more firmly than ever. Heidi jumped and bounded gaily by their side. In all this excitement the grandfather did not lose his judgment, and before long lifted Clara on his arm to carry her home. He knew that too much exertion would be dangerous, and rest was needed for the tired girl.

Peter, arriving in the village late that day, saw a large disputing crowd. They were all standing about an interesting object, and everybody pushed and fought for a chance to get nearest. It was no other than the chair.

"I saw it when they carried it up," Peter heard the baker say. "I bet it was worth at least five hundred francs. I should just like to know how it has happened."

"The wind might have blown it down," remarked Barbara, who was staring open-mouthed at the beautiful velvet cushions. "The uncle said so himself."

"It is a good thing if nobody else has done it," continued the baker. "When the gentleman from Frankfurt hears what has happened, he'll surely find out all about it, and I should pity the culprit. I am glad I haven't been up on the Alm for so long, else they might suspect me, as they would anybody who happened to be up there at the time."

Many more opinions were uttered, but Peter had heard enough. He quietly slipped away and went home. What if they should find out he had done it? A policeman might arrive any time now and they might take him away to prison. Peter's hair stood up on end at this alarming thought.

He was so troubled when he came home that he did not answer any questions and even refused his dish of potatoes. Hurriedly creeping into bed, he groaned.

"I am sure Peter has eaten sorrel again, and that makes him groan so," said his mother.

"You must give him a little more bread in the morning, Brigida. Take a piece of mine," said the compassionate grandmother.

When Clara and Heidi were lying in their beds that night, glancing up at the shining stars, Heidi remarked: "Didn't you think to-day, Clara, that it is fortunate God does not always give us what we pray for fervently, because He knows of something better?"

"What do you mean, Heidi?" asked Clara.

"You see, when I was in Frankfurt I prayed and prayed to come home again, and when I couldn't, I thought He had forgotten me. But if I had gone away so soon you would never have come here and would never have got well."

Clara, becoming thoughtful, said: "But, Heidi, then we could not pray for anything any more, because we would feel that He always knows of something better."

"But, Clara, we must pray to God every day to show we don't forget that all gifts come from Him. Grandmama has told me that God forgets us if we forget Him. But if some wish remains unfulfilled we must show our confidence in Him, for he knows best."

"How did you ever think of that?" asked Clara.

"Grandmama told me, but I know that it is so. We must thank God to-day that He has made you able to walk, Clara."

"I am glad that you have reminded me, Heidi, for I have nearly forgotten it in my excitement."

The children both prayed and sent their thanks up to heaven for the restoration of the invalid.

Next morning a letter was written to grandmama, inviting her to come up to the Alp within a week's time, for the children had planned to take her by surprise. Clara hoped then to be able to walk alone, with Heidi for her guide.

The following days were happier still for Clara. Every morning she awoke with her heart singing over and over again, "Now I am well! Now I can walk like other people!"

She progressed, and took longer walks every day. Her appetite grew amazingly, and the grandfather had to make larger slices of the bread and butter that, to his delight, disappeared so rapidly. He had to fill bowl after bowl of the foaming milk for the hungry children. In that way they reached the end of the week that was to bring the grandmama.

CHAPTER 23

Parting to Meet Again

A day before her visit the grandmama had sent a letter to announce her coming. Peter brought it up with him next morning. The grandfather was already before the hut with the children and his merry goats. His face looked proud, as he contemplated the rosy faces of the girls and the shining hair of his two goats.

Peter, approaching, neared the uncle slowly. As soon as he had delivered the letter, he sprang back shyly, looking about him as if he was afraid. Then with a leap he started off.

"I should like to know why Peter behaves like the Big Turk when he is afraid of the rod," said Heidi, watching his strange behavior.

"Maybe Peter fears a rod that he deserves," said the old man.

All the way Peter was tormented with fear. He could not help thinking of the policeman who was coming from Frankfurt to fetch him to prison.

It was a busy morning for Heidi, who put the hut in order for the expected visitor. The time went by quickly, and soon everything was ready to welcome the good grandmama.

The grandfather also returned from a walk, on which he

had gathered a glorious bunch of deep-blue gentians. The children, who were sitting on the bench, exclaimed for joy when they saw the glowing flowers.

Heidi, getting up from time to time to spy down the path, suddenly discovered grandmama, sitting on a white horse and accompanied by two men. One of them carried plenty of wraps, for without those the lady did not dare to pay such a visit.

The party came nearer and nearer, and soon reached the top.

"What do I see? Clara, what is this? Why are you not sitting in your chair? How is this possible?" cried the grandmama in alarm, dismounting hastily. Before she had quite reached the children she threw her arms up in great excitement:

"Clara, is that really you? You have red, round cheeks, my child! I hardly know you any more!" Grandmama was going to rush at her grandchild, when Heidi slipped from the bench, and Clara, taking her arm, they quietly took a little walk. The grandmama was rooted to the spot from fear. What was this? Upright and firm, Clara walked beside her friend. When they came back their rosy faces beamed. Rushing toward the children, the grandmother hugged them over and over again.

Looking over to the bench, she beheld the uncle, who sat there smiling. Taking Clara's arm in hers, she walked over to him, continually venting her delight. When she reached the old man, she took both his hands in hers and said:

"My dear, dear uncle! What have we to thank you for! This is your work, your care and nursing—"

"But our Lord's sunshine and mountain air," interrupted the uncle, smiling.

Then Clara called, "Yes, and also Schwänli's good, delicious milk. Grandmama, you ought to see how much goat-milk I can drink now; oh, it is so good!"

"Indeed I can see that from your cheeks," said the grandmama, smiling. "No, I hardly recognize you any more. You have become broad and round! I never dreamt that you could get so stout and tall! Oh, Clara, is it really true? I cannot look at you enough. But now I must telegraph your father to come. I shan't tell him anything about you, for it will be the greatest joy of all his life. My dear uncle, how are we going to manage it? Have you sent the men away?"

"I have, but I can easily send the goatherd."

So they decided that Peter should take the message. The uncle immediately whistled so loud that it resounded from all sides. Soon Peter arrived, white with fear, for he thought his doom had come. But he only received a paper that was to be carried to the post-office of the village.

Relieved for the moment, Peter set out. Now all the happy friends sat down round the table, and grandmama was told how the miracle had happened. Often the talk was interrupted by exclamations of surprise from grandmama, who still believed it was all a dream. How could this be her pale, weak little Clara? The children were in a constant state of joy, to see how their surprise had worked.

Meanwhile Mr. Sesemann, having finished his business in Paris, was also preparing a surprise. Without writing his mother he traveled to Ragatz on a sunny summer morning. He had arrived on this very day, some hours after his mother's departure, and now, taking a carriage, he drove to Mayenfeld.

The long ascent to the Alp from there seemed very weary and far to the traveller. When would he reach the goat-herd's hut? There were many little roads branching off in several directions, and sometimes Mr. Sesemann doubted if he had taken the right path. But not a soul was near, and no sound could be heard except the rustling of the wind and the hum of little insects. A merry little bird was singing on a larch-tree, but nothing more.

Standing still and cooling his brow, he saw a boy running down the hill at topmost speed. Mr. Sesemann called to him, but with no success, for the boy kept at a shy distance.

"Now, my boy, can't you tell me if I am on the right path to the hut where Heidi lives and the people from Frankfurt are staying?"

A dull sound of terror was the only reply. Peter shot off and rushed head over heels down the mountain-side, turning wild somersaults on his perilous way. His course resembled the course his enemy had taken some days ago.

"What a funny, bashful mountaineer!" Mr. Sesemann remarked to himself, thinking that the appearance of a stranger had upset this simple son of the Alps. After watching the downward course of the boy a little while, he soon proceeded on his way.

In spite of the greatest effort, Peter could not stop himself, and kept rolling on. But his fright and terror were still more terrible than his bumps and blows. This stranger was the policeman, that was a certain fact! At last, being thrown against a bush, he clutched it wildly.

"Good, here's another one!" a voice near Peter said. "I wonder who is going to be pushed down tomorrow, looking like a half-open potato-bag?" The village baker was making fun of him. For a little rest after his weary work, he had quietly watched the boy.

Peter regained his feet and slunk away. How did the baker know the chair had been pushed? He longed to go home to bed and hide, for there alone he felt safe. But he had to go up to the goats, and the uncle had clearly told him to come back as quickly as he could. Groaning, he limped away up to the Alp. How could he run now, with his fear and all his poor, sore limbs?

Mr. Sesemann had reached the hut soon after meeting Peter, and felt reassured. Climbing further, with renewed courage, he at last saw his goal before him, but not without long and weary exertion. He saw the Alm-hut above him, and the swaying fir-trees. Mr. Sesemann eagerly hurried to encounter his beloved child. They had seen him long ago from the hut, and a treat was prepared for him that he never suspected.

As he made the last steps, he saw two forms coming towards him. A tall girl, with light hair and rosy face, was leaning on Heidi, whose dark eyes sparkled with keen delight. Mr. Sesemann stopped short, staring at this vision. Suddenly big tears rushed from his eyes, for this shape before him recalled sweet memories. Clara's mother had looked exactly like this fair maiden. Mr. Sesemann at this moment did not know if he was awake or dreaming.

"Papa, don't you know me any more?" Clara called with beaming eyes. "Have I changed so much?"

Mr. Sesemann rushed up to her, folding her in his arms. "Yes, you *have* changed. How is it possible? Is it really true? Is it really you, Clara?" asked the over-joyed father, embracing her again and again, and then gazing at her, as she stood tall and firm by his side.

His mother joined them now, for she wanted to see the happiness of her son.

"What do you say to this, my son? Isn't our surprise finer than yours?" she greeted him. "But come over to our benefactor now, – I mean the uncle."

"Yes, indeed, I also must greet our little Heidi," said the gentleman, shaking Heidi's hand. "Well? Always fresh and happy on the mountain? I guess I don't need to ask, for no Alpine rose can look more blooming. Ah, child, what joy this is to me!"

With beaming eyes the child looked at the kind gentleman who had always been so good to her. Her heart throbbed in sympathy with his joy. While the two men, who had at last approached each other, were conversing, grandmama walked over to the grove. There, under the fir-trees, another surprise awaited her. A beautiful bunch of wondrously blue gentians stood as if they had grown there.

"How exquisite, how wonderful! What a sight!" she exclaimed, clapping her hands. "Heidi, come here! Have you brought me those? Oh, they are beautiful!"

The children had joined her, Heidi assuring her that it was another person's deed.

"Oh grandmama, up on the pasture it looks just like that," Clara remarked. "Just guess who brought you the flowers?"

At that moment a rustle was heard, and they saw Peter, who was trying to sneak up behind the trees to avoid the hut. Immediately the old lady called to him, for she thought that Peter himself had picked the flowers for her. He must be creeping away out of sheer modesty, the kind lady thought. To give him his reward, she called:

"Come here, my boy! don't be afraid."

Petrified with fear, Peter stood still. What had gone before had robbed him of his courage. He thought now that all was over with him. With his hair standing up on end and his pale face distorted by anguish, he approached.

"Come straight to me, boy," the old lady encouraged him. "Now tell me, boy, if you have done that."

In his anxiety, Peter did not see the grandmama's finger that pointed to the flowers. He only saw the uncle standing near the hut, looking at him penetratingly, and beside him the policeman, the greatest horror for him in the world. Trembling in every limb, Peter answered, "Yes!"

"Well, but what are you so frightened about?"

"Because – because it is broken and can never be mended again," Peter said, his knees tottering under him.

The grandmama now walked over to the hut: "My dear uncle," she asked kindly, "is this poor lad out of his mind?"

"Not at all," was the reply; "only the boy was the wind which blew away the wheel-chair. He is expecting the punishment he well deserves."

Grandmama was very much surprised, for she vowed that Peter looked far from wicked. Why should he have destroyed the chair? The uncle told her that he had noticed many signs of anger in the boy since Clara's advent on the Alp. He assured her that he had suspected the boy from the beginning.

"My dear uncle," the old lady said with animation, "we must not punish him further. We must be just. It was very hard on him when Clara robbed him of Heidi, who is and was his greatest treasure. When he had to sit alone day after day, it roused him to a passion which drove him to this wicked deed. It was rather foolish, but we all get so when we get angry."

The lady walked over to the boy again, who was still quivering with fear.

Sitting down on the bench, she began:

"Come, Peter, I'll tell you something. Stop trembling and listen. You pushed the chair down, to destroy it. You knew very well that it was wicked and deserved punishment. You tried very hard to conceal it, did you not? But if somebody thinks that nobody knows about a wicked deed, he is wrong; God always knows it. As soon as He finds that a man is trying to conceal an evil he has done, He wakens a little watchman in his heart, who keeps on pricking the person with a thorn till all his rest is gone. He keeps on calling to the evildoer: 'Now you'll be found out! Now your punishment is near!' – His joy has flown, for fear and terror take its place. Have you not just had such an experience, Peter?"

Peter nodded, all contrite. He certainly had experienced this.

"You have made a mistake," the grandmama continued, "by thinking that you would hurt Clara by destroying her chair. It has so happened that what you have done has been the greatest good for her. She would probably never have tried to walk, if her chair had been there. If she should stay here, she might even go up to the pasture every single day. Do you see, Peter? God can turn a misdeed to the good of the injured person and bring trouble on the offender. Have you understood me, Peter? Remember the little watchman when you long to do a wicked deed again. Will you do that?"

"Yes, I shall," Peter replied, still fearing the policeman, who had not left yet.

"So now that matter is all settled," said the old lady in conclusion. "Now tell me if you have a wish, my boy, for I am going to give you something by which to remember your friends from Frankfurt. What is it? What would you like to have?"

Peter, lifting his head, stared at the grandmama with round, astonished eyes. He was confused by this sudden change of prospect.

Being again urged to utter a wish, he saw at last that he was saved from the power of the terrible man. He felt as if the most crushing load had fallen off him. He knew now that it was better to confess at once, when something had gone wrong, so he said: "I have also lost the paper."

Reflecting a while, the grandmama understood and said: "That is right. Always confess what is wrong, then it can be settled. And now, what would you like to have?"

So Peter could choose everything in the world he wished. His brain got dizzy. He saw before him all the wonderful things in the fair in Mayenfeld. He had often stood there for hours, looking at the pretty red whistles and the little knives; unfortunately Peter had never possessed more than half what those objects cost.

He stood thinking, not able to decide, when a bright thought struck him.

"Ten pennies," said Peter with decision.

"That certainly is not too much," the old lady said with a smile, taking out of her pocket a big, round thaler, on top of which she laid twenty pennies. "Now I'll explain this to you. Here you have as many times ten pennies as there are weeks in the year. You'll be able to spend one every Sunday through the year."

"All my life?" Peter asked quite innocently.

The grandmama began to laugh so heartily at this that the two men came over to join her.

Laughingly she said: "You shall have it my boy; I will put it in my will and then you will do the same, my son. Listen! Peter the goatherd shall have a ten-penny piece weekly as long as he lives."

Mr. Sesemann nodded.

Peter, looking at his gift, said solemnly: "God be thanked!" Jumping and bounding, he ran away. His heart was so light that he felt he could fly.

A little later the whole party sat round the table holding a merry feast. After dinner, Clara, who was lively as never before, said to her father:

"Oh, Papa, if you only knew all the things grandfather did for me. It would take many days to tell you; I shall never forget them all my life. Oh, if we could please him only half as much as what he did for me."

"It is my greatest wish, too, dear child," said her father; "I have been trying to think of something all the time. We have to show our gratitude in some way."

Accordingly Mr. Sesemann walked over to the old man, and began: "My dear friend, may I say one word to you. I am sure you believe me when I tell you that I have not known any real joy for years. What was my wealth to me when I could not cure my child and make her happy! With the help of the Lord you have made her well. You have given her a new life. Please tell me how to show my gratitude to you. I know I shall never be able to repay you, but what is in my power I shall do. Have you any request to make? Please let me know."

The uncle had listened quietly and had looked at the happy father.

"Mr. Sesemann, you can be sure that I also am repaid by the great joy I experience at the recovery of Clara," said the uncle firmly. "I thank you for your kind offer, Mr. Sesemann. As long as I live I have enough for me and the child. But I have one wish. If this could be fulfilled, my life would be free of care."

"Speak, my dear friend," urged Clara's father.

"I am old," continued the uncle, "and shall not live many years. When I die I cannot leave Heidi anything. The child has no relations except one, who even might try to take advantage of her if she could. If you would give me the assurance, Mr. Sesemann, that Heidi will never be obliged to go into the world and earn her bread, you would amply repay me for what I was able to do for you and Clara."

"My dear friend, there is no question of that," began Mr. Sesemann; "the child belongs to us! I promise at once that we shall look after her so that there will not be any need of her ever earning her bread. We all know that she is not fashioned for a life among strangers. Nevertheless, she has made some true friends, and one of them will be here very shortly. Dr. Classen is just now completing his last business in Frankfurt. He intends to take your advice and live here. He has never felt so happy as with you and Heidi. The child will have two protectors near her, and I hope with God's will, that they may be spared a long, long time."

"And may it be God's will!" added the grandmama, who with Heidi had joined them, shaking the uncle tenderly by the hand. Putting her arms around the child, she said: "Heidi, I want to know if you also have a wish?"

"Yes indeed, I have," said Heidi, pleased.

"Tell me what it is, child!"

"I should like to have my bed from Frankfurt with the three high pillows and the thick, warm cover. Then grandmother will be able to keep warm and won't have to wear her shawl in bed. Oh, I'll be so happy when she won't have to lie with her head lower than her heels, hardly able to breathe!"

Heidi had said all this in one breath, she was so eager.

"Oh dear, I had nearly forgotten what I meant to do. I am so glad you have reminded me, Heidi. If God sends us happiness we must think of those who have many privations. I shall telegraph immediately for the bed, and if Miss Rottenmeier sends it off at once, it can be here in two days. I hope the poor blind grandmother will sleep better when it comes."

Heidi, in her happiness, could hardly wait to bring the old woman the good news. Soon it was resolved that everybody should visit the grandmother, who had been left alone so long. Before starting, however, Mr. Sesemann revealed his plans. He proposed to travel through Switzerland with his mother and Clara. He would spend the night in the village, so as to fetch Clara from the Alm next morning for the journey. From there they would go first to Ragatz and then further. The telegram was to be mailed that night.

Clara's feelings were divided, for she was sorry to leave the Alp, but the prospect of the trip delighted her.

When everything was settled, they all went down, the uncle carrying Clara, who could not have risked the lengthy walk. All the way down Heidi told the old lady of her friends in the hut; the cold they had to bear in winter and the little food they had.

Brigida was just hanging up Peter's shirt to dry, when the whole company arrived. Rushing into the house, she called to her mother: "Now they are all going away. Uncle is going, too, carrying the lame child."

"Oh, must it really be?" sighed the grandmother. "Have you seen whether they took Heidi away? Oh, if she only could give me her hand once more! Oh, I long to hear her voice once more!"

The same moment the door was flung open and Heidi held her tight.

"Grandmother, just think. My bed with the three pillows and the thick cover is coming from Frankfurt. Grandmama has said that it will be here in two days."

Heidi thought that grandmother would be beside herself with joy, but the old woman, smiling sadly, said:

"Oh, what a good lady she must be! I know I ought to be glad she is taking you with her, Heidi, but I don't think I shall survive it long."

"But nobody has said so," the grandmama, who had overheard those words, said kindly. Pressing the old woman's hand, she continued: "It is out of the question. Heidi will stay with you and make you happy. To see Heidi again, we will come up every year to the Alm, for we have many reasons to thank the Lord there."

Immediately the face of the grandmother lighted up, and she cried tears of joy.

"Oh, what wonderful things God is doing for me!" said the grandmother, deeply touched. "How good people are to trouble themselves about such a poor old woman as I. Nothing in this world strengthens the belief in a good Father in Heaven more than this mercy and kindness shown to a poor, useless little woman, like me."

"My dear grandmother," said Mrs. Sesemann, "before God in Heaven we are all equally miserable and poor; woe to us, if He should forget us! – But now we must say good-bye; next year we shall come to see you just as soon as we come up the Alp. We shall never forget you!" With that,

Mrs. Sesemann shook her hand. It was some time before she was allowed to leave, however, because the grandmother thanked her over and over again, and invoked all Heaven's blessings on her and her house.

Mr. Sesemann and his mother went on down, while Clara was carried up to spend her last night in the hut.

Next morning, Clara shed hot tears at parting from the beloved place, where such gladness had been hers. Heidi consoled her with plans for the coming summer, that was to be even more happy than this one had been. Mr. Sesemann then arrived, and a few last parting words were exchanged.

Clara, half crying, suddenly said: "Please give my love to Peter and the goats, Heidi! Please greet Schwänli especially from me, for she has helped a great deal in making me well. What could I give her?"

"You can send her salt, Clara. You know how fond she is of that," advised little Heidi.

"Oh, I will surely do that," Clara assented. "I'll send her a hundred pounds of salt as a remembrance from me."

It was time to go now, and Clara was able to ride proudly beside her father. Standing on the edge of the slope, Heidi waved her hand, her eyes following Clara till she had disappeared.

The bed has arrived. Grandmother sleeps so well every night now, that before long she will be stronger than ever. Grandmama has not forgotten the cold winter on the Alp and has sent a great many warm covers and shawls to the goatherd's hut. Grandmother can wrap herself up now and will not have to sit shivering in a corner.

In the village a large building is in progress. The doctor has arrived and is living at present in his old quarters. He has taken the uncle's advice and has bought the old ruins that sheltered Heidi and her grandfather the winter before. He is rebuilding for himself the portion with the fine apartment already mentioned. The other side is being prepared for

Heidi and her grandfather. The doctor knows that his friend is an independent man and likes to have his own dwelling. Bärli and Schwänli, of course, are not forgotten; they will spend the winter in a good solid stable that is being built for them.

The doctor and the Alm-Uncle become better friends every day. When they overlook the progress of the building, they generally come to speak of Heidi. They both look forward to the time when they will be able to move into the house with their merry charge. They have agreed to share together the pleasure and responsibility that Heidi brings them. The uncle's heart is filled with gratitude too deep for any words when the doctor tells him that he will make ample provision for the child. Now her grandfather's heart is free of care, for if he is called away, another father will take care of Heidi and love her in his stead.

At the moment when our story closes, Heidi and Peter are sitting in grandmother's hut. The little girl has so many interesting things to relate and Peter is trying so hard not to miss anything, that in their eagerness they are not aware that they are near the happy grandmother's chair. All summer long they have hardly met, and very many wonderful things have happened. They are all glad at being together again, and it is hard to tell who is the happiest of the group. I think Brigida's face is more radiant than any, for Heidi has just told her the story of the perpetual ten-penny piece. Finally the grandmother says: "Heidi, please read me a song of thanksgiving and praise. I feel that I must praise and thank the Lord for the blessings He has brought to us all!"

The End.

CLASSIC LITERATURE: WORDS AND PHRASES
*adapted from the **Collins English Dictionary***

Accoucheur NOUN a male midwife or doctor ❏ *I think my sister must have had some general idea that I was a young offender whom an Accoucheur Policemen had taken up (on my birthday) and delivered over to her* (*Great Expectations* by Charles Dickens)

addled ADJ confused and unable to think properly ❏ *But she counted and counted till she got that addled* (*The Adventures of Huckleberry Finn* by Mark Twain)

admiration NOUN amazement or wonder ❏ *lifting up his hands and eyes by way of admiration* (*Gulliver's Travels* by Jonathan Swift)

afeard ADJ afeard means afraid ❏ *shake it–and don't be afeard* (*The Adventures of Huckleberry Finn* by Mark Twain)

affected VERB affected means followed ❏ *Hadst thou affected sweet divinity* (*Doctor Faustus 5.2* by Christopher Marlowe)

aground ADV when a boat runs aground, it touches the ground in a shallow part of the water and gets stuck ❏ *what kep' you?–boat get aground?* (*The Adventures of Huckleberry Finn* by Mark Twain)

ague NOUN a fever in which the patient has alternate hot and cold shivering fits ❏ *his exposure to the wet and cold had brought on fever and ague* (*Oliver Twist* by Charles Dickens)

alchemy ADJ false or worthless ❏ *all wealth alchemy* (*The Sun Rising* by John Donne)

all alike PHRASE the same all the time ❏ *Love, all alike* (*The Sun Rising* by John Donne)

alow and aloft PHRASE alow means in the lower part or bottom, and aloft means on the top, so alow and aloft means on the top and in the bottom or throughout ❏ *Someone's turned the chest out alow and aloft* (*Treasure Island* by Robert Louis Stevenson)

ambuscade NOUN ambuscade is not a proper word. Tom means an ambush, which is when a group of people attack their enemies, after hiding and waiting for them ❏ *and so we would lie in ambuscade, as he called it* (*The Adventures of Huckleberry Finn* by Mark Twain)

amiable ADJ likeable or pleasant ❏ *Such amiable qualities must speak for themselves* (*Pride and Prejudice* by Jane Austen)

amulet NOUN an amulet is a charm thought to drive away evil spirits. ❏ *uttered phrases at once occult and familiar, like the amulet worn on the heart* (*Silas Marner* by George Eliot)

amusement NOUN here amusement means a strange and disturbing puzzle ❏ *this was an amusement the other way* (*Robinson Crusoe* by Daniel Defoe)

ancient NOUN an ancient was the flag displayed on a ship to show which country it belongs to. It is also called the ensign ❏ *her ancient and pendants out* (*Robinson Crusoe* by Daniel Defoe)

antic ADJ here antic means horrible or grotesque ❏ *armed and dressed after a very antic manner* (*Gulliver's Travels* by Jonathan Swift)

antics NOUN antics is an old word meaning clowns, or people who do silly things to make other people laugh ❏ *And point like antics at his triple crown* (*Doctor Faustus 3.2* by Christopher Marlowe)

appanage NOUN an appanage is a living

allowance ❏ *As if loveliness were not the special prerogative of woman–her legitimate appanage and heritage!* (*Jane Eyre* by Charlotte Brontë)

appended VERB appended means attached or added to ❏ *and these words appended* (*Treasure Island* by Robert Louis Stevenson)

approver NOUN an approver is someone who gives evidence against someone he used to work with ❏ *Mr. Noah Claypole: receiving a free pardon from the Crown in consequence of being admitted approver against Fagin* (*Oliver Twist* by Charles Dickens)

areas NOUN the areas is the space, below street level, in front of the basement of a house ❏ *The Dodger had a vicious propensity, too, of pulling the caps from the heads of small boys and tossing them down areas* (*Oliver Twist* by Charles Dickens)

argument NOUN theme or important idea or subject which runs through a piece of writing ❏ *Thrice needful to the argument which now* (*The Prelude* by William Wordsworth) .

artificially ADJ artfully or cleverly ❏ *and he with a sharp flint sharpened very artificially* (*Gulliver's Travels* by Jonathan Swift)

artist NOUN here artist means a skilled workman ❏ *This man was a most ingenious artist* (*Gulliver's Travels* by Jonathan Swift)

assizes NOUN assizes were regular court sessions which a visiting judge was in charge of ❏ *you shall hang at the next assizes* (*Treasure Island* by Robert Louis Stevenson)

attraction NOUN gravitation, or Newton's theory of gravitation ❏ *he predicted the same fate to attraction* (*Gulliver's Travels* by Jonathan Swift)

aver VERB to aver is to claim something strongly ❏ *for Jem Rodney,*

the mole catcher, averred that one evening as he was returning homeward (*Silas Marner* by George Eliot)

baby NOUN here baby means doll, which is a child's toy that looks like a small person ❏ *and skilful dressing her baby* (*Gulliver's Travels* by Jonathan Swift)

bagatelle NOUN bagatelle is a game rather like billiards and pool ❏ *Breakfast had been ordered at a pleasant little tavern, a mile or so away upon the rising ground beyond the green; and there was a bagatelle board in the room, in case we should desire to unbend our minds after the solemnity.* (*Great Expectations* by Charles Dickens)

bah EXCLAM Bah is an exclamation of frustration or anger ❏ *"Bah," said Scrooge.* (*A Christmas Carol* by Charles Dickens)

bairn NOUN a northern word for child ❏ *Who has taught you those fine words, my bairn?* (*Wuthering Heights* by Emily Brontë)

bait VERB to bait means to stop on a journey to take refreshment ❏ *So, when they stopped to bait the horse, and ate and drank and enjoyed themselves, I could touch nothing that they touched, but kept my fast unbroken.* (*David Copperfield* by Charles Dickens)

balustrade NOUN a balustrade is a row of vertical columns that form railings ❏ *but I mean to say you might have got a hearse up that staircase, and taken it broadwise, with the splinter-bar towards the wall, and the door towards the balustrades: and done it easy* (*A Christmas Carol* by Charles Dickens)

bandbox NOUN a large lightweight box for carrying bonnets or hats ❏ *I am glad I bought my bonnet, if it is only for the fun of having another bandbox* (*Pride and Prejudice* by Jane Austen)

barren NOUN a barren here is a stretch or expanse of barren land ❏ *a line* of upright stones, continued the length of the barren (*Wuthering Heights* by Emily Brontë)

basin NOUN a basin was a cup without a handle ❏ *who is drinking his tea out of a basin* (*Wuthering Heights* by Emily Brontë)

battalia NOUN the order of battle ❏ *till I saw part of his army in battalia* (*Gulliver's Travels* by Jonathan Swift)

battery NOUN a Battery is a fort or a place where guns are positioned ❏ *You bring the lot to me, at that old Battery over yonder* (*Great Expectations* by Charles Dickens)

battledore and shuttlecock NOUN The game battledore and shuttlecock was an early version of the game now known as badminton. The aim of the early game was simply to keep the shuttlecock from hitting the ground. ❏ *Battledore and shuttlecock's a wery good game vhen you an't the shuttlecock and two lawyers the battledores, in which case it gets too excitin' to be pleasant* (*Pickwick Papers* by Charles Dickens)

beadle NOUN a beadle was a local official who had power over the poor ❏ *But these impertinences were speedily checked by the evidence of the surgeon, and the testimony of the beadle* (*Oliver Twist* by Charles Dickens)

bearings NOUN the bearings of a place are the measurements or directions that are used to find or locate it ❏ *the bearings of the island* (*Treasure Island* by Robert Louis Stevenson)

beaufet NOUN a beaufet was a sideboard ❏ *and sweet-cake from the beaufet* (*Emma* by Jane Austen)

beck NOUN a beck is a small stream ❏ *a beck which follows the bend of the glen* (*Wuthering Heights* by Emily Brontë)

bedight VERB decorated ❏ *and bedight with Christmas holly stuck into the top.* (*A Christmas Carol* by Charles Dickens)

Bedlam NOUN Bedlam was a lunatic asylum in London which had statues carved by Caius Gabriel Cibber at its entrance ❏ *Bedlam, and those carved maniacs at the gates* (*The Prelude* by William Wordsworth)

beeves NOUN oxen or castrated bulls which are animals used for pulling vehicles or carrying things ❏ *to deliver in every morning six beeves* (*Gulliver's Travels* by Jonathan Swift)

begot VERB created or caused ❏ *Begot in thee* (*On His Mistress* by John Donne)

behoof NOUN behoof means benefit ❏ *"Yes, young man," said he, releasing the handle of the article in question, retiring a step or two from my table, and speaking for the behoof of the landlord and waiter at the door* (*Great Expectations* by Charles Dickens)

berth NOUN a berth is a bed on a boat ❏ *this is the berth for me* (*Treasure Island* by Robert Louis Stevenson)

bevers NOUN a bever was a snack, or small portion of food, eaten between main meals ❏ *that buys me thirty meals a day and ten bevers* (*Doctor Faustus 2.1* by Christopher Marlowe)

bilge water NOUN the bilge is the widest part of a ship's bottom, and the bilge water is the dirty water that collects there ❏ *no gush of bilge-water had turned it to fetid puddle* (*Jane Eyre* by Charlotte Brontë)

bills NOUN bills is an old term meaning prescription. A prescription is the piece of paper on which your doctor writes an order for medicine and which you give to a chemist to get the medicine ❏ *Are not thy bills hung up as monuments* (*Doctor Faustus 1.1* by Christopher Marlowe)

black cap NOUN a judge wore a black cap when he was about to sentence a prisoner to death ❏ *The judge* assumed the black cap, and the prisoner still stood with the same air and gesture. (*Oliver Twist* by Charles Dickens)

black gentleman NOUN this was another word for the devil ❑ *for she is as impatient as the black gentleman* (*Emma* by Jane Austen)

boot-jack NOUN a wooden device to help take boots off ❑ *The speaker appeared to throw a boot-jack, or some such article, at the person he addressed* (*Oliver Twist* by Charles Dickens)

booty NOUN booty means treasure or prizes ❑ *would be inclined to give up their booty in payment of the dead man's debts* (*Treasure Island* by Robert Louis Stevenson)

Bow Street runner PHRASE Bow Street runners were the first British police force, set up by the author Henry Fielding in the eighteenth century ❑ *as would have convinced a judge or a Bow Street runner* (*Treasure Island* by Robert Louis Stevenson)

brawn NOUN brawn is a dish of meat which is set in jelly ❑ *Heaped up upon the floor, to form a kind of throne, were turkeys, geese, game, poultry, brawn, great joints of meat, sucking-pigs* (*A Christmas Carol* by Charles Dickens)

bray VERB when a donkey brays, it makes a loud, harsh sound ❑ *and she doesn't bray like a jackass* (*The Adventures of Huckleberry Finn* by Mark Twain)

break VERB in order to train a horse you first have to break it ❑ *"If a high-mettled creature like this," said he, "can't be broken by fair means, she will never be good for anything"* (*Black Beauty* by Anna Sewell)

bullyragging VERB bullyragging is an old word which means bullying. To bullyrag someone is to threaten or force someone to do something they don't want to do ❑ *and a lot of loafers bullyragging him for sport* (*The Adventures of Huckleberry Finn* by Mark Twain)

but PREP except for (this) ❑ *but this, all pleasures fancies be* (*The Good-Morrow* by John Donne)

by hand PHRASE by hand was a common expression of the time meaning that baby had been fed either using a spoon or a bottle rather than by breast-feeding ❑ *My sister, Mrs. Joe Gargery, was more than twenty years older than I, and had established a great reputation with herself . . . because she had bought me up 'by hand'* (*Great Expectations* by Charles Dickens)

bye-spots NOUN bye-spots are lonely places ❑ *and bye-spots of tales rich with indigenous produce* (*The Prelude* by William Wordsworth)

calico NOUN calico is plain white fabric made from cotton ❑ *There was two old dirty calico dresses* (*The Adventures of Huckleberry Finn* by Mark Twain)

camp-fever NOUN camp-fever was another word for the disease typhus ❑ *during a severe camp-fever* (*Emma* by Jane Austen)

cant NOUN cant is insincere or empty talk ❑ *"Man," said the Ghost, "if man you be in heart, not adamant, forbear that wicked cant until you have discovered What the surplus is, and Where it is."* (*A Christmas Carol* by Charles Dickens)

canty ADJ canty means lively, full of life ❑ *My mother lived til eighty, a canty dame to the last* (*Wuthering Heights* by Emily Brontë)

canvas VERB to canvas is to discuss ❑ *We think so very differently on this point Mr Knightley, that there can be no use in canvassing it* (*Emma* by Jane Austen)

capital ADJ capital means excellent or extremely good ❑ *for it's capital, so shady, light, and big* (*Little Women* by Louisa May Alcott)

capstan NOUN a capstan is a device used on a ship to lift sails and anchors ❑ *capstans going, ships going out to sea, and unintelligible sea creatures* roaring curses over the bulwarks at respondent lightermen (*Great Expectations* by Charles Dickens)

case-bottle NOUN a square bottle designed to fit with others into a case ❑ *The spirit being set before him in a huge case-bottle, which had originally come out of some ship's locker* (*The Old Curiosity Shop* by Charles Dickens)

casement NOUN casement is a word meaning window. The teacher in Nicholas Nickleby misspells window showing what a bad teacher he is ❑ *W-i-n, win, d-e-r, der, winder, a casement.'* (*Nicholas Nickleby* by Charles Dickens)

cataleptic ADJ a cataleptic fit is one in which the victim goes into a trance-like state and remains still for a long time ❑ *It was at this point in their history that Silas's cataleptic fit occurred during the prayer-meeting* (*Silas Marner* by George Eliot)

cauldron NOUN a cauldron is a large cooking pot made of metal ❑ *stirring a large cauldron which seemed to be full of soup* (*Alice's Adventures in Wonderland* by Lewis Carroll)

cephalic ADJ cephalic means to do with the head ❑ *with ink composed of a cephalic tincture* (*Gulliver's Travels* by Jonathan Swift)

chaise and four NOUN a closed four-wheel carriage pulled by four horses ❑ *he came down on Monday in a chaise and four to see the place* (*Pride and Prejudice* by Jane Austen)

chamberlain NOUN the main servant in a household ❑ *In those times a bed was always to be got there at any hour of the night, and the chamberlain, letting me in at his ready wicket, lighted the candle next in order on his shelf* (*Great Expectations* by Charles Dickens)

characters NOUN distinguishing marks ❑ *Impressed upon all forms the characters* (*The Prelude* by William Wordsworth)

chary ADJ cautious ❑ *I should have been chary of discussing my guardian too freely even with her* (*Great Expectations* by Charles Dickens)

cherishes VERB here cherishes means cheers or brightens ❑ *some philosophic song of Truth that cherishes our daily life* (*The Prelude* by William Wordsworth)

chickens' meat PHRASE chickens' meat is an old term which means chickens' feed or food ❑ *I had shook a bag of chickens' meat out in that place* (*Robinson Crusoe* by Daniel Defoe)

chimeras NOUN a chimera is an unrealistic idea or a wish which is unlikely to be fulfilled ❑ *with many other wild impossible chimeras* (*Gulliver's Travels* by Jonathan Swift)

chines NOUN chine is a cut of meat that includes part or all of the backbone of the animal ❑ *and they found hams and chines uncut* (*Silas Marner* by George Eliot)

chits NOUN chits is a slang word which means girls ❑ *I hate affected, niminy-piminy chits!* (*Little Women* by Louisa May Alcott)

chopped VERB chopped means come suddenly or accidentally ❑ *if I had chopped upon them* (*Robinson Crusoe* by Daniel Defoe)

chute NOUN a narrow channel ❑ *One morning about day-break, I found a canoe and crossed over a chute to the main shore* (*The Adventures of Huckleberry Finn* by Mark Twain)

circumspection NOUN careful observation of events and circumstances; caution ❑ *I honour your circumspection* (*Pride and Prejudice* by Jane Austen)

clambered VERB clambered means to climb somewhere with difficulty, usually using your hands and your feet ❑ *he clambered up and down stairs* (*Treasure Island* by Robert Louis Stevenson)

clime NOUN climate ❑ *no season knows nor clime* (*The Sun Rising* by John Donne)

clinched VERB clenched ❑ *the tops whereof I could but just reach with my fist clinched* (*Gulliver's Travels* by Jonathan Swift)

close chair NOUN a close chair is a sedan chair, which is an covered chair which has room for one person. The sedan chair is carried on two poles by two men, one in front and one behind ❑ *persuaded even the Empress herself to let me hold her in her close chair* (*Gulliver's Travels* by Jonathan Swift)

clown NOUN clown here means peasant or person who lives off the land ❑ *In ancient days by emperor and clown* (*Ode on a Nightingale* by John Keats)

coalheaver NOUN a coalheaver loaded coal onto ships using a spade ❑ *Good, strong, wholesome medicine, as was given with great success to two Irish labourers and a coalheaver* (*Oliver Twist* by Charles Dickens)

coal-whippers NOUN men who worked at docks using machines to load coal onto ships ❑ *here, were colliers by the score and score, with the coal-whippers plunging off stages on deck* (*Great Expectations* by Charles Dickens)

cobweb NOUN a cobweb is the net which a spider makes for catching insects ❑ *the walls and ceilings were all hung round with cobwebs* (*Gulliver's Travels* by Jonathan Swift)

coddling VERB coddling means to treat someone too kindly or protect them too much ❑ *and I've been coddling the fellow as if I'd been his grandmother* (*Little Women* by Louisa May Alcott)

coil NOUN coil means noise or fuss or disturbance ❑ *What a coil is there?* (*Doctor Faustus 4.7* by Christopher Marlowe)

collared VERB to collar something is a slang term which means to capture.

In this sentence, it means he stole it [the money] ❑ *he collared it* (*The Adventures of Huckleberry Finn* by Mark Twain)

colling VERB colling is an old word which means to embrace and kiss ❑ *and no clasping and colling at all* (*Tess of the D'Urbervilles* by Thomas Hardy)

colloquies NOUN colloquy is a formal conversation or dialogue ❑ *Such colloquies have occupied many a pair of pale-faced weavers* (*Silas Marner* by George Eliot)

comfit NOUN sugar-covered pieces of fruit or nut eaten as sweets ❑ *and pulled out a box of comfits* (*Alice's Adventures in Wonderland* by Lewis Carroll)

coming out VERB when a girl came out in society it meant she was of marriageable age. In order to 'come out' girls were expecting to attend balls and other parties during a season ❑ *The younger girls formed hopes of coming out a year or two sooner than they might otherwise have done* (*Pride and Prejudice* by Jane Austen)

commit VERB commit means arrest or stop ❑ *Commit the rascals* (*Doctor Faustus 4.7* by Christopher Marlowe)

commodious ADJ commodious means convenient ❑ *the most commodious and effectual ways* (*Gulliver's Travels* by Jonathan Swift)

commons NOUN commons is an old term meaning food shared with others ❑ *his pauper assistants ranged themselves behind him; the gruel was served out; and a long grace was said over the short commons.* (*Oliver Twist* by Charles Dickens)

complacency NOUN here complacency means a desire to please others. To-day complacency means feeling pleased with oneself without good reason. ❑ *Twas thy power that raised the first complacency in me* (*The Prelude* by William Wordsworth)

complaisance NOUN complaisance was eagerness to please ❑ *we cannot wonder at his complaisance* (*Pride and Prejudice* by Jane Austen)

complaisant ADJ complaisant means polite ❑ *extremely cheerful and complaisant to their guest* (*Gulliver's Travels* by Jonathan Swift)

conning VERB conning means learning by heart ❑ *Or conning more* (*The Prelude* by William Wordsworth)

consequent NOUN consequence ❑ *as avarice is the necessary consequent of old age* (*Gulliver's Travels* by Jonathan Swift)

consorts NOUN concerts ❑ *The King, who delighted in music, had frequent consorts at Court* (*Gulliver's Travels* by Jonathan Swift)

conversible ADJ conversible meant easy to talk to, companionable ❑ *He can be a conversible companion* (*Pride and Prejudice* by Jane Austen)

copper NOUN a copper is a large pot that can be heated directly over a fire ❑ *He gazed in stupefied astonishment on the small rebel for some seconds, and then clung for support to the copper* (*Oliver Twist* by Charles Dickens)

copper-stick NOUN a copper-stick is the long piece of wood used to stir washing in the copper (or boiler) which was usually the biggest cooking pot in the house ❑ *It was Christmas Eve, and I had to stir the pudding for next day, with a copper-stick, from seven to eight by the Dutch clock* (*Great Expectations* by Charles Dickens)

counting-house NOUN a counting house is a place where accountants work ❑ *Once upon a time—of all the good days in the year, on Christmas Eve—old Scrooge sat busy in his countinghouse* (*A Christmas Carol* by Charles Dickens)

courtier NOUN a courtier is someone who attends the king or queen—a member of the court ❑ *next the ten courtiers;* (*Alice's Adventures in Wonderland* by Lewis Carroll)

covies NOUN covies were flocks of partridges ❑ *and will save all of the best covies for you* (*Pride and Prejudice* by Jane Austen)

cowed VERB cowed means frightened or intimidated ❑ *it cowed me more than the pain* (*Treasure Island* by Robert Louis Stevenson)

cozened VERB cozened means tricked or deceived ❑ *Do you remember, sir, how you cozened me* (*Doctor Faustus 4.7* by Christopher Marlowe)

cravats NOUN a cravat is a folded cloth that a man wears wrapped around his neck as a decorative item of clothing ❑ *we'd'a' slept in our cravats to-night* (*The Adventures of Huckleberry Finn* by Mark Twain)

crock and dirt PHRASE crock and dirt is an old expression meaning soot and dirt ❑ *and the mare catching cold at the door, and the boy grimed with crock and dirt* (*Great Expectations* by Charles Dickens)

crockery NOUN here crockery means pottery ❑ *By one of the parrots was a cat made of crockery* (*The Adventures of Huckleberry Finn* by Mark Twain)

crooked sixpence PHRASE it was considered unlucky to have a bent sixpence ❑ *You've got the beauty, you see, and I've got the luck, so you must keep me by you for your crooked sixpence* (*Silas Marner* by George Eliot)

croquet NOUN croquet is a traditional English summer game in which players try to hit wooden balls through hoops ❑ *and once she remembered trying to box her own ears for having cheated herself in a game of croquet* (*Alice's Adventures in Wonderland* by Lewis Carroll)

cross PREP across ❑ *The two great streets, which run cross and divide it into four quarters* (*Gulliver's Travels* by Jonathan Swift)

culpable ADJ if you are culpable for something it means you are to blame ❑ *deep are the sorrows that spring from false ideas for which no man is culpable.* (*Silas Marner* by George Eliot)

cultured ADJ cultivated ❑ *Nor less when spring had warmed the cultured Vale* (*The Prelude* by William Wordsworth)

cupidity NOUN cupidity is greed ❑ *These people hated me with the hatred of cupidity and disappointment.* (*Great Expectations* by Charles Dickens)

curricle NOUN an open two-wheeled carriage with one seat for the driver and space for a single passenger ❑ *and they saw a lady and a gentleman in a curricle* (*Pride and Prejudice* by Jane Austen)

cynosure NOUN a cynosure is something that strongly attracts attention or admiration ❑ *Then I thought of Eliza and Georgiana; I beheld one the cynosure of a ballroom, the other the inmate of a convent cell* (*Jane Eyre* by Charlotte Brontë)

dalliance NOUN someone's dalliance with something is a brief involvement with it ❑ *nor sporting in the dalliance of love* (*Doctor Faustus Chorus* by Christopher Marlowe)

darkling ADV darkling is an archaic way of saying in the dark ❑ *Darkling I listen* (*Ode on a Nightingale* by John Keats)

delf-case NOUN a sideboard for holding dishes and crockery ❑ *at the pewter dishes and delf-case* (*Wuthering Heights* by Emily Brontë)

determined ■ VERB here determined means ended ❑ *and be out of vogue when that was determined* (*Gulliver's Travels* by Jonathan Swift) ■ VERB determined can mean to have been learned or found especially by investigation or experience ❑ *All the sensitive feelings it wounded so cruelly, all the shame and misery it kept alive within my breast, became more poignant as I thought of this; and I determined that the life was unendurable* (*David Copperfield* by Charles Dickens)

Deuce NOUN a slang term for the Devil ❑ *Ah, I dare say I did. Deuce take me,* he added suddenly, *I know I did. I find I am not quite unscrewed yet.* (*Great Expectations* by Charles Dickens)

diabolical ADJ diabolical means devilish or evil ❑ *and with a thousand diabolical expressions* (*Treasure Island* by Robert Louis Stevenson)

direction NOUN here direction means address ❑ *Elizabeth was not surprised at it, as Jane had written the direction remarkably ill* (*Pride and Prejudice* by Jane Austen)

discover VERB to make known or announce ❑ *the Emperor would discover the secret while I was out of his power* (*Gulliver's Travels* by Jonathan Swift)

dissemble VERB hide or conceal ❑ *Dissemble nothing* (*On His Mistress* by John Donne)

dissolve VERB dissolve here means to release from life, to die ❑ *Fade far away, dissolve, and quite forget* (*Ode on a Nightingale* by John Keats)

distrain VERB to distrain is to seize the property of someone who is in debt in compensation for the money owed ❑ *for he's threatening to distrain for it* (*Silas Marner* by George Eliot)

Divan NOUN a Divan was originally a Turkish council of state–the name was transferred to the couches they sat on and is used to mean this in English ❑ *Mr Brass applauded this picture very much, and the bed being soft and comfortable, Mr Quilp determined to use it, both as a sleeping place by night and as a kind of Divan by day.* (*The Old Curiosity Shop* by Charles Dickens)

divorcement NOUN separation ❑ *By all pains which want and* divorcement hath (*On His Mistress* by John Donne)

dog in the manger, PHRASE this phrase describes someone who prevents you from enjoying something that they themselves have no need for ❏ *You are a dog in the manger, Cathy, and desire no one to be loved but yourself* (*Wuthering Heights* by Emily Brontë)

dolorifuge NOUN dolorifuge is a word which Thomas Hardy invented. It means pain-killer or comfort ❏ *as a species of dolorifuge* (*Tess of the D'Urbervilles* by Thomas Hardy)

dome NOUN building ❏ *that river and that mouldering dome* (*The Prelude* by William Wordsworth)

domestic PHRASE here domestic means a person's management of the house ❏ *to give some account of my domestic* (*Gulliver's Travels* by Jonathan Swift)

dunce NOUN a dunce is another word for idiot ❏ *Do you take me for a dunce? Go on?* (*Alice's Adventures in Wonderland* by Lewis Carroll)

Ecod EXCLAM a slang exclamation meaning 'oh God!' ❏ *"Ecod," replied Wemmick, shaking his head, "that's not my trade."* (*Great Expectations* by Charles Dickens)

egg-hot NOUN an egg-hot (see also 'flip' and 'negus') was a hot drink made from beer and eggs, sweetened with nutmeg ❏ *She fainted when she saw me return, and made a little jug of egg-hot afterwards to console us while we talked it over.* (*David Copperfield* by Charles Dickens)

encores NOUN an encore is a short extra performance at the end of a longer one, which the entertainer gives because the audience has enthusiastically asked for it ❏ *we want a little something to answer encores with, anyway* (*The Adventures of Huckleberry Finn* by Mark Twain)

equipage NOUN an elegant and impressive carriage ❏ *and besides, the equipage did not answer to any of*

their neighbours (*Pride and Prejudice* by Jane Austen)

exordium NOUN an exordium is the opening part of a speech ❏ *"Now, Handel," as if it were the grave beginning of a portentous business exordium, he had suddenly given up that tone* (*Great Expectations* by Charles Dickens)

expect VERB here expect means to wait for ❏ *to expect his farther commands* (*Gulliver's Travels* by Jonathan Swift)

familiars NOUN familiars means spirits or devils who come to someone when they are called ❏ *I'll turn all the lice about thee into familiars* (*Doctor Faustus* 1.4 by Christopher Marlowe)

fantods NOUN a fantod is a person who fidgets or can't stop moving nervously ❏ *It most give me the fantods* (*The Adventures of Huckleberry Finn* by Mark Twain)

farthing NOUN a farthing is an old unit of British currency which was worth a quarter of a penny ❏ *Not a farthing less. A great many back-payments are included in it, I assure you.* (*A Christmas Carol* by Charles Dickens)

farthingale NOUN a hoop worn under a skirt to extend it ❏ *A bell with an old voice–which I dare say in its time had often said to the house, Here is the green farthingale* (*Great Expectations* by Charles Dickens)

favours NOUN here favours is an old word which means ribbons ❏ *A group of humble mourners entered the gate: wearing white favours* (*Oliver Twist* by Charles Dickens)

feigned VERB pretend or pretending ❏ *not my feigned page* (*On His Mistress* by John Donne)

fence ◼ NOUN a fence is someone who receives and sells stolen goods ❏ *What are you up to? Ill-treating the boys, you covetous, avaricious, in-sa-ti-a-ble old fence?* (*Oliver Twist* by

Charles Dickens) ■ NOUN defence or protection ❏ *but honesty hath no fence against superior cunning* (*Gulliver's Travels* by Jonathan Swift)

fess ADJ fess is an old word which means pleased or proud ❏ *You'll be fess enough, my poppet* (*Tess of the D'Urbervilles* by Thomas Hardy)

fettered ADJ fettered means bound in chains or chained ❏ *"You are fettered," said Scrooge, trembling. "Tell me why?"* (*A Christmas Carol* by Charles Dickens)

fidges VERB fidges means fidgets, which is to keep moving your hands slightly because you are nervous or excited ❏ *Look, Jim, how my fingers fidges* (*Treasure Island* by Robert Louis Stevenson)

finger-post NOUN a finger-post is a sign-post showing the direction to different places ❏ *"The gallows," continued Fagin, "the gallows, my dear, is an ugly finger-post, which points out a very short and sharp turning that has stopped many a bold fellow's career on the broad highway."* (*Oliver Twist* by Charles Dickens)

fire-irons NOUN fire-irons are tools kept by the side of the fire to either cook with or look after the fire ❏ *the fire-irons came first* (*Alice's Adventures in Wonderland* by Lewis Carroll)

fire-plug NOUN a fire-plug is another word for a fire hydrant ❏ *The pony looked with great attention into a fire-plug, which was near him, and appeared to be quite absorbed in contemplating it* (*The Old Curiosity Shop* by Charles Dickens)

flank NOUN flank is the side of an animal ❏ *And all her silken flanks with garlands dressed* (*Ode on a Grecian Urn* by John Keats)

flip NOUN a flip is a drink made from warmed ale, sugar, spice and beaten egg ❏ *The events of the day, in combination with the twins, if not with the flip, had made Mrs. Micawber hysterical, and she shed tears as she replied* (*David Copperfield* by Charles Dickens)

flit VERB flit means to move quickly ❏ *and if he had meant to flit to Thrushcross Grange* (*Wuthering Heights* by Emily Brontë)

floorcloth NOUN a floorcloth was a hard-wearing piece of canvas used instead of carpet ❏ *This avenging phantom was ordered to be on duty at eight on Tuesday morning in the hall (it was two feet square, as charged for floorcloth)* (*Great Expectations* by Charles Dickens)

fly-driver NOUN a fly-driver is a carriage drawn by a single horse ❏ *The fly-drivers, among whom I inquired next, were equally jocose and equally disrespectful* (*David Copperfield* by Charles Dickens)

fob NOUN a small pocket in which a watch is kept ❏ *"Certain," replied the man, drawing a gold watch from his fob* (*Oliver Twist* by Charles Dickens)

folly NOUN folly means foolishness or stupidity ❏ *the folly of beginning a work* (*Robinson Crusoe* by Daniel Defoe)

fond ADJ fond means foolish ❏ *Fond worldling* (*Doctor Faustus 5.2* by Christopher Marlowe)

fondness NOUN silly or foolish affection ❏ *They have no fondness for their colts or foals* (*Gulliver's Travels* by Jonathan Swift)

for his fancy PHRASE for his fancy means for his liking or as he wanted ❏ *and as I did not obey quick enough for his fancy* (*Treasure Island* by Robert Louis Stevenson)

forlorn ADJ lost or very upset ❏ *you are from that day forlorn* (*Gulliver's Travels* by Jonathan Swift)

foster-sister NOUN a foster-sister was someone brought up by the same nurse or in the same household ❏ *I had been his foster-sister* (*Wuthering Heights* by Emily Brontë)

fox-fire NOUN fox-fire is a weak glow that is given off by decaying, rotten wood ❑ *what we must have was a lot of them rotten chunks that's called fox-fire* (*The Adventures of Huckleberry Finn* by Mark Twain)

frozen sea PHRASE the Arctic Ocean ❑ *into the frozen sea* (*Gulliver's Travels* by Jonathan Swift)

gainsay VERB to gainsay something is to say it isn't true or to deny it ❑ *"So she had," cried Scrooge. "You're right. I'll not gainsay it, Spirit. God forbid!"* (*A Christmas Carol* by Charles Dickens)

gaiters NOUN gaiters were leggings made of a cloth or piece of leather which covered the leg from the knee to the ankle ❑ *Mr Knightley was hard at work upon the lower buttons of his thick leather gaiters* (*Emma* by Jane Austen)

galluses NOUN galluses is an old spelling of gallows, and here means suspenders. Suspenders are straps worn over someone's shoulders and fastened to their trousers to prevent the trousers falling down ❑ *and home-knit galluses* (*The Adventures of Huckleberry Finn* by Mark Twain)

galoot NOUN a sailor but also a clumsy person ❑ *and maybe a galoot on it chopping* (*The Adventures of Huckleberry Finn* by Mark Twain)

gayest ADJ gayest means the most lively and bright or merry ❑ *Beth played her gayest march* (*Little Women* by Louisa May Alcott)

gem NOUN here gem means jewellery ❑ *the mountain shook off turf and flower, had only heath for raiment and crag for gem* (*Jane Eyre* by Charlotte Brontë)

giddy ADJ giddy means dizzy ❑ *and I wish you wouldn't keep appearing and vanishing so suddenly; you make one quite giddy.* (*Alice's Adventures in Wonderland* by Lewis Carroll)

gig NOUN a light two-wheeled carriage ❑ *when a gig drove up to the garden gate: out of which there jumped a fat gentleman* (*Oliver Twist* by Charles Dickens)

gladsome ADJ gladsome is an old word meaning glad or happy ❑ *Nobody ever stopped him in the street to say, with gladsome looks* (*A Christmas Carol* by Charles Dickens)

glen NOUN a glen is a small valley; the word is used commonly in Scotland ❑ *a beck which follows the bend of the glen* (*Wuthering Heights* by Emily Brontë)

gravelled VERB gravelled is an old term which means to baffle or defeat someone ❑ *Gravelled the pastors of the German Church* (*Doctor Faustus 1.1* by Christopher Marlowe)

grinder NOUN a grinder was a private tutor ❑ *but that when he had had the happiness of marrying Mrs Pocket very early in his life, he had impaired his prospects and taken up the calling of a Grinder* (*Great Expectations* by Charles Dickens)

gruel NOUN gruel is a thin, watery corn-meal or oatmeal soup ❑ *and the little saucepan of gruel* (Scrooge had a cold in his head) *upon the hob.* (*A Christmas Carol* by Charles Dickens)

guinea, half a NOUN a half guinea was ten shillings and sixpence ❑ *but lay out half a guinea at Ford's* (*Emma* by Jane Austen)

gull VERB gull is an old term which means to fool or deceive someone ❑ *Hush, I'll gull him supernaturally* (*Doctor Faustus 3.4* by Christopher Marlowe)

gunnel NOUN the gunnel, or gunwhale, is the upper edge of a boat's side ❑ *But he put his foot on the gunnel and rocked her* (*The Adventures of Huckleberry Finn* by Mark Twain)

gunwale NOUN the side of a ship ❑ *He dipped his hand in the water over the boat's gunwale* (*Great Expectations* by Charles Dickens)

Gytrash NOUN a Gytrash is an omen of misfortune to the superstitious, usually taking the form of a hound ❑ *I remembered certain of Bessie's tales, wherein figured a North-of-England spirit, called a 'Gytrash'* (*Jane Eyre* by Charlotte Brontë)

hackney-cabriolet NOUN a two-wheeled carriage with four seats for hire and pulled by a horse ❑ *A hackney-cabriolet was in waiting; with the same vehemence which she had exhibited in addressing Oliver, the girl pulled him in with her, and drew the curtains close.* (*Oliver Twist* by Charles Dickens)

hackney-coach NOUN a four-wheeled horse-drawn vehicle for hire ❑ *The twilight was beginning to close in, when Mr. Brownlow alighted from a hackney-coach at his own door, and knocked softly.* (*Oliver Twist* by Charles Dickens)

haggler NOUN a haggler is someone who travels from place to place selling small goods and items ❑ *when I be plain Jack Durbeyfield, the haggler* (*Tess of the D'Urbervilles* by Thomas Hardy)

halter NOUN a halter is a rope or strap used to lead an animal or to tie it up ❑ *I had of course long been used to a halter and a headstall* (*Black Beauty* by Anna Sewell)

hamlet NOUN a hamlet is a small village or a group of houses in the countryside ❑ *down from the hamlet* (*Treasure Island* by Robert Louis Stevenson)

hand-barrow NOUN a hand-barrow is a device for carrying heavy objects. It is like a wheelbarrow except that it has handles, rather than wheels, for moving the barrow ❑ *his sea chest following behind him in a hand-barrow* (*Treasure Island* by Robert Louis Stevenson)

handspike NOUN a handspike was a stick which was used as a lever ❑ *a bit of stick like a handspike* (*Treasure Island* by Robert Louis Stevenson)

haply ADV haply means by chance or perhaps ❑ *And haply the Queen-Moon is on her throne* (*Ode on a Nightingale* by John Keats)

harem NOUN the harem was the part of the house where the women lived ❑ *mostly they hang round the harem* (*The Adventures of Huckleberry Finn* by Mark Twain)

hautboys NOUN hautboys are oboes ❑ sausages and puddings resembling flutes and hautboys (*Gulliver's Travels* by Jonathan Swift)

hawker NOUN a hawker is someone who sells goods to people as he travels rather than from a fixed place like a shop ❑ *to buy some stockings from a hawker* (*Treasure Island* by Robert Louis Stevenson)

hawser NOUN a hawser is a rope used to tie up or tow a ship or boat ❑ *Again among the tiers of shipping, in and out, avoiding rusty chain-cables, frayed hempen hawsers* (*Great Expectations* by Charles Dickens)

headstall NOUN the headstall is the part of the bridle or halter that goes around a horse's head ❑ *I had of course long been used to a halter and a headstall* (*Black Beauty* by Anna Sewell)

hearken VERB hearken means to listen ❑ *though we sometimes stopped to lay hold of each other and hearken* (*Treasure Island* by Robert Louis Stevenson)

heartless ADJ here heartless means without heart or dejected ❑ *I am not heartless* (*The Prelude* by William Wordsworth)

hebdomadal ADJ hebdomadal means weekly ❑ *It was the hebdomadal treat to which we all looked forward from Sabbath to Sabbath* (*Jane Eyre* by Charlotte Brontë)

highwaymen NOUN highwaymen were people who stopped travellers and robbed them ❑ *We are highwaymen* (*The Adventures of Huckleberry Finn* by Mark Twain)

hinds NOUN hinds means farm hands, or people who work on a farm ❏ *He called his hinds about him* (*Gulliver's Travels* by Jonathan Swift)

histrionic ADJ if you refer to someone's behaviour as histrionic, you are being critical of it because it is dramatic and exaggerated ❏ *But the histrionic muse is the darling* (*The Adventures of Huckleberry Finn* by Mark Twain)

hogs NOUN hogs is another word for pigs ❏ *Tom called the hogs 'ingots'* (*The Adventures of Huckleberry Finn* by Mark Twain)

horrors NOUN the horrors are a fit, called delirium tremens, which is caused by drinking too much alcohol ❏ *I'll have the horrors* (*Treasure Island* by Robert Louis Stevenson)

huffy ADJ huffy means to be obviously annoyed or offended about something ❏ *They will feel that more than angry speeches or huffy actions* (*Little Women* by Louisa May Alcott)

hulks NOUN hulks were prison-ships ❏ *The miserable companion of thieves and ruffians, the fallen outcast of low haunts, the associate of the scourings of the jails and hulks* (*Oliver Twist* by Charles Dickens)

humbug NOUN humbug means nonsense or rubbish ❏ *"Bah," said Scrooge. "Humbug!"* (*A Christmas Carol* by Charles Dickens)

humours NOUN it was believed that there were four fluids in the body called humours which decided the temperament of a person depending on how much of each fluid was present ❏ *other peccant humours* (*Gulliver's Travels* by Jonathan Swift)

husbandry NOUN husbandry is farming animals ❏ *bad husbandry were plentifully anointing their wheels* (*Silas Marner* by George Eliot)

huswife NOUN a huswife was a small sewing kit ❏ *but I had put my huswife on it* (*Emma* by Jane Austen)

ideal ADJ ideal in this context means imaginary ❏ *I discovered the yell was not ideal* (*Wuthering Heights* by Emily Brontë)

If our two PHRASE if both our ❏ *If our two loves be one* (*The Good-Morrow* by John Donne)

ignis-fatuus NOUN ignis-fatuus is the light given out by burning marsh gases, which lead careless travellers into danger ❏ *it is madness in all women to let a secret love kindle within them, which, if unreturned and unknown, must devour the life that feeds it; and, if discovered and responded to, must lead ignis-fatuus-like, into miry wilds whence there is no extrication.* (*Jane Eyre* by Charlotte Brontë)

imaginations NOUN here imaginations means schemes or plans ❏ *soon drove out those imaginations* (*Gulliver's Travels* by Jonathan Swift)

impressible ADJ impressible means open or impressionable ❏ *for Marner had one of those impressible, self-doubting natures* (*Silas Marner* by George Eliot)

in good intelligence PHRASE friendly with each other ❏ *that these two persons were in good intelligence with each other* (*Gulliver's Travels* by Jonathan Swift)

inanity NOUN inanity is sillyness or dull stupidity ❏ *Do we not wile away moments of inanity* (*Silas Marner* by George Eliot)

incivility NOUN incivility means rudeness or impoliteness ❏ *if it's only for a piece of incivility like to-night's* (*Treasure Island* by Robert Louis Stevenson)

indigenae NOUN indigenae means natives or people from that area ❏ *an exotic that the surly indigenae will not recognise for kin* (*Wuthering Heights* by Emily Brontë)

indocible ADJ unteachable ❏ *so they were the most restive and indocible* (*Gulliver's Travels* by Jonathan Swift)

ingenuity NOUN inventiveness ❑ *entreated me to give him something as an encouragement to ingenuity* (*Gulliver's Travels* by Jonathan Swift)

ingots NOUN an ingot is a lump of a valuable metal like gold, usually shaped like a brick ❑ *Tom called the hogs 'ingots'* (*The Adventures of Huckleberry Finn* by Mark Twain)

inkstand NOUN an inkstand is a pot which was put on a desk to contain either ink or pencils and pens ❑ *throwing an inkstand at the Lizard as she spoke* (*Alice's Adventures in Wonderland* by Lewis Carroll)

inordinate ADJ without order. To-day inordinate means 'excessive'. ❑ *Though yet untutored and inordinate* (*The Prelude* by William Wordsworth)

intellectuals NOUN here intellectuals means the minds (of the workmen) ❑ *those instructions they give being too refined for the intellectuals of their workmen* (*Gulliver's Travels* by Jonathan Swift)

interview NOUN meeting ❑ *By our first strange and fatal interview* (*On His Mistress* by John Donne)

jacks NOUN jacks are rods for turning a spit over a fire ❑ *It was a small bit of pork suspended from the kettle hanger by a string passed through a large door key, in a way known to primitive housekeepers unpossessed of jacks* (*Silas Marner* by George Eliot)

jews-harp NOUN a jews-harp is a small, metal, musical instrument that is played by the mouth ❑ *A jews-harp's plenty good enough for a rat* (*The Adventures of Huckleberry Finn* by Mark Twain)

jorum NOUN a large bowl ❑ *while Miss Skiffins brewed such a jorum of tea, that the pig in the back premises became strongly excited* (*Great Expectations* by Charles Dickens)

jostled VERB jostled means bumped or pushed by someone or some people ❑ *being jostled himself into the kennel* (*Gulliver's Travels* by Jonathan Swift)

keepsake NOUN a keepsake is a gift which reminds someone of an event or of the person who gave it to them. ❑ *books and ornaments they had in their boudoirs at home: keepsakes that different relations had presented to them* (*Jane Eyre* by Charlotte Brontë)

kenned VERB kenned means knew ❑ *though little kenned the lamplighter that he had any company but Christmas!* (*A Christmas Carol* by Charles Dickens)

kennel NOUN kennel means gutter, which is the edge of a road next to the pavement, where rain water collects and flows away ❑ *being jostled himself into the kennel* (*Gulliver's Travels* by Jonathan Swift)

knock-knee ADJ knock-knee means slanted, at an angle. ❑ *LOT 1 was marked in whitewashed knock-knee letters on the brewhouse* (*Great Expectations* by Charles Dickens)

ladylike ADJ to be ladylike is to behave in a polite, dignified and graceful way ❑ *No, winking isn't ladylike* (*Little Women* by Louisa May Alcott)

lapse NOUN flow ❑ *Stealing with silent lapse to join the brook* (*The Prelude* by William Wordsworth)

larry NOUN larry is an old word which means commotion or noisy celebration ❑ *That was all a part of the larry!* (*Tess of the D'Urbervilles* by Thomas Hardy)

laths NOUN laths are strips of wood ❑ *The panels shrunk, the windows cracked; fragments of plaster fell out of the ceiling, and the naked laths were shown instead* (*A Christmas Carol* by Charles Dickens)

leer NOUN a leer is an unpleasant smile ❑ *with a kind of leer* (*Treasure Island* by Robert Louis Stevenson)

lenitives NOUN these are different kinds of drugs or medicines:

lenitives and palliatives were pain relievers; aperitives were laxatives; abstersives caused vomiting; corrosives destroyed human tissue; restringents caused constipation; cephalalgics stopped headaches; icterics were used as medicine for jaundice; apophlegmatics were cough medicine, and acoustics were cures for the loss of hearing ❑ *lenitives, aperitives, abstersives, corrosives, restringents, palliatives, laxatives, cephalalgics, icterics, apophlegmatics, acoustics* (*Gulliver's Travels* by Jonathan Swift)

lest CONJ in case. If you do something lest something (usually) unpleasant happens you do it to try to prevent it happening ❑ *She went in without knocking, and hurried upstairs, in great fear lest she should meet the real Mary Ann* (*Alice's Adventures in Wonderland* by Lewis Carroll)

levee NOUN a levee is an old term for a meeting held in the morning, shortly after the person holding the meeting has got out of bed ❑ *I used to attend the King's levee once or twice a week* (*Gulliver's Travels* by Jonathan Swift)

life-preserver NOUN a club which had lead inside it to make it heavier and therefore more dangerous ❑ *and with no more suspicious articles displayed to view than two or three heavy bludgeons which stood in a corner, and a 'life-preserver' that hung over the chimney-piece.* (*Oliver Twist* by Charles Dickens)

lighterman NOUN a lighterman is another word for sailor ❑ *in and out, hammers going in ship-builders' yards, saws going at timber, clashing engines going at things unknown, pumps going in leaky ships, capstans going, ships going out to sea, and unintelligible sea creatures roaring curses over the bulwarks at respondent lightermen* (*Great Expectations* by Charles Dickens)

livery NOUN servants often wore a uniform known as a livery ❑ *suddenly a footman in livery came running out of the wood* (*Alice's Adventures in Wonderland* by Lewis Carroll)

livid ADJ livid means pale or ash coloured. Livid also means very angry ❑ *a dirty, livid white* (*Treasure Island* by Robert Louis Stevenson)

lottery-tickets NOUN a popular card game ❑ *and Mrs. Philips protested that they would have a nice comfortable noisy game of lottery tickets* (*Pride and Prejudice* by Jane Austen)

lower and upper world PHRASE the earth and the heavens are the lower and upper worlds ❑ *the changes in the lower and upper world* (*Gulliver's Travels* by Jonathan Swift)

lustres NOUN lustres are chandeliers. A chandelier is a large, decorative frame which holds light bulbs or candles and hangs from the ceiling ❑ *the lustres, lights, the carving and the guilding* (*The Prelude* by William Wordsworth)

lynched VERB killed without a criminal trial by a crowd of people ❑ *He'll never know how nigh he come to getting lynched* (*The Adventures of Huckleberry Finn* by Mark Twain)

malingering VERB if someone is malingering they are pretending to be ill to avoid working ❑ *And you stand there malingering* (*Treasure Island* by Robert Louis Stevenson)

managing PHRASE treating with consideration ❑ *to think the honour of my own kind not worth managing* (*Gulliver's Travels* by Jonathan Swift)

manhood PHRASE manhood means human nature ❑ *concerning the nature of manhood* (*Gulliver's Travels* by Jonathan Swift)

man-trap NOUN a man-trap is a set of steel jaws that snap shut when trodden on and trap a person's leg

❏ *"Don't go to him," I called out of the window, "he's an assassin! A man-trap!"* (*Oliver Twist* by Charles Dickens)

maps NOUN charts of the night sky ❏ *Let maps to others, worlds on worlds have shown* (*The Good-Morrow* by John Donne)

mark VERB look at or notice ❏ *Mark but this flea, and mark in this* (*The Flea* by John Donne)

maroons NOUN A maroon is someone who has been left in a place which it is difficult for them to escape from, like a small island ❏ *if schooners, islands, and maroons* (*Treasure Island* by Robert Louis Stevenson)

mast NOUN here mast means the fruit of forest trees ❏ *a quantity of acorns, dates, chestnuts, and other mast* (*Gulliver's Travels* by Jonathan Swift)

mate VERB defeat ❏ *Where Mars did mate the warlike Carthigens* (*Doctor Faustus Chorus* by Christopher Marlowe)

mealy ADJ Mealy when used to describe a face meant palid, pale or colourless ❏ *I only know two sorts of boys. Mealy boys, and beef-faced boys* (*Oliver Twist* by Charles Dickens)

middling ADJ fairly or moderately ❏ *she worked me middling hard for about an hour* (*The Adventures of Huckleberry Finn* by Mark Twain)

mill NOUN a mill, or treadmill, was a device for hard labour or punishment in prison ❏ *Was you never on the mill?* (*Oliver Twist* by Charles Dickens)

milliner's shop NOUN a milliner's sold fabrics, clothing, lace and accessories; as time went on they specialized more and more in hats ❏ *to pay their duty to their aunt and to a milliner's shop just over the way* (*Pride and Prejudice* by Jane Austen)

minching un' munching PHRASE how people in the north of England

used to describe the way people from the south speak ❏ *Minching un' munching!* (*Wuthering Heights* by Emily Brontë)

mine NOUN gold ❏ *Whether both th'Indias of spice and mine* (*The Sun Rising* by John Donne)

mire NOUN mud ❏ *Tis my fate to be always ground into the mire under the iron heel of oppression* (*The Adventures of Huckleberry Finn* by Mark Twain)

miscellany NOUN a miscellany is a collection of many different kinds of things ❏ *under that, the miscellany began* (*Treasure Island* by Robert Louis Stevenson)

mistarshers NOUN mistarshers means moustache, which is the hair that grows on a man's upper lip ❏ *when he put his hand up to his mistarshers* (*Tess of the D'Urbervilles* by Thomas Hardy)

morrow NOUN here good-morrow means tomorrow and a new and better life ❏ *And now good-morrow to our waking souls* (*The Good-Morrow* by John Donne)

mortification NOUN mortification is an old word for gangrene which is when part of the body decays or 'dies' because of disease ❏ *Yes, it was a mortification–that was it* (*The Adventures of Huckleberry Finn* by Mark Twain)

mought PARTICIPLE mought is an old spelling of might ❏ *what you mought call me? You mought call me captain* (*Treasure Island* by Robert Louis Stevenson)

move VERB move me not means do not make me angry ❏ *Move me not, Faustus* (*Doctor Faustus 2.1* by Christopher Marlowe)

muffin-cap NOUN a muffin cap is a flat cap made from wool ❏ *the old one, remained stationary in the muffin-cap and leathers* (*Oliver Twist* by Charles Dickens)

mulatter NOUN a mulatter was another word for mulatto, which is a person with parents who are from different races ❏ *a mulatter, most as white as a white man* (*The Adventures of Huckleberry Finn* by Mark Twain)

mummery NOUN mummery is an old word that meant meaningless (or pretentious) ceremony ❏ *When they were all gone, and when Trabb and his men–but not his boy: I looked for him–had crammed their mummery into bags, and were gone too, the house felt wholesomer.* (*Great Expectations* by Charles Dickens)

nap NOUN the nap is the woolly surface on a new item of clothing. Here the surface has been worn away so it looks bare ❏ *like an old hat with the nap rubbed off* (*The Adventures of Huckleberry Finn* by Mark Twain)

natural ■ NOUN a natural is a person born with learning difficulties ❏ *though he had been left to his particular care by their deceased father, who thought him almost a natural.* (*David Copperfield* by Charles Dickens) ■ ADJ natural meant illegitimate ❏ *Harriet Smith was the natural daughter of some-body* (*Emma* by Jane Austen)

navigator NOUN a navigator was originally someone employed to dig canals. It is the origin of the word 'navvy' meaning a labourer ❏ *She ascertained from me in a few words what it was all about, comforted Dora, and gradually convinced her that I was not a labourer–from my manner of stating the case I believe Dora concluded that I was a navi-gator, and went balancing myself up and down a plank all day with a wheelbarrow–and so brought us together in peace.* (*David Copperfield* by Charles Dickens)

necromancy NOUN necromancy means a kind of magic where the magician speaks to spirits or ghosts to find out what will happen in the future ❏ *He surfeits upon cursed necro-mancy* (*Doctor Faustus chorus* by Christopher Marlowe)

negus NOUN a negus is a hot drink made from sweetened wine and water ❏ *He sat placidly perusing the newspaper, with his little head on one side, and a glass of warm sherry negus at his elbow.* (*David Copperfield* by Charles Dickens)

nice ADJ discriminating. Able to make good judgements or choices ❏ *consequently a claim to be nice* (*Emma* by Jane Austen)

nigh ADV nigh means near ❏ *He'll never know how nigh he come to getting lynched* (*The Adventures of Huckleberry Finn* by Mark Twain)

nimbleness NOUN nimbleness means being able to move very quickly or skillfully ❏ *and with incredible accuracy and nimbleness* (*Treasure Island* by Robert Louis Stevenson)

noggin NOUN a noggin is a small mug or a wooden cup ❏ *you'll bring me one noggin of rum* (*Treasure Island* by Robert Louis Stevenson)

none ADJ neither ❏ *none can die* (*The Good-Morrow* by John Donne)

notices NOUN observations ❏ *Arch are his notices* (*The Prelude* by William Wordsworth)

occiput NOUN occiput means the back of the head ❏ *saw off the occiput of each couple* (*Gulliver's Travels* by Jonathan Swift)

officiously ADJ kindly ❏ *the governess who attended Glumdalclitch very officiously lifted me up* (*Gulliver's Travels* by Jonathan Swift)

old salt PHRASE old salt is a slang term for an experienced sailor ❏ *a 'true sea-dog', and a 'real old salt'* (*Treasure Island* by Robert Louis Stevenson)

or ere PHRASE before ❏ *or ere the Hall was built* (*The Prelude* by William Wordsworth)

ostler NOUN one who looks after horses at an inn ❏ *The bill paid, and the waiter remembered, and the ostler not forgotten, and the chambermaid taken into consideration*

(*Great Expectations* by Charles Dickens)

ostry NOUN an ostry is an old word for a pub or hotel ❑ *lest I send you into the ostry with a vengeance* (*Doctor Faustus 2.2* by Christopher Marlowe)

outrunning the constable PHRASE outrunning the constable meant spending more than you earn ❑ *but I shall by this means be able to check your bills and to pull you up if I find you outrunning the constable.* (*Great Expectations* by Charles Dickens)

over ADJ across ❑ *It is in length six yards, and in the thickest part at least three yards over* (*Gulliver's Travels* by Jonathan Swift)

over the broomstick PHRASE this is a phrase meaning 'getting married without a formal ceremony' ❑ *They both led tramping lives, and this woman in Gerrard-street here, had been married very young, over the broomstick (as we say), to a tramping man, and was a perfect fury in point of jealousy.* (*Great Expectations* by Charles Dickens)

own VERB own means to admit or to acknowledge ❑ *It's my old girl that advises. She has the head. But I never own to it before her. Discipline must be maintained* (*Bleak House* by Charles Dickens)

page NOUN here page means a boy employed to run errands ❑ *not my feigned page* (*On His Mistress* by John Donne)

paid pretty dear PHRASE paid pretty dear means paid a high price or suffered quite a lot ❑ *I paid pretty dear for my monthly fourpenny piece* (*Treasure Island* by Robert Louis Stevenson)

pannikins NOUN pannikins were small tin cups ❑ *of lifting light glasses and cups to his lips, as if they were clumsy pannikins* (*Great Expectations* by Charles Dickens)

pards NOUN pards are leopards ❑ *Not charioted by Bacchus and his pards*

(*Ode on a Nightingale* by John Keats)

parlour boarder NOUN a pupil who lived with the family ❑ *and somebody had lately raised her from the condition of scholar to parlour boarder* (*Emma* by Jane Austen)

particular, a London PHRASE London in Victorian times and up to the 1950s was famous for having very dense fog–which was a combination of real fog and the smog of pollution from factories ❑ *This is a London particular . . . A fog, miss'* (*Bleak House* by Charles Dickens)

patten NOUN pattens were wooden soles which were fixed to shoes by straps to protect the shoes in wet weather ❑ *carrying a basket like the Great Seal of England in plaited straw, a pair of pattens, a spare shawl, and an umbrella, though it was a fine bright day* (*Great Expectations* by Charles Dickens)

paviour NOUN a paviour was a labourer who worked on the street pavement ❑ *the paviour his pickaxe* (*Oliver Twist* by Charles Dickens)

peccant ADJ peccant means unhealthy ❑ *other peccant humours* (*Gulliver's Travels* by Jonathan Swift)

penetralium NOUN penetralium is a word used to describe the inner rooms of the house ❑ *and I had no desire to aggravate his impatience previous to inspecting the penetralium* (*Wuthering Heights* by Emily Brontë)

pensive ADV pensive means deep in thought or thinking seriously about something ❑ *and she was leaning pensive on a tomb-stone on her right elbow* (*The Adventures of Huckleberry Finn* by Mark Twain)

penury NOUN penury is the state of being extremely poor ❑ *Distress, if not penury, loomed in the distance* (*Tess of the D'Urbervilles* by Thomas Hardy)

perspective NOUN telescope ❑ *a pocket perspective* (*Gulliver's Travels* by Jonathan Swift)

phaeton NOUN a phaeton was an open carriage for four people ❑ *often condescends to drive by my humble abode in her little phaeton and ponies* (*Pride and Prejudice* by Jane Austen)

phantasm NOUN a phantasm is an illusion, something that is not real. It is sometimes used to mean ghost ❑ *Experience had bred no fancies in him that could raise the phantasm of appetite* (*Silas Marner* by George Eliot)

physic NOUN here physic means medicine ❑ *there I studied physic two years and seven months* (*Gulliver's Travels* by Jonathan Swift)

pinioned VERB to pinion is to hold both arms so that a person cannot move them ❑ *But the relentless Ghost pinioned him in both his arms, and forced him to observe what happened next.* (*A Christmas Carol* by Charles Dickens)

piquet NOUN piquet was a popular card game in the C18th ❑ *Mr Hurst and Mr Bingley were at piquet* (*Pride and Prejudice* by Jane Austen)

plaister NOUN a plaister is a piece of cloth on which an apothecary (or pharmacist) would spread ointment. The cloth is then applied to wounds or bruises to treat them ❑ *Then, she gave the knife a final smart wipe on the edge of the plaister, and then sawed a very thick round off the loaf: which she finally, before separating from the loaf, hewed into two halves, of which Joe got one, and I the other.* (*Great Expectations* by Charles Dickens)

plantations NOUN here plantations means colonies, which are countries controlled by a more powerful country ❑ *besides our plantations in America* (*Gulliver's Travels* by Jonathan Swift)

plastic ADV here plastic is an old term meaning shaping or a power that was forming ❑ *A plastic power abode with me* (*The Prelude* by William Wordsworth)

players NOUN actors ❑ *of players which upon the world's stage be* (*On His Mistress* by John Donne)

plump ADV all at once, suddenly ❑ *But it took a bit of time to get it well round, the change come so uncommon plump, didn't it?* (*Great Expectations* by Charles Dickens)

plundered VERB to plunder is to rob or steal from ❑ *These crosses stand for the names of ships or towns that they sank or plundered* (*Treasure Island* by Robert Louis Stevenson)

pommel ■ VERB to pommel someone is to hit them repeatedly with your fists ❑ *hug him round the neck, pommel his back, and kick his legs in irrepressible affection!* (*A Christmas Carol* by Charles Dickens) ■ NOUN a pommel is the part of a saddle that rises up at the front ❑ *He had his gun across his pommel* (*The Adventures of Huckleberry Finn* by Mark Twain)

poor's rates NOUN poor's rates were property taxes which were used to support the poor ❑ *"Oh!" replied the undertaker; "why, you know, Mr. Bumble, I pay a good deal towards the poor's rates."* (*Oliver Twist* by Charles Dickens)

popular ADJ popular means ruled by the people, or Republican, rather than ruled by a monarch ❑ *With those of Greece compared and popular Rome* (*The Prelude* by William Wordsworth)

porringer NOUN a porringer is a small bowl ❑ *Of this festive composition each boy had one porringer, and no more* (*Oliver Twist* by Charles Dickens)

postboy NOUN a postboy was the driver of a horse-drawn carriage ❑ *He spoke to a postboy who was dozing under the gateway* (*Oliver Twist* by Charles Dickens)

post-chaise NOUN a fast carriage for two or four passengers ❑ *Looking round, he saw that it was a post-chaise, driven at great speed* (*Oliver Twist* by Charles Dickens)

postern NOUN a small gate usually at the back of a building ❑ *The little servant happening to be entering the fortress with two hot rolls, I passed through the postern and crossed the drawbridge, in her company* (*Great Expectations* by Charles Dickens)

pottle NOUN a pottle was a small basket ❑ *He had a paper-bag under each arm and a pottle of strawberries in one hand . . .* (*Great Expectations* by Charles Dickens)

pounce NOUN pounce is a fine powder used to prevent ink spreading on untreated paper ❑ *in that grim atmosphere of pounce and parchment, red-tape, dusty wafers, ink-jars, brief and draft paper, law reports, writs, declarations, and bills of costs* (*David Copperfield* by Charles Dickens)

pox NOUN pox means sexually transmitted diseases like syphilis ❑ *how the pox in all its consequences and denominations* (*Gulliver's Travels* by Jonathan Swift)

prelibation NOUN prelibation means a foretaste of or an example of something to come ❑ *A prelibation to the mower's scythe* (*The Prelude* by William Wordsworth)

prentice NOUN an apprentice ❑ *and Joe, sitting on an old gun, had told me that when I was 'prentice to him regularly bound, we would have such Larks there!* (*Great Expectations* by Charles Dickens)

presently ADV immediately ❑ *I presently knew what they meant* (*Gulliver's Travels* by Jonathan Swift)

pumpion NOUN pumpkin ❑ *for it was almost as large as a small pumpion* (*Gulliver's Travels* by Jonathan Swift)

punctual ADJ kept in one place ❑ *was not a punctual presence, but a spirit* (*The Prelude* by William Wordsworth)

quadrille ◼ NOUN a quadrille is a dance invented in France which is usually performed by four couples ❑ *However, Mr Swiveller had Miss Sophy's hand for the first quadrille (country-dances being low, were utterly proscribed)* (*The Old Curiosity Shop* by Charles Dickens) ◼ NOUN quadrille was a card game for four people ❑ *to make up her pool of quadrille in the evening* (*Pride and Prejudice* by Jane Austen)

quality NOUN gentry or upper-class people ❑ *if you are with the quality* (*The Adventures of Huckleberry Finn* by Mark Twain)

quick parts PHRASE quick-witted ❑ *Mr Bennet was so odd a mixture of quick parts* (*Pride and Prejudice* by Jane Austen)

quid NOUN a quid is something chewed or kept in the mouth, like a piece of tobacco ❑ *rolling his quid* (*Treasure Island* by Robert Louis Stevenson)

quit VERB quit means to avenge or to make even ❑ *But Faustus's death shall quit my infamy* (*Doctor Faustus 4.3* by Christopher Marlowe)

rags NOUN divisions ❑ *Nor hours, days, months, which are the rags of time* (*The Sun Rising* by John Donne)

raiment NOUN raiment means clothing ❑ *the mountain shook off turf and flower, had only heath for raiment and crag for gem* (*Jane Eyre* by Charlotte Brontë)

rain cats and dogs PHRASE an expression meaning rain heavily. The origin of the expression is unclear ❑ *But it'll perhaps rain cats and dogs to-morrow* (*Silas Marner* by George Eliot)

raised Cain PHRASE raised Cain means caused a lot of trouble. Cain is a character in the Bible who killed his brother Abel ❑ *and every time he got drunk he raised Cain around town* (*The Adventures of Huckleberry Finn* by Mark Twain)

rambling ADJ rambling means confused and not very clear ❑ *my* *head began to be filled very early with rambling thoughts* (Robinson Crusoe by Daniel Defoe)

raree-show NOUN a raree-show is an old term for a peep-show or a fairground entertainment ❑ *A raree-show is here, with children gathered round* (The Prelude by William Wordsworth)

recusants NOUN people who resisted authority ❑ *hardy recusants* (The Prelude by William Wordsworth)

redounding VERB eddying. An eddy is a movement in water or air which goes round and round instead of flowing in one direction ❑ *mists and steam-like fogs redounding everywhere* (The Prelude by William Wordsworth)

redundant ADJ here redundant means overflowing but Wordsworth also uses it to mean excessively large or too big ❑ *A tempest, a redundant energy* (The Prelude by William Wordsworth)

reflex NOUN reflex is a shortened version of reflexion, which is an alternative spelling of reflection ❑ *To cut across the reflex of a star* (The Prelude by William Wordsworth)

Reformatory NOUN a prison for young offenders/criminals ❑ *Even when I was taken to have a new suit of clothes, the tailor had orders to make them like a kind of Reformatory, and on no account to let me have the free use of my limbs.* (Great Expectations by Charles Dickens)

remorse NOUN pity or compassion ❑ *by that remorse* (On His Mistress by John Donne)

render VERB in this context render means give. ❑ *and Sarah could render no reason that would be sanctioned by the feeling of the community.* (Silas Marner by George Eliot)

repeater NOUN a repeater was a watch that chimed the last hour when a button was pressed–as a result it

was useful in the dark ❑ *And his watch is a gold repeater, and worth a hundred pound if it's worth a penny.* (Great Expectations by Charles Dickens)

repugnance NOUN repugnance means a strong dislike of something or someone ❑ *overcoming a strong repugnance* (Treasure Island by Robert Louis Stevenson)

reverence NOUN reverence means bow. When you bow to someone, you briefly bend your body towards them as a formal way of showing them respect ❑ *made my reverence* (Gulliver's Travels by Jonathan Swift)

reverie NOUN a reverie is a day dream ❑ *I can guess the subject of your reverie* (Pride and Prejudice by Jane Austen)

revival NOUN a religious meeting held in public ❑ *well I'd ben a-running' a little temperance revival thar' bout a week* (The Adventures of Huckleberry Finn by Mark Twain)

revolt VERB revolt means turn back or stop your present course of action and go back to what you were doing before ❑ *Revolt, or I'll in piecemeal tear thy flesh* (Doctor Faustus 5.1 by Christopher Marlowe)

rheumatics/rheumatism NOUN rheumatics [rheumatism] is an illness that makes your joints or muscles stiff and painful ❑ *a new cure for the rheumatics* (Treasure Island by Robert Louis Stevenson)

riddance NOUN riddance is usually used in the form good riddance which you say when you are pleased that something has gone or been left behind ❑ *I'd better go into the house, and die and be a riddance* (David Copperfield by Charles Dickens)

rimy ADJ rimy is an ADJECTIVE which means covered in ice or frost ❑ *It was a rimy morning, and very damp* (Great Expectations by Charles Dickens)

riper ADJ riper means more mature or older ❑ *At riper years to Wittenberg he went* (*Doctor Faustus chorus* by Christopher Marlowe)

rubber NOUN a set of games in whist or backgammon ❑ *her father was sure of his rubber* (*Emma* by Jane Austen)

ruffian NOUN a ruffian is a person who behaves violently ❑ *and when the ruffian had told him* (*Treasure Island* by Robert Louis Stevenson)

sadness NOUN sadness is an old term meaning seriousness ❑ *But I prithee tell me, in good sadness* (*Doctor Faustus 2.2* by Christopher Marlowe)

sailed before the mast PHRASE this phrase meant someone who did not look like a sailor ❑ *he had none of the appearance of a man that sailed before the mast* (*Treasure Island* by Robert Louis Stevenson)

scabbard NOUN a scabbard is the covering for a sword or dagger ❑ *Girded round its middle was an antique scabbard; but no sword was in it, and the ancient sheath was eaten up with rust* (*A Christmas Carol* by Charles Dickens)

schooners NOUN A schooner is a fast, medium-sized sailing ship ❑ *if schooners, islands, and maroons* (*Treasure Island* by Robert Louis Stevenson)

science NOUN learning or knowledge ❑ *Even Science, too, at hand* (*The Prelude* by William Wordsworth)

scrouge VERB to scrouge means to squeeze or to crowd ❑ *to scrouge in and get a sight* (*The Adventures of Huckleberry Finn* by Mark Twain)

scrutore NOUN a scrutore, or escritoire, was a writing table ❑ *set me gently on my feet upon the scrutore* (*Gulliver's Travels* by Jonathan Swift)

scutcheon/escutcheon NOUN an escutcheon is a shield with a coat of arms, or the symbols of a family name, engraved on it ❑ *On the scutcheon we'll have a bend* (*The Adventures of Huckleberry Finn* by Mark Twain)

sea-dog PHRASE sea-dog is a slang term for an experienced sailor or pirate ❑ *a 'true sea-dog', and a 'real old salt,'* (*Treasure Island* by Robert Louis Stevenson)

see the lions PHRASE to see the lions was to go and see the sights of London. Originally the phrase referred to the menagerie in the Tower of London and later in Regent's Park ❑ *We will go and see the lions for an hour or two–it's something to have a fresh fellow like you to show them to, Copperfield* (*David Copperfield* by Charles Dickens)

self-conceit NOUN self-conceit is an old term which means having too high an opinion of oneself, or deceiving yourself ❑ *Till swollen with cunning, of a self-conceit* (*Doctor Faustus chorus* by Christopher Marlowe)

seneschal NOUN a steward ❑ *where a grey-headed seneschal sings a funny chorus with a funnier body of vassals* (*Oliver Twist* by Charles Dickens)

sensible ADJ if you were sensible of something you are aware or conscious of something ❑ *If my children are silly I must hope to be always sensible of it* (*Pride and Prejudice* by Jane Austen)

sessions NOUN court cases were heard at specific times of the year called sessions ❑ *He lay in prison very ill, during the whole interval between his committal for trial, and the coming round of the Sessions.* (*Great Expectations* by Charles Dickens)

shabby ADJ shabby places look old and in bad condition ❑ *a little bit of a shabby village named Pikesville* (*The Adventures of Huckleberry Finn* by Mark Twain)

shay-cart NOUN a shay-cart was a small cart drawn by one horse ❑ *"I were at the Bargemen t'other night, Pip;"*

whenever he subsided into affection, he called me Pip, and whenever he relapsed into politeness he called me Sir; "when there come up in his shay-cart Pumblechook." (Great Expectations by Charles Dickens)

shilling NOUN a shilling is an old unit of currency. There were twenty shillings in every British pound ❑ *"Ten shillings too much," said the gentleman in the white waistcoat.* (*Oliver Twist* by Charles Dickens)

shines NOUN tricks or games ❑ *well, it would make a cow laugh to see the shines that old idiot cut* (*The Adventures of Huckleberry Finn* by Mark Twain)

shirking VERB shirking means not doing what you are meant to be doing, or evading your duties ❑ *some of you shirking lubbers* (*Treasure Island* by Robert Louis Stevenson)

shiver my timbers PHRASE shiver my timbers is an expression which was used by sailors and pirates to express surprise ❑ *why, shiver my timbers, if I hadn't forgotten my score!* (*Treasure Island* by Robert Louis Stevenson)

shoe-roses NOUN shoe-roses were roses made from ribbons which were stuck on to shoes as decoration ❑ *the very shoe-roses for Netherfield were got by proxy* (*Pride and Prejudice* by Jane Austen)

singular ADJ singular means very great and remarkable or strange ❑ *"Singular dream," he says* (*The Adventures of Huckleberry Finn* by Mark Twain)

sire NOUN sire is an old word which means lord or master or elder ❑ *She also defied her sire* (*Little Women* by Louisa May Alcott)

sixpence NOUN a sixpence was half of a shilling ❑ *if she had only a shilling in the world, she would be very lilkely to give away sixpence of it* (*Emma* by Jane Austen)

slavey NOUN the word slavey was used when there was only one servant in

a house or boarding-house–so she had to perform all the duties of a larger staff ❑ *Two distinct knocks, sir, will produce the slavey at any time* (*The Old Curiosity Shop* by Charles Dickens)

slender ADJ weak ❑ *In slender accents of sweet verse* (*The Prelude* by William Wordsworth)

slop-shops NOUN slop-shops were shops where cheap ready-made clothes were sold. They mainly sold clothes to sailors ❑ *Accordingly, I took the jacket off, that I might learn to do without it; and carrying it under my arm, began a tour of inspection of the various slop-shops.* (*David Copperfield* by Charles Dickens)

sluggard NOUN a lazy person ❑ *"Stand up and repeat 'Tis the voice of the sluggard,'" said the Gryphon.* (*Alice's Adventures in Wonderland* by Lewis Carroll)

smallpox NOUN smallpox is a serious infectious disease ❑ *by telling the men we had smallpox aboard* (*The Adventures of Huckleberry Finn* by Mark Twain)

smalls NOUN smalls are short trousers ❑ *It is difficult for a large-headed, small-eyed youth, of lumbering make and heavy countenance, to look dignified under any circumstances; but it is more especially so, when superadded to these personal attractions are a red nose and yellow smalls* (*Oliver Twist* by Charles Dickens)

sneeze-box NOUN a box for snuff was called a sneeze-box because sniffing snuff makes the user sneeze ❑ *To think of Jack Dawkins — lummy Jack — the Dodger — the Artful Dodger — going abroad for a common twopenny-halfpenny sneeze-box!* (*Oliver Twist* by Charles Dickens)

snorted VERB slept ❑ *Or snorted we in the Seven Sleepers' den?* (*The Good-Morrow* by John Donne)

snuff NOUN snuff is tobacco in powder form which is taken by sniffing ❑

as he thrust his thumb and fore-finger into the proffered snuff-box of the undertaker: which was an ingenious little model of a patent coffin. (*Oliver Twist* by Charles Dickens)

soliloquized VERB to soliloquize is when an actor in a play speaks to himself or herself rather than to another actor ❏ *"A new servitude! There is something in that," I soliloquized (mentally, be it understood; I did not talk aloud)* (*Jane Eyre* by Charlotte Brontë)

sough NOUN a sough is a drain or a ditch ❏ *as you may have noticed the sough that runs from the marshes* (*Wuthering Heights* by Emily Brontë)

spirits NOUN a spirit is the nonphysical part of a person which is believed to remain alive after their death ❏ *that I might raise up spirits when I please* (*Doctor Faustus 1.5* by Christopher Marlowe)

spleen ◼ NOUN here spleen means a type of sadness or depression which was thought to only affect the wealthy ❏ *yet here I could plainly discover the true seeds of spleen* (*Gulliver's Travels* by Jonathan Swift) ◼ NOUN irritability and low spirits ❏ *Adieu to disappointment and spleen* (*Pride and Prejudice* by Jane Austen)

spondulicks NOUN spondulicks is a slang word which means money ❏ *not for all his spondulicks and as much more on top of it* (*The Adventures of Huckleberry Finn* by Mark Twain)

stalled of VERB to be stalled of something is to be bored with it ❏ *I'm stalled of doing naught* (*Wuthering Heights* by Emily Brontë)

stanchion NOUN a stanchion is a pole or bar that stands upright and is used as a buidling support ❏ *and slid down a stanchion* (*The Adventures of Huckleberry Finn* by Mark Twain)

stang NOUN stang is another word for pole which was an old measurement ❏ *These fields were intermingled*

with woods of half a stang (*Gulliver's Travels* by Jonathan Swift)

starlings NOUN a starling is a wall built around the pillars that support a bridge to protect the pillars ❏ *There were states of the tide when, having been down the river, I could not get back through the eddy-chafed arches and starlings of old London Bridge* (*Great Expectations* by Charles Dickens)

startings NOUN twitching or night-time movements of the body ❏ *with midnight's startings* (*On His Mistress* by John Donne)

stomacher NOUN a panel at the front of a dress ❏ *but send her aunt the pattern of a stomacher* (*Emma* by Jane Austen)

stoop VERB swoop ❏ *Once a kite hovering over the garden made a swoop at me* (*Gulliver's Travels* by Jonathan Swift)

succedaneum NOUN a succedaneum is a substitute ❏ *But as a succedaneum* (*The Prelude* by William Wordsworth)

suet NOUN a hard animal fat used in cooking ❏ *and your jaws are too weak For anything tougher than suet* (*Alice's Adventures in Wonderland* by Lewis Carroll)

sultry ADJ sultry weather is hot and damp. Here sultry means unpleasant or risky ❏ *for it was getting pretty sultry for us* (*The Adventures of Huckleberry Finn* by Mark Twain)

summerset NOUN summerset is an old spelling of somersault. If someone does a somersault, they turn over completely in the air ❏ *I have seen him do the summerset* (*Gulliver's Travels* by Jonathan Swift)

supper NOUN supper was a light meal taken late in the evening. The main meal was dinner which was eaten at four or five in the afternoon ❏ *and the supper table was all set out* (*Emma* by Jane Austen)

surfeits VERB to surfeit in something is to have far too much of it, or to overindulge in it to an unhealthy degree ❑ *He surfeits upon cursed necromancy* (*Doctor Faustus chorus* by Christopher Marlowe)

surtout NOUN a surtout is a long close-fitting overcoat ❑ *He wore a long black surtout reaching nearly to his ankles* (*The Old Curiosity Shop* by Charles Dickens)

swath NOUN swath is the width of corn cut by a scythe ❑ *while thy hook Spares the next swath* (*Ode to Autumn* by John Keats)

sylvan ADJ sylvan means belonging to the woods ❑ *Sylvan historian* (*Ode on a Grecian Urn* by John Keats)

taction NOUN taction means touch. This means that the people had to be touched on the mouth or the ears to get their attention ❑ *without being roused by some external taction upon the organs of speech and hearing* (*Gulliver's Travels* by Jonathan Swift)

Tag and Rag and Bobtail PHRASE the riff-raff, or lower classes. Used in an insulting way ❑ *"No," said he; "not till it got about that there was no protection on the premises, and it come to be considered dangerous, with convicts and Tag and Rag and Bobtail going up and down."* (*Great Expectations* by Charles Dickens)

tallow NOUN tallow is hard animal fat that is used to make candles and soap ❑ *and a lot of tallow candles* (*The Adventures of Huckleberry Finn* by Mark Twain)

tan VERB to tan means to beat or whip ❑ *and if I catch you about that school I'll tan you good* (*The Adventures of Huckleberry Finn* by Mark Twain)

tanyard NOUN the tanyard is part of a tannery, which is a place where leather is made from animal skins ❑ *hid in the old tanyard* (*The Adventures of Huckleberry Finn* by Mark Twain)

tarry ADJ tarry means the colour of tar or black ❑ *his tarry pig-tail* (*Treasure Island* by Robert Louis Stevenson)

thereof PHRASE from there ❑ *By all desires which thereof did ensue* (*On His Mistress* by John Donne)

thick with, be PHRASE if you are 'thick with someone' you are very close, sharing secrets–it is often used to describe people who are planning something secret ❑ *Hasn't he been thick with Mr Heathcliff lately?* (*Wuthering Heights* by Emily Brontë)

thimble NOUN a thimble is a small cover used to protect the finger while sewing ❑ *The paper had been sealed in several places by a thimble* (*Treasure Island* by Robert Louis Stevenson)

thirtover ADJ thirtover is an old word which means obstinate or that someone is very determined to do want they want and can not be persuaded to do something in another way ❑ *I have been living on in a thirtover, lackadaisical way* (*Tess of the D'Urbervilles* by Thomas Hardy)

timbrel NOUN timbrel is a tambourine ❑ *What pipes and timbrels?* (*Ode on a Grecian Urn* by John Keats)

tin NOUN tin is slang for money/cash ❑ *Then the plain question is, an't it a pity that this state of things should continue, and how much better would it be for the old gentleman to hand over a reasonable amount of tin, and make it all right and comfortable* (*The Old Curiosity Shop* by Charles Dickens)

tincture NOUN a tincture is a medicine made with alcohol and a small amount of a drug ❑ *with ink composed of a cephalic tincture* (*Gulliver's Travels* by Jonathan Swift)

tithe NOUN a tithe is a tax paid to the church ❑ *and held farms which, speaking from a spiritual point of view, paid highly-desirable tithes* (*Silas Marner* by George Eliot)

towardly ADJ a towardly child is dutiful or obedient ❏ *and a towardly child* (*Gulliver's Travels* by Jonathan Swift)

toys NOUN trifles are things which are considered to have little importance, value, or significance ❏ *purchase my life from them by some bracelets, glass rings, and other toys* (*Gulliver's Travels* by Jonathan Swift)

tract NOUN a tract is a religious pamphlet or leaflet ❏ *and Joe Harper got a hymn-book and a tract* (*The Adventures of Huckleberry Finn* by Mark Twain)

train-oil NOUN train-oil is oil from whale blubber ❏ *The train-oil and gunpowder were shoved out of sight in a minute* (*Wuthering Heights* by Emily Brontë)

tribulation NOUN tribulation means the suffering or difficulty you experience in a particular situation ❏ *Amy was learning this distinction through much tribulation* (*Little Women* by Louisa May Alcott)

trivet NOUN a trivet is a three-legged stand for resting a pot or kettle ❏ *a pocket-knife in his right; and a pewter pot on the trivet* (*Oliver Twist* by Charles Dickens)

trot line NOUN a trot line is a fishing line to which a row of smaller fishing lines are attached ❏ *when he got along I was hard at it taking up a trot line* (*The Adventures of Huckleberry Finn* by Mark Twain)

troth NOUN oath or pledge ❏ *I wonder, by my troth* (*The Good-Morrow* by John Donne)

truckle NOUN a truckle bedstead is a bed that is on wheels and can be slid under another bed to save space ❏ *It rose under my hand, and the door yielded. Looking in, I saw a lighted candle on a table, a bench, and a mattress on a truckle bedstead.* (*Great Expectations* by Charles Dickens)

trump NOUN a trump is a good, reliable person wo can be trusted ❏ This lad Hawkins is a trump, I perceive (*Treasure Island* by Robert Louis Stevenson)

tucker NOUN a tucker is a frilly lace collar which is worn around the neck ❏ *Whereat Scrooge's niece's sister the plump one with the lace tucker: not the one with the roses blushed.* (*A Christmas Carol* by Charles Dickens)

tureen NOUN a large bowl with a lid from which soup or vegetables are served ❏ *Waiting in a hot tureen!* (*Alice's Adventures in Wonderland* by Lewis Carroll)

turnkey NOUN a prison officer; jailer ❏ *As we came out of the prison through the lodge, I found that the great importance of my guardian was appreciated by the turnkeys, no less than by those whom they held in charge.* (*Great Expectations* by Charles Dickens)

turnpike NOUN the upkeep of many roads of the time was paid for by tolls (fees) collected at posts along the road. There was a gate to prevent people travelling further along the road until the toll had been paid. ❏ *Traddles, whom I have taken up by appointment at the turnpike, presents a dazzling combination of cream colour and light blue; and both he and Mr. Dick have a general effect about them of being all gloves.* (*David Copperfield* by Charles Dickens)

twas PHRASE it was ❏ *twas but a dream of thee* (*The Good-Morrow* by John Donne)

tyrannized VERB tyrannized means bullied or forced to do things against their will ❏ *for people would soon cease coming there to be tyrannized over and put down* (*Treasure Island* by Robert Louis Stevenson)

'un NOUN 'un is a slang term for one– usually used to refer to a person ❏ *She's been thinking the old 'un* (*David Copperfield* by Charles Dickens)

undistinguished ADJ undiscriminating or incapable of making a distinction

between good and bad things ❑
*their undistinguished appetite to
devour everything* (Gulliver's Travels
by Jonathan Swift)

use NOUN habit ❑ *Though use make
you apt to kill me* (The Flea by John
Donne)

vacant ADJ vacant usually means
empty, but here Wordsworth uses it
to mean carefree ❑ *To vacant
musing, unreproved neglect* (The
Prelude by William Wordsworth)

valetudinarian NOUN one too concerned
with his or her own health. ❑ *for
having been a valetudinarian all his
life* (Emma by Jane Austen)

vamp VERB vamp means to walk or
tramp to somewhere ❑ *Well, vamp
on to Marlott, will 'ee* (Tess of the
D'Urbervilles by Thomas Hardy)

vapours NOUN the vapours is an old
term which means unpleasant and
strange thoughts, which make the
person feel nervous and unhappy
❑ *and my head was full of
vapours* (Robinson Crusoe by
Daniel Defoe)

vegetables NOUN here vegetables means
plants ❑ *the other vegetables are in
the same proportion* (Gulliver's
Travels by Jonathan Swift)

venturesome ADJ if you are venturesome you are willing to take risks ❑
*he must be either hopelessly stupid or
a venturesome fool* (Wuthering
Heights by Emily Brontë)

verily ADJ verily means really or truly
❑ *though I believe verily* (Robinson
Crusoe by Daniel Defoe)

vicinage NOUN vicinage is an area or
the residents of an area ❑ *and to
his thought the whole vicinage was
haunted by her.* (Silas Marner by
George Eliot)

victuals NOUN victuals means food ❑
grumble a little over the victuals
(The Adventures of Huckleberry
Finn by Mark Twain)

vintage NOUN vintage in this context
means wine ❑ *Oh, for a draught of*

vintage! (Ode on a Nightingale by
John Keats)

virtual ADJ here virtual means
powerful or strong ❑ *had virtual
faith* (The Prelude by William
Wordsworth)

vittles NOUN vittles is a slang word
which means food ❑ *There never
was such a woman for givin' away
vittles and drink* (Little Women by
Louisa May Alcott)

voided straight PHRASE voided
straight is an old expression which
means emptied immediately ❑ *see
the rooms be voided straight* (Doctor
Faustus 4.1 by Christopher
Marlowe)

wainscot NOUN wainscot is wood panel
lining in a room so wainscoted
means a room lined with wooden
panels ❑ *in the dark wainscoted
parlor* (Silas Marner by George
Eliot)

walking the plank PHRASE walking
the plank was a punishment in
which a prisoner would be made to
walk along a plank on the side of
the ship and fall into the sea,
where they would be abandoned ❑
*about hanging, and walking the
plank* (Treasure Island by Robert
Louis Stevenson)

want VERB want means to be lacking
or short of ❑ *The next thing wanted
was to get the picture framed*
(Emma by Jane Austen)

wanting ADJ wanting means lacking or
missing ❑ *wanting two fingers of
the left hand* (Treasure Island by
Robert Louis Stevenson)

wanting, I was not PHRASE I was not
wanting means I did not fail ❑ *I
was not wanting to lay a founda-
tion of religious knowledge in his
mind* (Robinson Crusoe by Daniel
Defoe)

ward NOUN a ward is, usually, a child
who has been put under the
protection of the court or a
guardian for his or her protection ❑
I call the Wards in Jarndyce. The

are caged up with all the others. (*Bleak House* by Charles Dickens)

waylay VERB to waylay someone is to lie in wait for them or to intercept them ❑ *I must go up the road and waylay him* (*The Adventures of Huckleberry Finn* by Mark Twain)

weazen NOUN weazen is a slang word for throat. It actually means shrivelled ❑ *You with a uncle too! Why, I knowed you at Gargery's when you was so small a wolf that I could have took your weazen betwixt this finger and thumb and chucked you away dead* (*Great Expectations* by Charles Dickens)

wery ■ ADV very ❑ *Be wery careful o' vidders all your life* (*Pickwick Papers* by Charles Dickens) ■ *See* wibrated

wherry NOUN wherry is a small swift rowing boat for one person ❑ *It was flood tide when Daniel Quilp sat himself down in the wherry to cross to the opposite shore.* (*The Old Curiosity Shop* by Charles Dickens)

whether PREP whether means which of the two in this example ❑ *we came in full view of a great island or continent (for we knew not whether)* (*Gulliver's Travels* by Jonathan Swift)

whetstone NOUN a whetstone is a stone used to sharpen knives and other tools ❑ *I dropped pap's whetstone there too* (*The Adventures of Huckleberry Finn* by Mark Twain)

wibrated VERB in Dickens's use of the English language 'w' often replaces 'v' when he is reporting speech. So here 'wibrated' means 'vibrated'. In Pickwick Papers a judge asks Sam Weller (who constantly confuses the two letters) 'Do you spell it with a 'v' or a 'w'?' to which Weller replies 'That depends upon the taste and fancy of the speller, my Lord' ❑ *There are strings . . . in the human heart that had better not be wibrated'* (*Barnaby Rudge* by Charles Dickens)

wicket NOUN a wicket is a little door in a larger entrance ❑ *Having rested here, for a minute or so, to collect a*

good burst of sobs and an imposing show of tears and terror, he knocked loudly at the wicket; (*Oliver Twist* by Charles Dickens)

without CONJ without means unless ❑ *You don't know about me, without you have read a book by the name of The Adventures of Tom Sawyer* (*The Adventures of Huckleberry Finn* by Mark Twain)

wittles ■ NOUN vittles is a slang word which means food ❑ *I live on broken wittles–and I sleep on the coals* (*David Copperfield* by Charles Dickens) ■ *See* wibrated

woo VERB courts or forms a proper relationship with ❑ *before it woo* (*The Flea* by John Donne)

words, to have PHRASE if you have words with someone you have a disagreement or an argument ❑ *I do not want to have words with a young thing like you.* (*Black Beauty* by Anna Sewell)

workhouse NOUN workhouses were places where the homeless were given food and a place to live in return for doing very hard work ❑ *And the Union workhouses? demanded Scrooge. Are they still in operation?* (*A Christmas Carol* by Charles Dickens)

yawl NOUN a yawl is a small boat kept on a bigger boat for short trips. Yawl is also the name for a small fishing boat ❑ *She sent out her yawl, and we went aboard* (*The Adventures of Huckleberry Finn* by Mark Twain)

yeomanry NOUN the yeomanry was a collective term for the middle classes involved in agriculture ❑ *The yeomanry are precisely the order of people with whom I feel I can have nothing to do* (*Emma* by Jane Austen)

yonder ADV yonder means over there ❑ *all in the same second we seem to hear low voices in yonder!* (*The Adventures of Huckleberry Finn* by Mark Twain)